NO DUKES ALLOWED

THE KENT'S ROW DUCHESSES

BOOK ONE

JESS MICHAELS

The last few years have brought on a great deal of physical and emotional pain. I even considered not writing anymore. So to everyone who encouraged and enjoyed and held me in my suffering, thank you.

But especially to Mackenzie Walton, who always makes me better and tells me I was good to start with. If I could craft the perfect editor, you would be it.

And to Michael. Always. Even in your own challenges, you are my champion. I couldn't do any part of this without your love and advice and support.

PROLOGUE

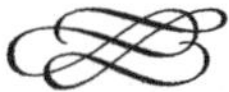

Summer 1814

Valaria St. Clare, Duchess of Gooding, had to believe that if one was given a rulebook to marriage, hating one's husband would have been at the top of a list of what not to do.

And yet, as she stared across their ballroom at him, surrounded by his cronies, hate was what she felt. Silas was drinking heavily, laughing and crowing and telling boisterous and embarrassing stories that echoed in the room so everyone could hear.

If she had found the nerve to go to his side and gently suggest he lower his tone, she knew what his response would have been. To tell her it was his birthday and he would do what he pleased. And everyone would laugh and she would fake a smile and no one would know that Silas *always* did as he pleased.

Certainly tonight would be no different.

Her stomach turned and she dropped her gaze a moment. When she lifted it again, she found one of Silas's best mates stepping up to her side. The Duke of Blackvale. He was tall and very handsome and of course rich and powerful. Silas didn't waste his time on anyone who wasn't. He boasted of his influential circle of friends often enough.

But unlike those others in her husband's group, she didn't despise Blackvale. He was…different from the rest. And so she forced a smile in welcome.

"Blackvale," she said. "Are you enjoying the party?"

"It seems Si is," Blackvale said with a long look across the room. His expression was something settled between concern and humor at Silas's increasingly boorish behavior.

"Hmm," Valaria returned, noncommittal. She was very good, after all, at hiding what she felt. "We have not seen you around as much lately. Have you been busy?"

"Yes," he said with a sigh. "My brother has been managing one of the estates and had some issue, so I had to ride to the rescue. But it's resolved now and I should be in London more for the next few months."

There was a little flutter in Valaria's chest. If Blackvale was in town, he was with Silas. They had been friends a very long time despite their different personalities. She sometimes looked at Blackvale, who seemed to have a deep sense of responsibility to duty, friends and family, and wondered how in the world they were friends. But then again, they had become chums when they were very young.

"I'm sure Silas will be pleased," she said.

He held her stare for a moment. Perhaps a moment too long, and she ducked her head, uncertain what he was looking for as those light brown eyes moved slowly over her face. He cleared his throat and his voice was suddenly a little thick. "Yes."

She glanced back up at him and she found he was now focused on Silas, who had slugged back yet another drink. She shivered at the state he would be in by the time they retired to bed. Her stomach turned at the thought.

"He's getting a bit sloppy there, isn't he?" Blackvale mused, almost to himself.

She shrugged. "Perhaps he'll pass out and limit any damage he might do to his reputation by—" She cut herself off with a sigh as she watched Silas stagger toward the back of the ballroom, muttering something she couldn't hear as he mounted the table. She sighed. "By dancing on the table."

Blackvale shook his head. "He really needs to be more careful what he allows. Excuse me, Your Grace, I will take care of this. Perhaps I can get him tucked into bed."

Valaria fought to keep her excitement from her face at the idea. If Silas went to his bed, it kept him out of hers. Blackvale didn't know the gift he offered with his suggestion and offer of help.

"That might be best," Valaria said lightly. He executed a small nod, but before he left she said, "B-Blackvale?"

He turned back. "Your Grace?"

"You are a good friend," she said softly.

His lips parted as if he hadn't expected the compliment, then he smiled. "And you are a good wife."

He left her then and she blinked back tears. The man had no idea how wrong he was. And she hoped he never would.

CHAPTER 1

Spring 1815

It was a well-known fact that when one wanted to put a dowager duchess out to pasture, one placed her on Kent's Row.

It was a fine street, of course, with tree-lined walkways and brightly colored doors to welcome those who came to call at the neatly kept townhouses. Still, there was no denying its purpose, which Valaria felt keenly as her carriage rumbled to a stop in front of one of the tall homes, sunlight dancing off the bright Roman cement walls.

Number 106. That was hers now, her home after two years of living at a far finer residence of her late husband, Silas St. Clare, Duke of Gooding. For some women, especially of her tender years, the switch to the smaller abode might have been a little shocking. After all, most of the duchesses on the Row were in their sixties or even older. They were not expected to dance or twirl or laugh too loudly anymore.

And yet as the carriage door was opened and her footman helped her out, Valaria tilted back her fine bonnet and breathed a sigh of…*relief*…at this new home. A place where she could hide.

Being put out to pasture sounded perfectly fine to her.

Of course she told herself that, but then the grief washed over her and she gripped the edge of the carriage door briefly before it passed. Then she forced a smile as her new butler, Higgins, came down the short set of stairs to greet her.

"Your Grace," he said, executing a small bow. "Welcome home."

Her smile wavered slightly but she managed to maintain the mask as she inclined her head toward this man she had met but once before today. Her old butler had remained at the duke's residence, after all. Along with almost all her familiar servants, save for her personal maid, Fanny.

"Thank you so much, Higgins," she said. "I'm sure the new staff has done a wonderful job preparing the home for me. I look forward to seeing it now that it is filled with furniture and life."

"Indeed, Your Grace," he said, and motioned toward the door. "I shall give you a tour straight away if you are not too tired from your journey."

She gave a small laugh. "The twenty minutes across London, you mean? Yes, I think I can manage."

She was about to follow his gentle direction into the house when she saw two ladies coming up the street together at a rapid clip. It was evident by their focused stares in her direction that they were coming to her.

Her stomach turned a little at the attention, but she cast a quick glance toward Higgins. "Neighbors?" she asked softly.

"Yes, Your Grace."

He drew a breath as if to identify her impending guests, but before he could, Valaria gasped, "Why, that is the Duchess of Turnbridge and the Duchess of Sidmouth. They are of an age with me—are they visiting someone here?"

Higgins shook his head. "No, madam. They both live on the Row. Two and three houses down, respectively, on the other side of the Dowager Duchess of Winchester, who is your direct neighbor to the north."

Valaria's eyes went wide at the mention of one of the most respected dowagers in London, but she could not ask more because the two ladies arrived at last, in a smiling cloud of perfume and perfectly coifed hair and beautiful gowns.

"Your Grace," the Duchess of Sidmouth said, stretching out an elegant hand in greeting. "Good afternoon, and welcome to Kent's Row."

Valaria shook the offered hand. "Good afternoon, Your Graces. How kind of you to welcome me."

And it was kind, though she had to assume this direct approach was also driven by a desire to have the first look at their new neighbor. She could see curtains along the row were drawn back, other dowagers watching this exchange and, Valaria was certain, judging her.

Her stomach turned at what they might see. What she might show accidentally. This was her new life, after all, but could it truly be a happy one after everything she had endured...and done? Could she have a future with the secrets of the past just waiting to haunt her?

She realized the women were still talking and forced herself to focus.

"I am the Duchess of Sidmouth, but you'll find many of the dowagers don't stand on ceremony here. Too much Your Gracing gets very confusing. So I am Flora."

Valaria smiled at Flora. She was petite and curvaceous, with dark red hair that hung in little ringlets around her pretty face.

"You and I came out the same year, I think," Valaria said.

Flora nodded. "We did, indeed. I always admired your beautiful gowns. And you may not recall it, because that year was such a crush of debutantes, but you were of help to me—"

Valaria caught her breath. "I do remember! Someone had spilled wine on your gown, wasn't it?"

"A rival," Flora agreed. "Someone interested in my eventual husband's fortune. She purposefully spilled the wine to keep me away, and you just appeared out of nowhere and swept me off and cleaned me up."

"It was Prudence Foster, wasn't it?" Valaria said with a scrunch of her nose. "Wretched thing." She did not add that Prudence had made a great game out of Valaria's life afterward. She had been the one to laugh loudest and make the snidest expressions when anything went wrong.

"Yes, wretched thing," Flora said with a shake of her head. "At any rate, I never forgot your kindness, even though I didn't get to speak to you much afterward thanks to the Season's schedule. But we are remedying that." She glanced at her companion. "And this is the Duchess of Tunbridge."

"Bernadette," the other lady said. She seemed shyer, as her dark eyes drifted away from Valaria's face. But she was uncommonly lovely with her dark hair arranged perfectly to frame an oval face. She wore a pretty yellow gown that made everything seem a bit sunnier.

"Your Grace," Valaria said.

"Flora spoke so highly of you when we realized you were moving into the Row that I couldn't wait to meet you. Though you may find I am certainly much closer to fitting in with our neighbors," Bernadette said. "As I came out three years before you two."

"You make it sound as though you are ancient," Flora said with a laugh.

"Sometimes I am made to feel that being just south of thirty *is* ancient, my dear," Bernadette said. "At any rate, we saw you arrive as we were having tea, and Flora could not wait one moment but to greet you."

"Not a moment," Flora agreed, and her eyes danced with real pleasure. "After all, it isn't every day we get a new duchess on the Row, and when we do, she is never our age."

"Not that we don't enjoy our older neighbors," Bernadette hastened to add. "They are nothing but kind. But there is something about having friends close by who are of an age with oneself."

Valaria blinked. Friends. She hadn't had many of those in the last two years. By design. And here these two women were chattering away to her like it was a given that they would be thus.

Something that could easily change, she knew. She found herself taking a slight step back and glancing back apologetically at Higgins, who had moved away from their group but was still waiting for her now at the top of the stairs.

"You must forgive me," she said. "It is such a busy day."

Flora opened her mouth as if to say something, but Bernadette interrupted. "Of course it is. And we have intruded in our excitement. But now you have been welcomed and we will leave you to your settling in."

"With our insistence that you join us for tea tomorrow," Flora added.

Bernadette shot her a look. "You cannot strong arm the poor woman into joining us. You will frighten her away with your insistence."

"I will not." Flora shook her head. "You aren't so easy to scare are you, Your Grace?"

Valaria swallowed because the question, however teasingly meant, carried a weight neither of these ladies could understand. She put on the mask she so often wore with others and forced a laugh. "Not at all. I would be...pleased to join you for tea tomorrow."

"Excellent!" Flora said, tossing Bernadette a triumphant look. "At my home, which is three doors down from yours." She motioned down the lane. "Three o'clock."

"I'll be there," Valaria agreed.

That settled, Bernadette caught Flora's arm and began to drag her away. "We'll let you settle yourself. Good afternoon!"

They headed off, heads close together, talking and laughing as they strolled arm in arm. Valaria stared at them a moment. They seemed genuinely fond of each other. And genuinely interested in her. A strange sensation after years of putting up carefully crafted walls so no one would see the truth of her life.

But the idea of perhaps being allowed friends in this new life was bewitching, indeed. She would just have to be careful about it. And if there was anyone who knew the ins and outs of being careful, it was her.

"Are you ready, Your Grace?" Higgins called out gently.

She smoothed her hands along the front of her gown and pivoted to face him. "I am. And thank you for your patience. Now lead the way."

He did so and she followed, feeling a bit of a lightness to her step as she did. One she didn't fully trust, but oh, how she welcomed it.

Callum Osgood, Duke of Blackvale, made his way through the crowd at his club, scanning the room for friends. Not cronies, not acquaintances...he looked for *friends*. They were a commodity he'd come to value all the more in the past few months.

He found one as he moved toward the fireplace with its enormous mantel where one of those friends, Theo, the Duke of Lightmorrow, was having a drink. Lightmorrow's gaze lit up and he waved to indicate that Callum should join him.

He did so with a grin he didn't have to force. After the pair had shaken hands, Callum looked around. "I must say I do prefer Fitzhugh's to any other club."

Theo grinned. "As do I. I know one cannot avoid White's and the like, but the company here is far more lively and genuine. I suppose it reflects the ownership."

"I suppose it does," Callum agreed as both men looked toward the bar where Fitzhugh, himself, stood, seemingly unimpressed by everything around him. The man did have an air of mystery around him. One Callum rather envied. It seemed everyone always knew his business. Whether he liked it or not.

"So what brings you out tonight?" Theo asked, and motioned to one of the footmen, who brought a whisky over for Callum.

Callum took a sip. "Whatever brings anyone out to these kinds of places. Boredom?"

Theo's brow wrinkled ever so slightly. "I ask because this is the first time you have come out since..."

His friend trailed off, and Callum finished his drink in one swig. "Since Silas's death?"

He flinched as he said those words. It was still so shocking, what had happened. At midnight that night he had been laughing with his friend, by eight the next morning, he had received word that Silas was dead. A drunken accident with his horse, they had said, which seemed so unreal. How could everything have ended so horribly and quickly?

Theo inclined his head slightly. "Yes. I'm not saying I'm sorry to see you. It's been eight weeks. It seems a long enough time to mourn a friend, after all."

Callum stared into his empty glass as if he could will it to fill again. "Hmmm," he mused. "Sometimes it seems forever and sometimes like it was yesterday."

Theo patted his shoulder gently. "I am sure that's true. But somehow the world goes on. After all, I heard that the new duke took over the estate in London today."

"Silas's cousin?" Callum said, jerking his head up. "God's teeth, I remember Franklin as a boy, always following Si and me everywhere, tattling on us at will. He has yearned for this title his entire life. I suppose he's happy now."

"I couldn't say," Theo said. "I wasn't as close to the family as you were."

Callum ignored the slight strain to Theo's voice. He'd always hated it that his two closest friends had not gotten on. They were both dear to him. But he thought many times that perhaps they kept from being less than cordial only because of him.

He sighed and then wrinkled his brow as a thought occurred to him. "And what of the duchess? Does that mean that Valaria has been relegated to some other estate? So soon into her mourning?"

The very idea of it hit him in the chest. Valaria, the wife of his best friend, having to reorganize her life in the midst of what had to be terrible pain. He couldn't help but think of her blue-gray eyes, ones that seemed to pierce through a man. They had always held that lilt of sadness, that briefest glimpse into a soul with so many layers.

Not that he'd allowed himself to make that much of a study of her. She was his friend's wife, after all. He cared about her because he cared about Silas. That hadn't changed. Perhaps it had to become even stronger, in fact, since Silas was no longer there to protect her.

"I heard they moved her to the Row," Theo said, and dragged Callum from his musings.

He couldn't have heard that right. It was impossible. "The Row?" he repeated. "*Kent's Row?*"

Theo shrugged. "It's what I heard."

"But Kent's Row is for the older ladies," Callum said.

"It's become a little corner of dowagers," Theo corrected him. "And she is that now. Though I agree that most of the women on the Row are far above her years. In fact, there's only a handful of younger ladies there. I cannot imagine how boring it is for them."

Callum stared into the fire, his brows knitting. Once again, he couldn't help but think about Valaria. It wasn't that they'd talked that often, though when they did he had enjoyed it. How could one not? Valaria was beautiful, but also bright. Occasionally she gave this tiny smile and...

No, he cut the thought off. At any rate, she normally passed through rooms where Silas gathered with his friends, never intruding upon their masculine pursuits. At balls and parties, she busied herself with friends and only danced with Silas. She was never impolite, but she made no effort to come out of her shell with gentlemen.

And yet Callum still felt an intensely protective instinct as he thought of her, relegated to her grief alone, out amongst ladies who mostly couldn't understand the ins and outs of young widowhood.

"I ought to call on her," he mused out loud.

Theo leaned back, resting his empty glass on the mantelpiece. "Ought you to?"

"To pay my respects," Callum said, and hated how he heard justification in his tone. Like he was doing something wrong and trying to make it right. "To make sure she's settling in comfortably. After all, there are few people in the world who could understand her thoughts and feelings right now."

"And you think you are one of them."

He willed away the sting behind his eyes. "Silas was like a brother to me," he said softly. "I know some part of her pain at least." He cleared his throat. "I ought to pay my respects, if nothing else. I owe that to Silas, do I not? He was one of my closest friends."

There was a slight flutter to Theo's expression. One he always got when this topic was raised, either before or since Silas's death. "Yes. He was that, though you were markedly different men."

"I suppose we were," Callum agreed. "But when one has been friends practically since birth, that is bound to happen from time to time. At any rate, I will call on her tomorrow, I think."

Theo tilted his head and suddenly his expression was a little playful. Rakish, even, as his friend was known to be. "Are you certain this decision is only to do with loyalty to Silas?"

"What does that mean?" Callum said, perhaps more strongly than he meant to.

"Nothing," Theo said with a laugh. "But the dowager is a very attractive woman. And one I know you have taken notice of for some time, even if you try to pretend otherwise."

Callum pursed his lips. So his interest had been marked. Wonderful. "For Christ's sake, Lightmorrow, you're being disgusting. The woman's husband died eight weeks ago. I would be a complete scoundrel to have an ulterior motive in checking on her. Even if her husband weren't a friend."

Theo held up his hands but didn't even bother to look chagrined. "Of course, of course. Forgive me. Though I do think the world is sometimes better for a scoundrel."

"That's because you are one," Callum muttered.

Theo didn't argue, and his laughter echoed as he slapped Callum's shoulder again. "I won't torment you about this for now. Why don't we play a round of billiards, instead?"

Callum huffed out a breath, but he nodded and followed Theo from the room. His rake of a companion might give him shite about it, but Callum knew his motives were true when it came to Valaria. Attraction, if that's what there was, didn't have to mean bad behavior.

And it wouldn't. He could control himself.

CHAPTER 2

Although Valaria had fretted about her tea with Bernadette and Flora after she'd settled in the day before, it turned out there was no reason. She sat in Flora's parlor the following afternoon and felt...well, it was almost relaxed. Not entirely, but something close to it.

And she could admit, at least to herself, that it wasn't a feeling she'd had in a very long time. It helped that the two women were such good friends and that they could be talkative. In the span of an hour, Valaria had come to realize that though Bernadette was the oldest of their little threesome, she was also the most innocent. She blushed easily and would steer the topic away from points of discomfort if she saw them.

Flora, on the other hand, was breezy and open and playful. She made no secret the fact that she had been very happy in her marriage to the late Duke of Sidmouth, despite their vast thirty-year age difference. She smiled warmly when she spoke of him and seemed to have no regrets whatsoever.

Valaria tried not to hate her for that.

"We've prattled on for so long," Bernadette said at last, and reached across to grab Valaria's hand for a brief squeeze. "Tell us about yourself."

Valaria shifted and withdrew her hand slowly. "I'm not sure what there is to tell that you wouldn't already know. I'm a…a very recent widow, only a couple of months. My husband died in an accident." She swallowed. "A tragic accident."

"I recall when it happened," Flora said, her expression truly stricken. "I cannot imagine. And you found him? I'm so very sorry."

Valaria felt herself go a little numb as shifted into the responses she had trained herself to give over the last eight weeks. "Thank you."

Bernadette's brow wrinkled slightly, and for a moment she stared at Valaria. A little too hard, like she could see something Valaria didn't wish to share. Then she smiled. "Certainly we are far more than our pasts or husbands. Will you tell us of your likes? Your pursuits?"

That should have been a kinder topic. Valaria could see she meant it as one, and yet the pressure in her chest only seemed to increase. The fact was, she didn't have an answer. The last two years of her life since her marriage she had been…isolated. Her movements watched and judged, her pursuits limited and spoiled by the reactions of a man who…

No. She cut that thought off in her mind. She was not going down that path, not in front of these women who were practically strangers. She couldn't risk the reaction those thoughts sometimes created.

She forced a smile instead. "Oh, I think I'm fairly typical in my pursuits. I do needlepoint and read."

Flora tilted her head. "Do I recall you being proficient in…what instrument was it…oh Lord, why can't I recall? Everyone used to talk about how beautifully you played."

The reaction Valaria had been trying to avoid overwhelmed her and she blinked at the tears that filled her eyes. "The harp-lute. Yes, I once played. But I…I stopped."

"That's a shame," Flora said. "Bernadette is wonderful on the pianoforte."

"She is too kind. I am passable on the pianoforte. I never practice enough," Bernadette insisted with a smile.

Flora shot her a look before she continued, "And I sing." She hesitated. "Though I would not say well."

Bernadette laughed, but Valaria could sense the other woman reading her again. "Well, it is best we do not make a triplet, then. No use frightening the poor servants." She pushed to her feet. "Flora, speaking of reading, I have that book I borrowed from you. I finished it last night. We could go fetch it."

Flora's brow knitted. "I…fetch it now? Could that not wait?"

"I will forget if I don't return it to you now," Bernadette insisted with a meaningful stare.

Valaria swallowed. This was her opportunity for the escape she found herself craving. She got to her feet, as well. "You know, I should get back to my home. We are still settling in and there is much to be decided and worked on that requires my input."

"Of course, we understand," Bernadette said. "But I hope we will regularly make time to be together. There is a vast difference between being a young widow and a widow of advancing years. And though I do love our older neighbors and I hope we'll have a gathering soon where you can meet them all, I think I see a kindred spirit in you, Valaria. A person I'd love to call friend."

Valaria caught her breath at the genuine expression of welcome and acceptance on both the women's faces. She'd almost forgotten what that felt like. She nodded slowly. "I-I would very much like that."

Flora's wide smile was instantaneous and she caught both of Valaria's hands briefly. "Excellent news. Come, let us see you out."

Valaria allowed it, and after she'd waved her goodbyes, she could feel the two women watching her as she made her way back down the lane toward her own door. There was relief in the meeting ending. She was not yet fully trusting of her own reactions to people after so long separating herself.

And yet...there had been something so lovely about the time spent. It was certainly impossible not to like the two dowager duchesses, and to feel welcomed into their little circle. They had painted a picture for her of a future of friendship. Independence. A future where she might be, dare she hope, happy?

She found herself smiling at the idea as she turned into her drive, but the expression fell at what she found there. A carriage was parked before her door and she recognized the crest emblazed on the side. Blackvale. Which could only mean that Silas's best friend, the Duke of Blackvale, had come to call.

Without sending word ahead of his intention, of course. Without giving her a chance to say no. Because men like him, like her husband, they didn't think of these things. They didn't care.

She lifted her chin and stiffened her spine, hoping she could control the sudden pounding of her heart so he would not see her weakness and pounce upon it. She moved toward the door, but before she could reach it, it opened and Blackvale, himself, stepped out with Higgins at his heels.

"Yes, I understand. I don't know how that could have happened, but I shall—"

He said no more because he looked down the stairs at that moment and his gaze met hers. Valaria hated how she made note of his appearance. It was a failing she'd always had when it came to this man, even though she knew that physical beauty in a person meant less than nothing when it came to actual goodness. But he was undeniably handsome with his lean, lanky frame, well-defined jawline, light brown eyes and the mop of brown curls that always seemed rakishly imperfect.

"Valaria," he breathed, and then blinked. "Forgive me, Your Grace. I did not expect to see you."

She folded her arms. "I don't know why. You came to my home.

Unannounced, I might add. Why else would you do that except to see me?"

His brow wrinkled at her peppery tone. "I—yes, how foolish of me. I did intend to see you, but not unannounced. I sent word last night that I intended to call, but the message must have been misdelivered by my courier. He was taking care of several missives at once, you see, and perhaps he lost track of the one for you."

She worried her lip. That was a reasonable explanation, but not one she was ready to accept entirely. She knew the men of his kind too well. And she also knew not to upset them, so she forced herself to soften her tone. "Well, I suppose that must happen. As you can see, though, I was not at home."

He nodded. "Yes, your butler told me you were off to visit a few of the other dowagers here on the row. I hope you had a nice time."

He smiled and her heart did the strangest little patter that she forced herself to ignore. Nervousness would do that. It meant nothing else.

"What did you want here, Blackvale?" she asked.

"I was only checking in on you, Your Grace." He glanced back toward the house. "I did not have an appointment, so I know I may be intruding, but might we have a moment? Just to talk."

She glanced at Higgins, still waiting at the door. The butler met her stare evenly and looked at the ready to help her dismiss this man. That fact gave her a little strength. This was her house, not Silas's. She was in charge. If she let this man in, it was because she chose to allow him entry. And she could revoke that permission just as swiftly.

She examined Blackvale's face. He did look earnestly interested in talking to her. But he wasn't being lewd in his attentions, like some of Silas's friends had been in the weeks since his death. Making little comments about her needing company. She shuddered just thinking about it.

But Blackvale had never been like those other men. No, he'd been nothing but polite to her over the years. Kind when they spoke. He was a gentleman of the truest sense, at least by appearance and public behavior. For now, she would choose to believe that was his true character.

And if she let him in, she knew it was more likely this would be finished and she could ensure he didn't return.

"Your Grace?" he said softly.

She motioned toward the door. "Of course. Please, come in."

He followed her inside and she gave Higgins a slight smile. "I apologize for the trouble, Higgins." She glanced back at Blackvale. "Would you like tea, Your Grace?"

"Thank you, no. I think you just came from tea, so I would not trouble you."

She blinked. Silas would have *demanded* tea. Although he also would never have allowed her to take tea outside of the house, either.

She entered the parlor and Blackvale followed. She felt him at her back, the heat of him, the presence, even though he didn't get too close. Still, her heart beat faster and she gripped her hands into fists to stop them from shaking as she sat in one of the chairs and motioned for him to take the settee across from her.

He did so and then he just…looked at her. She shifted beneath that focused regard. "What was it you wished to discuss?"

He blinked as if he'd been pulled from deep thoughts. "Yes, of course. I only wanted to check that you were settling in well. I know you relocated only yesterday."

Her lips pinched. "And who told you about my situation?"

"Theo." He shook his head. "Forgive me, the Duke of Lightmorrow."

"I know who Theo is," she said softly, and to her surprise, there was a slight twitch to his cheek. "Lightmorrow is a gossip. Which must mean that people are talking about me."

Blackvale swallowed. "I would not sport with your intelligence and say that wasn't true, Your Grace. You know there has been interest in your situation since..." He hesitated and his voice cracked as he continued, "Since Silas's death."

For a moment, she felt a cacophony of reactions to his genuine emotions. First was surprise. Men didn't often show their hearts, and yet it was plain that Blackvale was truly pained by the loss of his old friend. Her second emotion was anger. Silas didn't deserve such loyalty and grief. Especially not from a man like this. One who seemed, at least outwardly, to be the opposite of her husband.

But the last emotion that washed over her was more surprising. She felt...envy. Jealousy that Blackvale could feel something so pure toward Silas. That he was not damaged by her husband's cruelty and could experience a normal progression of grief for his friend. Something so unlike the tangled and complicated path of her own.

"I suppose it makes sense that I am their current topic," she said, turning her face so he wouldn't see her emotions too plainly. They would reveal too much, she feared.

"I can understand why that focused regard would be difficult, but if it helps, I don't think anyone was saying anything in a negative light. Just that you had moved from the main house here to the Row." He frowned. "I am surprised that Franklin would insist on such a thing."

"No, you aren't," she said softly, and now she did meet his eyes. "You've known the new duke as long as you knew Silas. You know who and what he is. That he waited two months to overrun the household and push me out was an exercise in great restraint for him."

His nostrils flared. "He did it cruelly?"

She laughed, though she felt no humor. "It wasn't done kindly, at the very least."

Anger flickered across his handsome features and she found herself tensing against it, even though it didn't seem to be directed at her. "I will speak to him on your behalf, I will demand—"

She reached across the gap of space between them and briefly touched his forearm. There was a surprising crackle of awareness that ripped through her when she did, so she snatched her hand away. It had done its duty, at any rate, silencing him as he simply…stared at her.

"I appreciate your intentions," she said gently. "But moving from the home I shared with Silas looks to be a blessing, not a curse, in the end. There were too many memories there. Here, at least, I can begin to move on."

She knew he would interpret her words in one way, rather than the way she meant them. And his expression relaxed, as she hoped it would. He nodded. "I can understand that."

"I hope that answers your questions," she said, and glanced toward the door.

He followed her gaze and then his eyes returned to her. "Your Grace, I would like to offer my services."

She stared at him. "Services?"

"Yes," he said. "Silas was one of my dearest friends, after all. And since his heir is not behaving in the most gentlemanly fashion, I think the duty must fall to me to offer you support and ensure your comfort."

Valaria pursed her lips. "That's very kind, but I could not accept."

"Why not?" he asked, pushing but not cruelly. "I am of rank, I am connected to a great many people who were connected to Silas. During this difficult time, I could truly be of service."

"It would trouble you," Valaria said, but she could see that Blackvale was not convinced.

"I would *like* to be of service," he said, this time softer. With more pain. "Please. Let me."

One thing became crystal clear in that moment: the Duke of Blackvale was not going to be turned from this idea by her kindness. He needed it. And that meant she might have to try something sharper, something colder to turn him from the dangerous path he was now treading down.

A path that could lead to her ruin.

CHAPTER 3

Callum had felt Valaria's discomfort from the moment he saw her. It was plain on her face, in her gaze, which she darted away from his constantly. He'd written it off as grief, perhaps even her finding it difficult to see him when they had both been so close to Silas.

But now something else entered that remarkable blue-gray stare of hers. Something cold. Something hard. A wall came down between them in an instant and he found himself regretting that she felt a need to build it. Especially since he was almost certain that her reason for erecting it was...fear.

She feared him. And he had no idea why. Their past interactions had never been cruel. He could recall them all down to the very detail. So why would she be fearful?

"I assure you, Your Grace, there is no need for your *interference*," she said.

He flinched at her emphasis on that word before he pushed to his feet and moved away from her. Perhaps she only needed a moment to gather herself, to think about his offer of support. While he did so, he looked around the parlor. He'd been too distracted by her presence to do so earlier.

The room was sparsely decorated beyond the furniture, but it was a pleasant room. Sunny and comfortable. "It is a lovely home," he offered.

She drew in a long breath. "I am still settling in. But I believe it will be. Surely, though, you must see that my comfort has been seen to, Your Grace."

"But not by Franklin," he said slowly, facing her. "Was it your brothers?"

She folded her arms. "Why are you so determined to pry into my affairs?"

He wrinkled his brow. "I'm not."

"You very much are, asking all your impertinent questions."

"I'm only concerned about your well-being, Valaria."

She shook her head. "You ought not to call me that."

"You are correct. I apologize, Your Grace." He saw her flinch at the honorific. "It seems you like your appropriate address as duchess just as little."

She pushed from the chair and pivoted on him. "And none of those things are your business, *Callum*." She arched a brow as she said his first name. Hearing her say it was overwhelming, even if she meant it as a curse rather than a kindness. "I can be as impertinent as you."

"If you wish to call me by my given name, it troubles me little, Your Grace. I would like to be your friend, and many of my friends call me Callum."

"We aren't friends," she insisted. "You were Silas's friend. Now, perhaps you mean your intrusive behavior with the best of intentions. I will grant you that."

"With great difficulty, it seems," he said softly.

She ignored him. "I am comfortable in my new home. I am not sorry that Franklin has taken his place and will likely never intrude upon me again. As for my brothers, they will also not bother me."

He tilted his head. "When I inquired about them, it was to ask if you had their support."

Once again, a flash of pain washed over her lovely face. God, it was a lovely face. She cleared her throat. "I am fine, Your Grace. I need no support. Not from *anyone*."

She lifted her chin, her spine ramrod straight. She looked everything an icy queen. Except that her lower lip trembled ever so slightly. A tiny indication of her vulnerability. Of her emotion.

She motioned to the door. "I do thank you for calling, Your Grace. And for your sentiments and your offer of support."

She was dismissing him. And he moved toward the door and the foyer with her at his heels. But when they reached the exit, he turned and looked at her carefully. "I would like to call again, Your Grace."

Her nostrils flared and her fists tightened at her sides, but then she inclined her head. "There is no way I could refuse such a kind offer. But I do hope you'll make sure your courier actually delivers your request to call next time."

"I will," he assured her. "Good day, Your Grace."

"Good day, Your Grace," she repeated.

He stepped out into the warmth of the late spring air and drew a deep breath of it before he got into the waiting carriage. He pulled the curtain back as it began to move and saw her standing on the top step, watching him, arms folded and breeze stirring her brown locks around her cheeks.

He settled back against the carriage seat with a sigh. Perhaps he ought to have left it at that. The duchess did not wish his assistance and she had a right to her privacy.

But he knew something was amiss. And until he understood what it was and made certain she did not require his help, he felt compelled to press his assistance a little longer.

God help him.

~

As soon as Blackvale's carriage rumbled away on the street, Valaria turned on her heel and went back into the house, her breath short. She hurried upstairs and flung herself into her bedroom, slamming the door behind her. Stepping over trunks and boxes that had yet to be unpacked, she collapsed onto her bed where she stared up at the ceiling as she huffed out angry breath after angry breath.

Who she was angry at, well, that was debatable. She was angry at Callum, first and foremost. He had intruded upon her space, filling it with his presence and his questions. She was angry at Silas for creating a scenario where she couldn't just thank the man for his offer and never fear what his apparent persistence would reveal.

But mostly she was angry with herself. For not being able to manage Callum better. For being so impacted by his presence and his attention and his…his bigness that filled up her parlor and made it and her feel small in its presence. She was angry at herself for not being able to better put him off.

She pulled her pillow over her face with a cry of frustration.

"I beg your pardon, Your Grace."

Valaria jolted to a seated position and the pillow fell away, revealing her maid, Fanny, at the door which led to the adjoining dressing room. With any other servant, she would have been humiliated at being seen in such a state, but over the years Fanny had seen her in far worse. The two had formed a true friendship and so she didn't try to pretend Fanny hadn't seen exactly what she'd seen.

"Having a good scream out, are we?" Fanny pressed as she entered the room and picked up the pillow that had fallen to the floor.

"A bit of one, yes," Valaria admitted.

"Your tea with the other duchesses could not have been so very bad, could it?" Fanny asked with a little smile.

Valaria shook her head. "No, not at all. They were very kind and I was able to avoid any questions that might lead to the kind of follow-up you and I wish to avoid. I would have called it an almost complete success of a day until I got home. We had a visitor, Fanny."

The maid shifted. "From your tone and pale face, not one you wished to see. Tell me it is not the new duke, come to pry into places he'd best leave alone."

"Franklin gives not a whit about his late cousin," Valaria said with a wave of her hand, "and is likely too busy making terrible decor choices in my favorite parlor to think one bit about me or Silas." She pushed from the bed. "No, this visitor is far more dangerous, because, for some reason, he *did* care for the late duke. Did you ever encounter the Duke of Blackvale?"

Fanny hesitated.

"One of Silas's oldest friends," Valaria supplied. "The tallest, most frustratingly handsome man in London with a mop of hair that looks like someone's fingers have combed through it...perhaps not his own."

There was a light of recognition in Fanny's gaze. "Yes, I think I did pass through a room with you at some point and encounter the man you're describing. The late duke called him Cal, I think."

"And he called my husband Si." She clenched her hands at her sides. "Thick as thieves, they were. And Blackvale had a weakness to Silas that I could never explain. An inability to see his lesser traits." She rolled her eyes. "So all Callum recalls is the best of him. And he feels some obligation to look after me, he says."

Fanny swallowed. "I see. Do you think he is the type to ask...to ask certain kinds of questions?"

"Yes," Valaria burst out, fluttering her hands around her as she paced across the room. "He will do nothing but ask questions and intrude and see through me if I try to hide things."

"Can you put him off?" Fanny asked.

"I tried," Valaria said on a heavy sigh that felt like it came from the depths of her very soul. "But he intends to call again, he says. And I have no idea how to manage him."

"Then we'll have to figure that out," Fanny said, worrying her hands before her. "After all, there are a great many ways to control a man. Coldness, boring him, avoiding him..."

Valaria cleared her throat, and that interrupted Fanny's continued suggestions on how to bring a man to heel. "I can only hope I'm getting ahead of myself. He wished to check on my welfare. I ensured him I was fine. Now that he is relieved of what he considered a duty, perhaps he'll simply forget all about me. After all, he must have far more pressing concerns on his mind."

Fanny seemed to consider it. "Yes, we will hope he'll move on then. And if he doesn't, I promise you, Your Grace, together we will find a way to put him off." She smiled brightly, though Valaria wondered if that was just Fanny's way of comforting her. "Now, I had some thoughts about how we might best organize your gowns. Would you like to look at what I have in mind?"

Valaria nodded and followed her maid into the dressing room. But all the while they were discussing the ins and outs of how to organize her new life, she couldn't help but think of Callum.

And how he didn't seem the kind of man who would forget all about her and whatever promise he'd made in his head to protect her.

CHAPTER 4

Callum had never felt so out of sorts in his entire life as he had in the two days since his encounter with Valaria. She had made herself perfectly clear, after all, that she didn't want his assistance. And though he knew he would likely offer it again, he wasn't trying to bother her. And yet he kept thinking about her. He was thinking about her now as he strolled the aisles of Mattigan's Bookshop, trying to focus on the titles before him and not her.

"Blackvale," came a voice behind him. He pivoted and felt his smile fall. It was the new Duke of Gooding, Silas's cousin, who was saying his name. If there was a color that would describe the man before him, it was taupe. He was a forgettable man and had lived a forgettable life. Callum recalled him following Silas around as a boy, trying to make an impression, toadying about and glaring at Callum for being his cousin's closer friend. And tattling on them. Oh, how he'd love to get the two of them in trouble.

But today the man looked positively lit up. Callum's stomach turned at the idea that he was...*crowing* about his new position. One that had been "earned" by the death of someone Callum cared for.

"Gooding," he choked out, hating to hear that title on his tongue and not have it be Si. "I have not seen you since the funeral."

"Yes," Franklin said with a little sniff. "I suppose it has been that long. Thankfully I am out of mourning and back in the world. Finding my place."

Callum nodded slowly. "Yes, I've heard you took your place very recently, pushing your cousin's wife out to Kent's Row."

Discomfort washed over Franklin's visage and he shifted. "Well, it was time, wasn't it? She was settled well, bordering on too well."

Anger rippled through Callum and he clenched his fists at his sides. "Is there a level of compensation that you feel is too high for a woman who lost her husband before she even reached her thirtieth year? I hadn't heard of that. How telling."

Franklin let out his breath slowly. "That isn't what I meant. I was simply surprised to hear that you knew and wondered if she was talking about it, complaining. After all, she was the one who requested that she exit the ducal home."

Callum clenched his jaw. Valaria had already said that she had been pushed out and not with a great deal of finesse. He felt a swelling desire to press the subject. To confront this man who strutted around in his glee at his change of fortune that had caused so much pain to others. But then he thought of Valaria's concern that she was a topic of gossip. He would only create more of that by carrying on in this way.

So he bit his tongue and drew a breath to settle himself before he said, "I'm sure that is a great comfort to you."

"What good would it have done for her to stay?" Franklin asked with a shrug. "She only would have sat around in a parlor, reading books and counting out the days until she was in half-black and then color. She can more comfortably do that on the Row, I'd wager. At least she'll be surrounded by other ladies in the same position." He shook his head. "I was just about to go. I only wanted to say good day, Blackvale. I'm certain we'll see each other out and about much more now that I am duke and we are equals."

"I'm sure," Callum said, and arched a brow. "Good day."

Franklin huffed out a breath and hurried from the shop, leaving

Callum staring after him. The man was an arse. Not a villain, perhaps, but truly a fool.

Callum returned to the shelves and stared at the books before him. Franklin had said something about Valaria reading books in her mourning and at least Callum knew that she probably *would* pass some of the quiet time reading. He knew she liked the pastime —they had spoken of books once or twice in their brief conversations during Silas's life.

Perhaps that was one way he could help her, actually. It would not be proper for her to come out to a bookshop and browse, but she might like a few new titles. He moved to the front, where the proprietor, Mr. Mattigan, stood behind a raised counter.

"Ah, Your Grace," he said, his smile widening. "A pleasure to see you. Are you finding what you'd like or would you like to place a special order?"

"Perhaps both, depending on what you tell me next," Callum said. "What do you have that is brand new? Something sought after."

Mattigan's eyes lit up. "A man after my own heart. Let me show you!"

He stepped down to join Callum, drawing him back into the stacks. Callum smiled as he followed because this, at least, felt like it was actually doing something for Valaria. And picturing her reaction when she received the gift gave him far more pleasure than he liked to admit.

As a widow supposedly in mourning, Valaria had very little she was allowed to do in the eyes of Society. She could have small gatherings with friends, which she had begun to do every day with Flora and Bernadette since her arrival on the Row a few days ago. She was growing closer to them each time they spent time together. And if she walked in the park near her home or in one of the larger parks in the heart of London, people only gave her sad looks rather than judged her.

But those two things felt like her only options and she was beginning to go out of her skull at home. There were only so many times a person could reorganize a library or fiddle in their garden. She wanted to go to exhibitions and readings, to museums and salons! Hell, she would have accepted an invitation to a ball, and she *hated* a ball.

Of course, all that nervous energy was made worse by the fact that she was constantly waiting for Callum to show back up at her door with more offers of help. More of his broad shouldered, smoldering distraction that was so bloody dangerous.

But he had not made himself known in several days, and she supposed that he might have listened to her after all and marked his obligation to her as concluded. She ignored the faint sting of that as she paced into her study and looked at the letters she had to answer. She'd been leaving them for days. While she appreciated the kind words of distant friends and relatives, their assumption that she was deep in painful mourning only made her lack of feeling for Silas even more obvious and guilt-inducing.

She didn't deserve their comfort. And if any of them knew what she had thought, what she had done…they would withdraw that comfort immediately.

But there was no avoiding the duty, so she pushed her shoulders back and started toward the desk. Before she reached it, though, there was a light knock on the partly open door behind her. She turned to find Higgins there with a package wrapped in brown paper tied with a blue bow. "This just arrived, Your Grace," he said, coming into the room.

She motioned to the desk, her heart pounding. "A gift, how unexpected! Put it here, thank you!"

The butler did as he had been asked and then inclined his head and departed when Valaria said she needed nothing further. Once the door had been closed, she untied the ribbon and pushed away the paper wrapping. Her mouth dropped open. It was a stack of books, all new to her, but on the top was a highly sought-after copy of *Guy Mannering,* an adventure story with thieves and smugglers, as well as a struggle over inheritance. Everyone had talked about it relentlessly the last few months, though finding a copy was difficult since it continued to sell out at every store.

She clutched the book to her chest and as she did so a folded note fell onto the desktop. She picked it up and read her name in an efficient, masculine hand. She swallowed hard. Her first guess at the gifter could not be correct.

But when she unfolded the brief note, she found she was. The books were from Callum and he had written,

---

Valaria,

I recalled your love of reading and I hope that these will help pass the hours. I especially enjoyed Guy Mannering*. It is worth the excitement around it. Perhaps we can speak about it when next we meet.*

— BLACKVALE

She stared at the words and then the books. She could not think of a time that Silas had ever engaged in her love of reading. He only grumbled when she had her mind in the worlds that words created, but he would *never* have thought to give her a book. That Callum *had* felt…intimate in some way. Like he knew something about her, even though he didn't, not really. Plenty of people liked books.

"Still, it was very generous," she murmured, and let her finger run along the length of the silky ribbon that had once bound the package. It meant he was thinking about her, perhaps not with the same intrusive fervor that she occasionally found herself thinking of him. But she still shivered at the thought.

Slowly she took the new book over to the fire and sat down to read. The letters could wait, and so could her continued confusion over Callum. For now she would do as he suggested and escape into the world of adventure.

She would just have to decide later how to respond to his gift if and when she saw him again. And decide if she had to see it as a potential danger, or just a kindness that she hadn't had to earn, but had been given openly.

As dangerous as that idea was.

CHAPTER 5

It had been two days since she'd received Callum's gift of books and Valaria's anticipation of her next visit from him had only increased. Every time the bell at her door jingled, her heart leapt quite against her will. But he hadn't come. He hadn't written. He'd gone as silent as he had been in the few days before the delivery of his gift.

It seemed he had forgotten all about her, after all. That should have made Valaria happy. She ought to have been celebrating that fact and yet, as she sat on a picnic blanket in the park near Kent's Row with Flora and Bernadette, she couldn't help feeling...

Annoyed. Frustrated. Neglected.

"Oh, that is a very sour look," Flora teased gently, reaching across the blanket to touch her hand. "Do you not like the wine?"

Valaria blinked and smiled at her friend. "I'm sorry. I was wool-gathering, I admit. The wine is wonderful." She took a sip to accentuate the point. "This is just the first time I've been out with friends since Silas's death and I feel a little out of sorts."

Bernadette's expression softened. "Of course you do. Grief is difficult that way. It can strike at the most unexpected moments."

Valaria pursed her lips together. Let her friends think that her hesitation was grief and not that every time someone looked at her, she wondered if they could read guilt in her expression. That the black gown she was forced to wear to signify mourning felt like chains across her shoulders, pulling her down and down and down forever.

Let them think what would keep them from judging and hating her.

"It was so kind of you to invite me," Valaria said. "And this park is perfectly…" She trailed off without finishing her sentence because in that moment two men came walking up the path toward her and her party.

"Perfectly…?" Bernadette encouraged her to continue.

"Callum," Valaria choked out, and then blinked as she forced her attention back to the duchesses. "I'm sorry, I just caught a glimpse of an old friend of my late husband's, the Duke of Blackvale. He seems to be strolling our park with the Duke of Lightmorrow."

Bernadette straightened a little and moved her head to seek out the gentlemen through the groups of people blocking their view. "Lightmorrow?"

"Do you know them?" Valaria asked, and hated how her voice trembled as the men grew nearer and Callum's gaze fell on her. He lifted his brow and then tilted his hat before they crossed the lawn toward them.

"Oh, a little," Bernadette said, and her hands fluttered in her lap. "Lightmorrow's father and mine were neighbors in the country. I used to see him in the summer sometimes. I doubt he would recall me."

Valaria couldn't speak more on the subject for the men had reached them. The ladies all rose to greet them.

"Your Graces," Callum said with a bow that Lightmorrow repeated. "What a fine day for a picnic. Such a grand idea."

"It was, indeed. Good afternoon." Valaria managed half a curtsey out of propriety. "Do you know my companions? May I present the Duchess of Sidmouth and the Duchess of Tunbridge."

"Etta," Lightmorrow said as he stepped up to take Bernadette's hand and lift it to his lips briefly. "It's been an age."

Bernadette's cheeks were flame red now and she nodded. "It has been, Theo...Your Grace. A delight to see you."

He smiled at her, then turned his attention to Valaria and Flora. "And Your Graces. Good afternoon. Duchess Gooding, I am so sorry about your recent loss. I knew Silas a little."

Valaria wrinkled her brow as she nodded her thanks. There was something faintly in Lightmorrow's tone that told her he might not be entirely fond of her late husband. Which made her like him slightly more.

"What brings you to the park this fine afternoon, gentlemen?" Flora asked. "You are a long way from St. James or Hyde, which would seem close to both your homes."

Valaria sent Flora a side glance. Her friend was correct, of course. Valaria had just been too distracted by the arrival of the men to ponder it. Was this Callum's attempt to casually check on her again? To intrude ever so politely, despite her telling him she didn't need his help? Or to demand thanks for the books, which she hadn't told her friends about yet? She didn't know why she'd kept them a secret exactly.

Except she didn't want questions. And now he might create them.

Callum didn't look at Flora when he answered, but his light brown eyes settled on Valaria instead. "We have an old friend who lives in Greystown, which is just a short ride over. He mentioned the beauty of this park, and here we are."

Valaria pursed her lips. She didn't think he was telling the truth, but there was no easy way to call him on the lie. Not without creating a scene in front of her friends and even *more* questions from them.

"Well, we should leave you two to it then," she said instead, giving the sweetest smile she could muster before she turned away as a dismissal.

"That is much appreciated, but seeing you three here gives me the very best idea. I would love to host you all for supper tonight."

Valaria snapped her gaze back toward him at that suggestion. "I am in mourning, Your Grace."

It was said so sharply that both the duchesses and the Duke of Lightmorrow stared at her as if she'd sprouted a second head. Callum looked less troubled and continued to hold her gaze evenly and calmly.

"I realize that," he said gently. "But this would only be a small gathering of friends. Nothing very different than what you've done in the park today. Certainly not something untoward." He held up his hands. "But certainly I would never cause you discomfort if the invitation feels wrong to you."

Slowly Valaria looked at Flora and Bernadette. They were watching her with the same close, weighing expression that they'd each had when she first had tea with them upon her arrival to the Row. She knew whatever she said, the answer to Callum's invitation would create a reaction.

And that was why she feared she couldn't avoid saying yes. She would have to say she would go and then dance a fine line with him yet again.

"I would not speak for the others—" she began softly.

Bernadette was the one who spoke. "I don't think either Flora or I have plans tonight. Do we?"

Flora shook her head. "In fact, no. And I've heard you have a wonderful cook, Your Grace," she said, directing her comment to Callum. "Is it true you stole him out from under Prinny, himself?"

"A gentleman never tells," Callum said. He winked at Flora when he said it and that created a pit in Valaria's stomach, especially when her friend laughed in response.

Valaria shifted. Since both her friends had said yes, it was difficult to refuse. After all, her lack of appearance for mourning was more meant to restrict her from public events. A supper with friends was more than acceptable, especially after two months of "grief".

"If Flora and Bernadette can attend, I...would...be happy to do the same," she ground out through clenched teeth.

Callum's expression lit up. "Wonderful." Valaria waited for him to mention his gift of the books, but he didn't. He simply tipped his hat and said, "I look forward to seeing you all there."

"As do I," Lightmorrow said with a smile for the group. "Now come along, Callum, we've troubled these ladies enough. Good afternoon, Your Graces." His gaze drifted to Bernadette. "Etta."

"Good day," Bernadette and Flora said in unison.

Valaria pursed her lips and watched as the two dukes made their way off together, talking as they went. They'd gone a short distance when Callum looked back over his shoulder at her. His gaze found hers and then he smiled before he continued along his route away.

She huffed out a breath despite herself and plunked back down on the picnic blanket to retrieve her wine, which she drank in one heady gulp.

She looked up to find Flora and Bernadette staring at her. She stiffened. Damn the Duke of Blackvale. Not only was he creating discomfort for her, he was threatening this tenuous friendship she was building with Flora and Bernadette.

The two women retook their places on the blanket, and Bernadette refilled Valaria's wine as Flora reached out to cover her hand.

"Is everything...well?" Flora asked carefully. Like Valaria was glass and could be broken too easily. Right now she felt like it. And she couldn't afford to be glass. She had to be a steel sword, a brick-and-mortar wall.

"Of course," she lied with a smile.

"You were a bit...sharp with the Duke of Blackvale," Bernadette said, as carefully as Flora had addressed her. "Do you not like him?"

Valaria swallowed. There was a question. Did she *like* Callum? She'd known him two years—he had been a constant presence around her home before Silas's death. She'd watched him, at first with anxiety and eventually with interest on how such a steady man could remain friends with such a volatile one. And then he'd come into her life as a widow so very unexpectedly. Made himself a part of her existence in ways she didn't like to think about.

"I really don't know him well enough to like or dislike the duke," she said when it was clear her silence was creating as much a problem as her words would. "He was Silas's friend, not mine. I am...surprised he has taken such an interest in me. I doubt we spoke five times in the years I was married, beyond a polite 'good day' and a little small talk about the weather and the roads and...and books."

Except she remembered each one down to the detail. Apparently he did, as well.

"I think it's kind of him to worry after your well-being," Flora said with a sigh. "I know my dear Stuart would have been pleased to know his friends or family gave a whit about me." Her face fell. "Which they most certainly do not. If the Duke of Blackvale wants to stand in your late husband's stead and be certain you are well, that seems like a good thing."

Valaria stared at the two women across the blanket from her. They were so kind and after months...years...of isolation and silence. They welcomed her in, perhaps at first because of whatever past kindness she had done for Flora, but also because they seemed to genuinely like her. That was such a rare thing in her recent life that she suddenly wished to do something foolish.

She wanted to tell them the truth.

The truth of her marriage, the truth of her broken heart, the truth of the fear that clouded her every dream and so many of her waking moments. She wanted to spill herself onto the picnic blanket and finally be free of the words that seemed to echo in her head constantly.

She blinked the foolish thought away. If she did that, she wouldn't feel better. No, everything would be worse. Not only would these women hate her afterward, but she would threaten her own life and the lives of others. So she swallowed the truth, choked it back like she had for so long and forced a smile.

"I realize the Duke of Blackvale seems to have my best interest at heart. I do...I do appreciate that, I assure you. But I think there is another issue for us to discuss which is more pressing than my minimal relationship with Blackvale. Isn't that right...*Etta*?"

Bernadette shifted on the blanket as Flora grinned at her and topped off her wine.

"That is true, Bernadette. I didn't know you were so well acquainted with the Duke of Lightmorrow! Do tell."

"There is nothing to tell," Bernadette insisted. "As I said earlier, Theo's father and mine had adjoining estates in the country and we knew each other as children. I was sometimes called Etta then, by my grandfather. I'm surprised he recalls it at all, since he only could have met the man once. I'm certain he was just being polite."

"I'm certain," Flora giggled.

Bernadette's cheeks were flaming and she swatted lightly at Flora. Valaria couldn't help but laugh with them, even though she felt a little on the outside of their easy rapport. After all, if Bernadette wished to look at Lightmorrow through batting lashes, she could. If Flora wanted to push them together, which was definitely what her playful expression implied, that was fine, as well. They were both free in a way Valaria wasn't. And that had nothing to do with the long months of mourning left ahead of her. She would likely never feel free enough to flirt or play like that.

Her future might not be entirely lonely. She felt certain she would be friends with these two women, and she could fill her life with music and art and other pursuits that pleased her now that there was no one standing over her shoulder to stop her.

But there were some doors that would be...would *always* be...closed.

~

Callum paced the floor of the parlor, pausing only occasionally at the fire to stare at the crackling flames. He pivoted to start his march across the room once more when Theo cleared his throat.

"For God's sake, you'll wear a path in the carpet." He held out the drink Callum had abandoned on the sideboard a short time before. "Sip your drink and try not to act like a lost puppy."

Callum glared at him and took the glass. "I'm not a lost puppy."

Theo tilted his head. "This woman has truly gotten under your skin," he murmured. "How? You barely know her."

Callum let out a long sigh. For a moment he considered playing like he didn't know who Theo was talking about, but it would only drag out the inevitable. And if there was anyone he could trust to discuss a testy subject, it was this man.

"I think you know I always felt an attraction to her," he said slowly. "Valaria. I suppose that made me a bastard."

"You didn't act on it," Theo said with a shrug. "*That* would have made you a bastard. Though perhaps Silas wouldn't have given a damn."

Callum pursed his lips. Most of the time he might have defended Silas's memory against the arrows Theo seemed determined to sling. But in this case, he couldn't.

"Silas made no secret of his affairs, no," he agreed. "I tried to talk about it with him a few times, but he made the point that many a man of rank has dalliances on the side. And he was…not wrong."

Of course, it had all felt wrong. Callum couldn't have imagined stepping out on Valaria. On any woman he called wife. When he took those vows, he would take them with a serious intent. His fun outside his own home would be finished. And he hoped he would find a bride who desired him enough that there would be no sense of loss in that fact.

"Do you think that's why she is so reticent to have your help?" Theo asked. "Or your presence at all? Does she know about Silas's mistresses?"

Callum pondered that question. "I don't know. I suppose she might. And if she blamed his cronies for his behavior and included me in their ranks, perhaps it would explain why she wants me to stay away." He shook his head. "I see that she's in pain and I want to ease it."

"That isn't your duty," Theo said gently. "Friend to her late husband or not."

Callum shrugged, and was happy when his butler, Morris, entered the room. "The Duchesses Tunbridge, Sidmouth and Gooding, Your Graces."

He stepped away and the ladies entered the room one by one, looking lovely in their finery. Valaria came in last, her gown a black satin that flowed over her curves. There were a few touches to it, including stitched flowers on her shoulder and the hem.

"Welcome, ladies," he said, shaking off his initial reaction to having her here. "May I pour some drinks for you before supper?"

He moved to the sideboard and poured sherry for the Duchess of Sidmouth and madeira for the Duchess of Tunbridge. When he turned his attention to Valaria, she bent her head. "Nothing for me, thank you."

Without saying more, she stepped away, walking to the double doors that led to the terrace and staring through their glass as if she were planning her escape.

Callum pursed his lips and watched her, even as he joined Theo and his other two guests. Theo's suggestion that perhaps Valaria avoided him because she thought him involved in some way with Silas's infidelity kept returning to his mind. Had she loved his late friend so deeply that her pain could not allow her to be protected by him?

And if he could speak to her on the subject, would he be able to ease her mind? After all, with Franklin puffed up on his own new power and her brothers apparently estranged from her, she might need assistance in the future. He wanted to offer it to her.

He returned his attention to the group and found Theo watching him, one eyebrow arched in playful accusation. He glared back. Theo might believe otherwise, but his attraction to Valaria was not in any way at play in his behavior. He could separate his mind from his cock, even if his friend wasn't capable.

"I think I will take a bit of air before supper," Valaria said from the terrace. Without waiting for a response, she stepped out of the room.

For a moment the other two duchesses exchanged a look, but they seemed to resolve any hesitations about what to do regarding Valaria, for they both returned to careful conversation with Theo. Callum waited a moment, staring at the door where she had gone, anxiety and drive to follow rising up in his chest. Finally, he couldn't deny it anymore.

He huffed out a breath and moved toward the terrace. "I-I will go make certain Her Grace is well."

He thought he heard Theo say his name, but he ignored it as he stepped outside and pulled the doors shut behind him. He had always loved this terrace. It was wide, wrapping around most of the back of the house so that someone who exited a parlor at one end could meet with someone who had exited from another. Certainly assignations had occurred out here because of that access, but he wasn't thinking of that as he peered around the darkness for Valaria. No small feat considering her black dress would help her easily melt into the shadows.

He could not find her and at last said, "Valaria?"

There was silence and he repeated her name. With a sigh, she stepped from the space at the corner of the terrace and folded her arms. "What do you want, Your Grace?"

He wrinkled his brow. "Were you…hiding from me?"

She pursed her lips. "I came out here for a moment alone."

He looked back toward the parlor he had exited. Inside he could see the duchesses still engaged in conversation with Theo. He could go back, but this was an opportunity to resolve at least some issue between him and Valaria.

So he moved half a step toward her and tried to ignore her sharp intake of breath when he did so.

"Have I done something to offend you, Your Grace?" he asked softly.

"No," she answered swiftly. Too swiftly, considering she also turned her face so that her expression was hidden again by shadow.

"Valaria," he said, more sharply. A demand rather than a request.

She seemed to understand that because she narrowed her gaze at him. "I don't understand what you want from me, Callum. Is it thanks for your gift? Will that appease you?"

He stared. "I did not send you the books so that you would thank me," he explained slowly. "I did it entirely for your pleasure. If I was wrong in doing so, I apologize."

She bent her head. "I…did enjoy them. I read *Guy Mannering* in but a few hours. I was entirely engrossed and that was…well, it was very nice."

"Good. I'm glad."

"And?"

"And nothing," he insisted, gentling his tone. "I don't want anything from you."

She didn't look like she believed him when she glanced up at him through a hooded gaze.

He shifted and continued, "I understand why trusting me might be difficult on some level. Silas was imperfect, I-I know that. I know he might have done some things that hurt you—"

She skittered backward, her blue-gray eyes wide in the faint light from the house. "What do you mean? What do you know?"

He sucked in a quick breath. So she *was* hurt by Silas's affairs. And for a brief moment, he hated his friend for causing that upset. "I know that some men cannot be satisfied only by what they have at home. Even when they should be in every way. Even when what they have is so…so perfect."

Her mouth dropped open and her gaze flitted to his lips briefly. But then the wall came back down and her expression turned cold.

She folded her arms again, rebuilding that shield she so desperately wanted to keep between them.

"You don't know anything about our relationship, Callum. Know that is a fact that will *never* change." She lifted her chin. "You want to interfere with me, I suppose out of either kindness or a masculine need for control over everything. The motive doesn't really matter, because the outcome will be the same. I have spent a lifetime under the thumb of one man or another and I will never return to that life."

She moved toward him and she would have looked so strong but for the fact that her lower lip was trembling ever so slightly. He caught his breath at the little hint of her vulnerability.

"I did enjoy the books, but please don't misconstrue that to mean that I want your...presence. I don't want anyone's presence. I don't want..." Her breath hitched. "I don't want..."

A tear suddenly trickled from her eye. She gasped and lifted her fingers to it, a look of almost shock on her face. He pulled the clean handkerchief from his pocket and moved toward her, close enough that he could hand her the cloth. Too close, now that he was here and he could feel the faint hint of her body heat. She stared up at him, eyes sparkling in the light. And he wanted her.

Because he'd always wanted her. Bastard that he was.

"Valaria," he said softly as he took her hand and tried to make it only about comfort.

She wasn't wearing gloves and neither was he, so when he touched her, it was the first time his skin had ever brushed hers. It was everything he'd ever hoped and dreamed about. Like the softest silk, and she caught her breath as her fingers clenched against his briefly.

"I didn't mean to cause you pain," he whispered, moving even closer. Now her skirts brushed against his boots and her breath stirred against his chin as she stared up at him. "I'm sorry."

She looked at him like she hardly understood those words. Like she'd never heard them before. And perhaps she hadn't. Silas had never been one for apologies.

"Callum," she murmured, and then shook her head, as if there were no words.

He found himself lowering his mouth toward her and realized she was tilting hers up. His mind screamed at him to stop. To be prudent and right, but he couldn't listen. Couldn't focus on anything except her, only her, always her.

And his mouth took hers and it was everything.

CHAPTER 6

Valaria's lips were soft beneath Callum's, so very soft. For a moment he just reveled in the touch of them. But then she made a soft sound at the back of her throat and slightly parted them, which changed everything. He wrapped an arm around her waist, drawing her against him gently as he traced the crease of her lips. God, she was sweet, like honeyed wine. He never wanted to stop drowning in that flavor.

She placed her hands against his chest, palms flat, and for a moment he thought she might push him away. He felt the flutter of hesitation in the flex of her fingers, but then she tilted her head just a fraction and darted her tongue out to touch his.

He was trying not to lose control. He had already gone way too far, but this woman had been a drug in his system from the first moment he touched her. And he was beginning to be pulled under by the drive to have more and more of her.

He splayed his fingers against her back and took a little more, their tongues dueling in an endless dance of pleasure and desire and heat. She made that soft sigh again, and the sound of her pleasure put his body on edge like it had never been before.

But before the kiss could advance further, before even more

imprudence could reign, her hands fisted against his chest and she did push. He immediately released her, stepping back as he panted in heavy breaths. They stared at each other in the dim light that filtered onto the terrace from the house.

She shook her head, her eyes wide and wild. Her mouth opened and shut a few times, like she was seeking something to say. But then she pushed past him and walked back across the terrace, back to the door into the parlor where their friends waited. She never looked back.

"Fuck," he muttered, and crossed to the terrace wall to look out over the garden below. His entire body shook and he fought to regain some small semblance of control.

Control he had thrown away and now...well, now there would be consequences. Not the least of which was the guilt he felt in taking advantage of a woman in mourning, his late best friend's wife. What kind of man did that make him?

"The worst kind," he grumbled, and moved toward the parlor. He looked through the window as he approached. Valaria had gone inside and she now stood with the others. She had a glass of madeira in her hand, she seemed untroubled as she spoke to Theo and the duchesses.

But when he entered the room, she glanced over her shoulder at him. Her cheeks paled, her pupils dilated, her hands shook ever so slightly. He had done that.

And he hated himself for it.

Valaria had never thanked Silas for much, but tonight she felt in his debt. After years of putting on a mask and pretending not to feel fear or pain or heartbreak or anger, she was very good at it. And so she'd been able to mask her panic...and other feelings...as she shared supper with the group. It hadn't been easy...but she'd done it.

And now she sat at the table, the empty dessert plates not yet taken away, and she knew her face was unreadable. But her mind was racing, just as it had been for the last hour.

She'd kissed Callum. Well, he'd kissed her? It was hard to recall anything but the feel of his lips against hers, the taste of him when he pressed his tongue to hers, the way his arms had felt around her.

It would have been easier if it had all been distasteful. If she could hate him for taking such liberties. But she didn't. He had been kind to her, he had touched her and she had...*wanted.* Wanted the kiss, wanted the touch...wanted him. It had been years since she'd felt that tug of desire. Since the beginning of her marriage, before Silas had revealed all his true colors and made her loathe him. And even then, the wanting had been a faint tug, not this cascading waterfall of need that had thrown her off guard and made her want to run away so that she wouldn't be so off kilter.

"What do you think, Valaria?"

She blinked as she realized that Bernadette was speaking to her and that the entire table was watching her, expecting some kind of response to whatever was being asked.

"I apologize," she said, and didn't have to force her blush. "I have been caught woolgathering, I fear. What was the question?"

"Charades, Your Grace," the Duke of Lightmorrow said, his tone gentle. "We were debating what activity would be best for after supper entertainment and Etta was asking your opinion on charades."

Valaria cast her glance again at Callum. He was gliding a finger along the rim of his glass, his posture as uncomfortable as her own felt. If she had to go into a parlor with him and play games...oh, she wasn't certain she wouldn't combust with all the tangled emotions going on inside of her.

She sighed. "I do love charades. Though I wouldn't say I'm the best at them. But...I'm afraid I must be the worst guest. I have not been out in company for so long, I'm feeling a bit overwhelmed.

And it's led to a headache. I would not ask that the other duchesses leave the fun, but I think I should return home."

Flora was seated on her left and she caught Valaria's hand. "Oh dearest, you should have said something earlier. Being out in company must be complicated for you. Mourning is not an easy thing. We shall escort you home. I'm sure the gentlemen understand."

Callum's mouth tightened slightly, but he inclined his head. "Of course we do."

Lightmorrow nodded. "We shall be bereft without your feminine company, but somehow we will soldier on until the next time we are together."

Bernadette laughed softly at his playful words, but Valaria couldn't bring herself to do the same. She hoped that would be taken as a reaction to her pretended headache and that no one would feel the tension now coursing between her and Callum.

"Let me have your carriage fetched," Theo said, casting a quick look down the table at Callum. He got up and the ladies did the same, which made Callum move to his feet, as well.

He cleared his throat as he came around the table toward her. "Let me escort you, Your Grace."

He held out a hand to her and she could hardly breathe as she thought of how those same outstretched fingers she had felt clenching against her back as he held her so gently such a short time before.

She swallowed and took his hand, allowing him to tuck her fingers into the crook of his arm as they followed the others from the dining room. He moved slowly, and soon they were a few strides behind the others.

"I'm...I'm sorry, Valaria," he said softly, his voice rough.

She shook her head. "It...we ought not speak of it."

He stopped at the entrance to the foyer where the others were gathered, chatting as they waited for the carriage the ladies had traveled in together.

"I think we must." He released her and turning to face her straight on.

She stared up at him, into those pale brown eyes that were so filled with guilt and desire. Such a potent mix. Such a dangerous one. And yet the fact that she saw that he still wanted her was…thrilling.

"But not tonight," she said.

He shook his head and glanced toward their friends. "No. Most definitely not. Tomorrow?"

She shut her eyes briefly. There was no way to avoid the conversation. And perhaps this could play in her favor. If this man felt guilt for betraying his late friend, would that not end his drive to take care of her? Protect her?

A little regret stung her at that thought, but she pushed it aside. It was for the best. A man like the Duke of Blackvale would find out her secrets eventually if he stayed near her. She couldn't let that happen.

"Tomorrow is fine," she choked out. "Call on me at eleven. I'll be ready for you."

The carriage pulled up then and she moved away from him, feeling his presence at her back with every step. He took her hand to help her into the carriage behind Bernadette and Flora, his gaze holding steady with hers when she settled into her seat. His warmth still tingling her palm even when he released her and shut them in for the short ride back to Kent's Row.

She drew her first full breath since the kiss once they began to move.

"Seeing how rattled you are, I think we ought not to have pushed for this night out," Flora said, taking her hand. Valaria almost wished she hadn't, because it lessened the impact of Callum's touch.

"It wasn't your fault," Valaria said. "I assure you."

"Did…did something happen on the terrace when Blackvale went to check on you?" Bernadette asked softly.

Valaria tensed. And there it was. She had tried so hard to hide what she felt, but she'd failed. She sighed. "It's nothing. Just my…my mistakes have come to roost."

Flora's brow lowered in concern. "I realize we are new friends, but I hope you know you can talk to us about whatever is going on."

Valaria looked at them, both leaning forward on the edge of the carriage seat across from her, looking nothing but truly concerned for her welfare. What a strange thing to find when she'd spent the last two years of her life feeling so isolated.

And she wanted, in that wild moment, to tell them everything. To fall into their friendly arms and lighten her burden. But she couldn't, just as she hadn't been able to when she felt that desire to connect with these two women earlier. After all, the lightness would be temporary and it would only lead to more anguish for all involved.

"I-I'm being silly. Overwrought thanks to a headache," she whispered. "Don't concern yourselves."

Bernadette reached out and gently covered her hand. "One day, perhaps, you'll be more comfortable to share your troubles. But until then, is there anything we can do to help?"

The carriage was slowing as it reached the Kent's Row neighborhood. Valaria placed her free hand on top of Bernadette's and smiled at her, then at Flora. "Not yet. But perhaps soon?"

Her willingness to allow for a future where she might let them in seemed to appease her friends. Flora mercifully changed the subject to the delicious soup that had started their meal earlier in the evening, and Valaria relaxed as much as she could when thoughts of Callum haunted every corner of her mind.

Tomorrow would come, and sooner than she hoped for it. She had no idea what would happen when she was alone with him and they talked openly about the shocking kiss that she could still feel against her tingling lips.

But once she had, she might need friends at that point. For advice…and for protection from the desires she didn't want to feel and the man who inspired them.

~

Callum stepped back into the foyer and found Theo waiting for him, arms crossed against his chest, one eyebrow arched in judgment.

"What did you do?" he asked before Callum could even close the door.

Callum sighed. "Something I think you would approve of. Rake that you are."

Theo's eyes went wide. "I can think of nothing you could have done that would be rakish while we were all gathered at a supper together. Unless…" He trailed off. "You didn't."

Callum swallowed. God, he hated how observant Theo was. It was unforgiveable in these circumstances when he didn't *really* want to have to confess what he'd done. "What is your guess? I'll tell you if you're right."

"You were outside with the Duchess of Gooding for a short time. But long enough to…did you kiss her?"

"Goddamn it, Theo," Callum grunted as he returned to the parlor where they'd started their night and poured himself a far too large glass of whisky.

"I'm right, though. I can see it in your eyes." Theo shook his head as he entered the room behind him. "What were you thinking?"

"I wasn't thinking. I was acting like a rake and a rogue and a bastard." He downed half the liquor in one heated swig and took a moment to catch his breath from it. "Fucking hell."

"How was it?" Theo asked.

Callum slammed the drink down. "That's…that's not a question that I should—"

"Oh, come now. You've had eyes for that woman for years. You acted like it was fine and rational and that you could ignore those desires, but here you are. So stop trying to be a monk with no heat in your blood and be honest."

"It was..." Callum pursed his lips. "It was lovely. And very wrong. You saw her face when she left."

"Yes, she was rather off kilter. Which must mean she enjoyed it too."

Callum didn't want to consider that option. It was a little too tempting. "Or she was so offended she could hardly stand to be in a room with me."

Theo pondered that briefly and then shook his head. "No, if she was offended she wouldn't have stayed after you did it. She would have slapped you, which I assume she didn't."

"No," Callum agreed quietly, thinking of how Valaria's lips had moved beneath his own. How she'd made such a soft exhalation of pleasure that made him burn and ache for her. "But whether or not the lady liked it or I liked it isn't the material point, is it? She is only at the beginning of her mourning period, I was her husband's close friend. It was wrong of me. And that is what I'll tell her when I call on her tomorrow morning."

"You're...calling on her tomorrow," Theo repeated slowly. "You're going to her home to be alone with her and talk to her about kissing her on the terrace."

God's teeth, when his friend said it that way, it sounded like a very bad idea. It sounded like a situation ripe for further seduction.

Callum pushed away thoughts of that and straightened his shoulders. Like he could physically make himself behave. "I am going to apologize for liberties I've taken and see if I can make amends."

Theo was quiet a long moment, his gaze flitting over Callum's face for what felt like far too long. Then he shrugged. "There is nothing more I'd like to do than tease you further about this, but you have such a hangdog expression that there's hardly any fun in it."

"I feel guilty because I should," Callum said softly. "I have betrayed a long-held friendship and crossed a line with a woman who already mistrusts me."

"You said she enjoyed it. Did she kiss you back?" Theo asked.

Callum could have dodged the question for a while, but he knew Theo. This wouldn't stop until he had the answers he demanded.

"Yes," Callum grumbled.

Theo nodded slowly. "You know, not every lady actually mourns during a mourning period. I've personally helped several widows through their first year or isolation."

Callum swallowed. "As fascinating as your utter debauchery is, Theo, I doubt I'm going to be in that position. She could barely accept a few books from me."

"You gave her a...a *gift*?" Theo said, and now his eyes were wide.

"As I said, I made a mistake during a moment of high emotion." Callum waved his hand and hoped it would dismiss the entire subject. "I'm assuming it was the same for her. We will discuss it and move on. End of story."

"But—"

"End of story," he repeated, and set his now-empty glass on the sideboard. "Please."

Theo held up his hands in surrender. "So you say. I'll honor that. But I hope you know you can talk to me about this again if you need to do so."

For a moment, Callum considered saying something glib. It would have made him more comfortable. But then he thought of all the times he wished he'd been more honest or more direct with Silas, and instead he reached out to squeeze Theo's shoulder.

"I appreciate it. I do." He released his friend. "Now, what do you say we go play a hand of cards since the ladies have left us early?"

"An excellent notion," Theo said, and slung his arm around Callum's shoulders as they left the room together.

As Callum tried not to think of things Theo made him imagine when it came to his conversation with Valaria the next day.

CHAPTER 7

Valaria paced her parlor at ten forty-five the next day, watching her clock tick mercilessly slowly. She had been ready for an hour and had tried to fill her time first by organizing her small library, then by reading...but it was all for naught. She couldn't focus or pretend that she wasn't desperately nervous to see Callum.

Or that the butterflies in her stomach were only because of that nervousness. She was also...*thrilled* at the idea of seeing him. She had thought of nothing but the weight of his mouth on hers since the previous night. And it didn't matter how dangerous that desire was, how deeply it might damage her. She still relived his kiss with a hunger that frightened her.

She glanced at the clock again. Had only three minutes passed? She was going to expire from anticipation before she was done.

She pivoted to pace her parlor again and found that Higgins had stepped into the entryway. "I beg your pardon, Your Grace," he said. "But the Duke of Blackvale has arrived."

Her heart began to pound and she clasped her hands before herself in the hopes her servant wouldn't see that she'd begun to tremble almost out of control. "I see. You may show him in."

Higgins nodded and departed, reappearing but a moment later to announce Callum. She heard his title, watched as he stepped around her butler and into the room. Dear God, he was handsome. So tall and lanky and perfectly pulled together. And that jawline, she so wanted to trace it with her fingertips. But she felt like she was behind glass. Everything seemed muffled and off kilter.

"Your Grace?"

She blinked as Higgins' voice brought her back to reality. "I'm sorry?"

"Would you like tea or some other kind of refreshment?" he repeated.

"Tea, Your Grace?" She glanced at Callum.

He shifted slightly, his gaze focused on hers. "Whisky?" he returned with a nervous chuckle.

She flinched. Callum might mean that as a playful quip, but she couldn't help but think of Silas and his whisky. Silas and what happened after too many whiskies. She shook her head at Higgins. "Nothing for now, thank you."

The butler departed the room and Callum shifted. "I apologize for the joke. It's obviously far too early in the day for a drink. I'm… er…a little tense."

"You?"

He tilted his head. "You think it hard to believe?"

She stared at him, drinking in the lean length of his body, the casual confidence with which he always held himself. His handsome face with all those fascinating angles had certainly caused more than one stir amongst ladies in a ballroom or parlor. And now that she'd felt the brush of his lips to hers, she had to imagine he'd certainly kissed many women before her. He would kiss a great deal more once he'd long forgotten her and whatever obligation he'd convinced himself he had to her.

She looked back at the door, which was still open. "I…I don't know my new servants well enough to be comfortable having this conversation so openly." She motioned for the terrace doors. "Would you take a walk in the garden with me?"

He inclined his head. "It's a fine day. I would be pleased to walk with you, Your Grace."

She shifted at the softness to his tone. The way he moved toward her, as if he would offer his arm. She ignored it and moved to the terrace doors to open them into the surprising warmth of the late spring day. He said nothing, but followed her out and down the short steps which led to her small garden below.

Yes, this seemed a safe option for their conversation. They wouldn't have to talk openly in front of someone who might whisper her secrets, but they wouldn't be in a closed room that would certainly feel too confined after their previous encounter. Out here she could control him.

She glanced at him, walking beside her, hands clasped behind his back. No. No one would ever control this man. But she could control herself. And that would have to be enough.

~

Callum could feel the tension coursing through Valaria even though she was trying to pretend to be relaxed and comfortable. It was in the stiffness of her shoulders, the way she kept fluttering her hands from one position to another as they walked through her garden.

He drew a breath. "It's a pretty place."

"What?" She looked around. "I-I suppose it is. I've been so consumed by organizing inside, I haven't spent much time out here."

She stopped, and together they took in their surroundings. The well-maintained crushed gravel pathway was buffeted by lush green grass and bushes and lined by daffodils and tulips that had likely only bloomed in the last day or so, thanks to the warmer weather.

"It *is* lovely," she murmured, almost more to herself than to him.

But then she glanced at him, though she didn't meet his gaze. "I-I do find it hard to believe that you would be nervous around me."

He realized she was answering his question from back in the parlor and drew a long breath. "And why is that?"

"Because you are well-known for your prowess with women," she said, and her cheeks flamed with high color. He couldn't help but mark the prettiness of that pink even though her answer troubled him.

"Well-known? I…who said that?"

"Silas," she burst out, clenching her hands at her sides. "He made a point to ramble on about it endlessly any time you came up in conversation."

He wrinkled his brow, hit by both confusion at this answer and his irritation that followed. Why in the world would Silas bring up Callum bedding women to his wife? A lady. A lady who clearly didn't want to hear those stories, true or not. It seemed untoward and rude to her to do so. Plus, it had clearly colored her view of him.

She sighed. "So how can one little kiss with me make you nervous?"

"There is a vast difference between being a little rakish now and then with ladies who appreciate a man who plays that role and kissing the widow of one's best friend just months after his death." He shook his head. "To—to corner her on a terrace to kiss her after you told her you wanted nothing from her."

She stared up at him, her expression confused now. "You—you act as though you forced me."

He shifted. She had kissed him back, but that didn't necessarily mean he hadn't gone too far. "Did I?" he whispered.

She shook her head immediately. "No, Callum. You didn't."

He tensed. That was the first time she had used his given name with any warmth and he felt the power of it work through him. There was sudden tension in the air, very much like the tension that had hung between them the previous night. And in that moment he saw a flutter of...desire cross her lovely face. Desire that called to his own.

And it was so very wrong.

He took a step back, creating the space he hadn't been strong enough to create before. "I-I was still incorrect in how I handled myself," he said, to himself as much as to her. "You are in mourning. Si was my friend."

"And he's dead," she said, more sharply than he had expected. "There is no betraying him anymore. If there ever was."

"What does that mean?"

The desire was gone, replaced with the fear that she had always exhibited when he approached her. Like she had gone too far. She glanced away from him. "You are correct that we shouldn't have kissed. It was a lapse in judgment, one I must never repeat, Your Grace."

He swallowed. "I will admit to you that I am more disappointed than I should be." Her eyes widened, but he continued before she could say anything. "But I will respect your wishes, Your Grace."

"You will?" Her voice was so small, so laced with disbelief that he drew back. Was she so accustomed to her desires being stomped over that she couldn't believe he would allow her those boundaries?

Or was her disbelief solely about him?

Either way, he didn't like that she had no faith she would be listened to.

He stepped even farther away. "I'll give you some space now," he said. "Because I fear I've taken up too much of your time as it is. Thank you for seeing me today. And excuse me."

She still looked utterly confused at his retreat. She opened and shut her mouth as if searching for something to say but coming up with nothing.

He took a few strides toward the house, but then stopped and looked back at her. "I-I do hope that if we see each other, you might still call me friend. And not avoid me."

She looked into his eyes and nodded. "Of course. Good—good day, Callum."

"Valaria," he said, and then walked away from her with the knowledge he might be walking away for good.

~

Valaria entered the foyer in time to see Callum riding off the drive and onto the street. Riding away from her. She shivered at the image of him vanishing onto the busy road, gone... perhaps forever.

"Higgins said the duke left almost as fast as he came," Fanny said.

Valaria turned to find her maid stepping off the last stair with a relieved expression. "Y-Yes. I was expecting an ordeal with him today, but he...he only apologized and then left."

"Apologized?" Fanny repeated. "For what?"

Valaria froze. She had not told her maid about the kiss. They might be close thanks to what they had endured together, but she was not of a mind to reveal something so personal even to her.

She shrugged. "Just something a little untoward that happened last night at the supper at his home. Nothing of note."

Except the kiss was certainly of note. And so was this afternoon when Callum had respected her wishes without so much as an argument. She'd almost...wanted one from him. Wanted him to say that he didn't want to walk away from her.

"If he was untoward and apologized, does that mean you have found the key to getting rid of him?" Fanny asked, hope in her tone.

"I think so," Valaria breathed. "I don't think the duke will darken our doors again."

She said the words and heard Fanny's murmured, "Good." Her maid said something else before she walked away, back to her duties, most likely, but Valaria didn't hear any of it.

Because she ought to have been as pleased as Fanny was about Callum's ultimate departure. But somehow she was not.

CHAPTER 8

Almost a week had passed since Callum had walked out of Valaria's townhouse on Kent's Row, and yet he had not stopped thinking about her. He should have. He should have put a period on the brief sentence that had been their renewed acquaintance and moved on to other things, other pursuits.

But he couldn't. He thought of her while he readied himself in the morning, he thought of her when he went about his day, he thought of her when he was at balls or parties or his club. He certainly thought of her at night while pulled himself off.

And he thought of her now, sitting in Theo's parlor after a night of gambling at their club.

"God, when are you going to end this brood? It's gone on for what feels like a lifetime," Theo said as he plopped down on the settee next to Callum and handed over a bottle for them to share.

Callum took a swig and handed the bottle back. "I'm not having a brood," he insisted softly.

Lied. He was certainly having a brood. The broodiest brood he'd ever brooded.

Theo snorted. "Obviously this is still about the Duchess of

Gooding. And since I was able to pry out of you that your conversation with her did not go terribly, I can't understand why you are still so stuck on this subject."

Callum dipped his head back against the cushion and stared at the ceiling. "I shouldn't be. But I feel frustrated. Uncomfortable. And I can't place why." He huffed out a breath. "I suppose it is just guilt over what still feels like a betrayal of Silas."

Theo was quiet a moment. "Yes. Silas."

Callum looked at him. "Why did you hate him?"

"Hate him?" Theo held up his hands. "I didn't hate—" He cut himself off. "Oh, bloody hell, the man is dead. Yes, I hated him."

"Well," Callum breathed, "so it's out at last. The truth."

"I'm sorry if it hurts you, because *you* I most definitely do not hate." Theo patted Callum's knee briefly. "But I never understood why the hell you were so close to someone so markedly different from you."

Callum shut his eyes as thoughts of his childhood bombarded him briefly. He pushed them away. "You're different from me, as well. I just wish I understood your hesitation about him. Your avoidance. Your contempt."

Theo pondered his half-empty glass a moment. "I saw that man be needlessly cruel to others many a time, Callum. He wore a mask and when it slipped, he was ugly beneath. For some reason, he was very careful not to show you that part of himself."

There was a moment's silence as Callum considered that. There was a kneejerk reaction in him that said he should defend Silas against this accusation. But when that faded a little, he could think of a few times in their friendship when Si had been...less than kind. Almost always when he drank, and Callum had always found some way to excuse the behavior.

Was it possible he had been so blind to not see that was actually who his friend was?

He cleared his throat. "Why wouldn't he show me the truth of him?"

Theo tilted his head. "Because he knew if he did, you would have called him out. You would have ended the friendship, and if there is one thing I knew about Silas, he valued that friendship. Now, whether that was mercenary or genuine, I have no idea. Perhaps I am not the best judge, biased as I am about the subject. But he didn't want you to know what he was."

Scrubbing a hand over his face, Callum got up and paced away to the window to stare out into the dark. "If you are right, it speaks low of me that I would not be able to see past any mask he wore."

"People get very good at hiding," Theo said. "My father was like that. Though he put the greatest share of the monster in him onto the shoulders of us in his family."

Callum looked at him. Theo was rarely open about his past and now there was an expression of bright pain on his face as he spoke. Callum felt the waves of it…but he also recognized it. It was the same expression that had been on Valaria's face whenever she spoke of Silas. Whenever she tried to push Callum away.

He drew back a fraction. "Do you…do you think that Silas might have been cruel to Valaria that same way?"

"If he was cruel to Valaria," Theo said gently, "it would have been worse. Because she had nowhere to run." His jaw tightened. "But she's free now and you have agreed to give her space, so why does what she suffered or not suffered matter to you?"

Callum clenched his hands at his sides. "Because if I stood by and did nothing—"

"Because you didn't know," Theo said.

"But if something like that happened, I *should* have known," Callum insisted, and felt the truth of it so deep within his chest that it felt like the guilt was intertwined with his muscle and sinew. "I should have known and I-I should have come to her aid. Protected her."

Theo moved toward him. "I don't know anything about the life that Valaria and Silas shared," he said. "Perhaps I lay too much of my own past on what I saw. But I do know that whatever was between them, for good or for ill, it isn't your responsibility, Callum. *She* isn't your responsibility."

"Then why does she feel like she is?"

Theo dropped his gaze away. "You wanted her."

Callum tensed. "It was one kiss."

"Before you kissed her," Theo said with a snort. "I think you wanted her from the moment you saw her, didn't you? Worse, you *like* her."

Callum felt his nostrils flare as those words sank in. And felt so true. He did like Valaria. He liked her intelligent gaze and her rare smiles. And if he was honest, he'd liked her for a long time. Perhaps more than he should have as her husband's best friend. "And what do I do about that if you are right?" he asked.

Theo's lips parted. "I…don't know. I'm adept at avoiding such attachment, not actually dealing with it."

"Well, perhaps avoiding it is what I should continue to do," Callum said, going back to the bottle on the table in front of the settee and taking a long drink of it in the hopes it would eventually blot out this conversation. Or at least soften it later. "For both our sakes."

~

Although Callum's gift of books had kept her entertained for a few extra days, Valaria's pleasure in them had faded considerably since he had last exited her home, their kiss dismissed and never to be repeated. Space was what she had said she desired, but getting what one wanted wasn't always fun. And being alone to ponder every mistake one had ever made was worse.

That feeling of being trapped was exactly how she ended up at Hyde Park in the middle of the day, strolling around the path that danced beside the edge of the Serpentine. It had been a cool morning, so the park was not heavily populated at present and she felt she could breathe again. Like she had not been put in the grave beside Silas to molder after all.

"Is this better, Your Grace?" Fanny asked at her side.

She smiled at her maid. "So much better. This was a wonderful idea. Humans weren't meant to be entirely cooped up inside, I don't think. Or at least I wasn't. Stepping out, getting some air, seeing some nature, what harm could come of—"

She cut off the thought because her gaze had shifted up the path and there she saw a man coming toward them on a horse. She flinched briefly as images of a dark and rainy night flooded her mind. But she pushed them away and saw that the man on the animal was one she instantly recognized from his posture and gait, even if she shouldn't.

"Blackvale," she breathed, and drank in the sight of him. He did know how to sit a horse, in his full riding gear and top hat, with his hessians gleaming in the afternoon sun that peeked out from around the clouds to taunt her.

Fanny followed her stare and her eyes widened. "Oh dear. And he's coming this way."

"We shall be polite," Valaria insisted, and wished her heart weren't beating so drattedly loud. God, could Fanny hear it? Would Callum be able to?

Fanny stepped back as Callum brought his horse to a halt next to them and swung down. His gaze was intense on Valaria's face as he stammered, "Your—your Grace."

"Your Grace," she repeated with a slight incline of her head. "I did not expect to see you in the park."

He glanced at her maid and then moved a fraction closer. He dropped his voice. "I hope you know I also was not planning to see you here, Valaria. I was not trying to intrude upon the privacy you requested."

There was something truly troubled in both his tone and the way he would not meet her gaze with his own. She found herself wondering what had changed in him, and wishing he were back to that playful…if slightly pushy…man who had kissed her.

"I did not believe you were," she reassured him gently. "After all, Hyde Park is a popular place. You cannot be expected to alter your entire life so that you don't cross paths with me."

He nodded and some of the worry left his face. "And yet I would not trouble you further. I'll leave you and your companion to the park."

He turned as if to go back to his horse and she knew if she left it be that he would go. But she didn't want that exactly. After all, she had been unable to get him out of her mind, no matter what she did to try to make it so. He was just *there* and what had happened between them had happened. But if she faced it, faced him, then perhaps the pulsing connection would fade. Become more commonplace.

"Your Grace, when you departed my home last week, you said that if we saw each other you hoped we could still meet as friends.," she called out. "There is no reason for us not to do so. Why don't you walk with me a moment?"

She saw Fanny's wild stare in her direction and knew her maid would have something to say about this later. But for now she ignored it.

"I…" he began, and glanced toward his horse. "Of course. I would be pleased to join you."

She wasn't certain whether to be relieved by his agreement or hate herself for putting them in this situation when she knew she should stay far away from this man. But then again, he would suspect less of her behavior if she were casually polite, wouldn't he?

He walked beside her, one hand tangled in the lead for his horse and they were in what could only be described as an awkward silence for a bit of time. Awkward enough that Valaria could not take it anymore.

"I am glad the weather broke at last," she said, hating herself for being so inane. And yet that was exactly what she must be to break this spell.

He looked around. "Yes. I will take any sunshine I can get during a London spring. Your…your new home bears up well in the bad weather?"

She drew back a little at the true concern in his voice. "Er, yes. It seems the place was well-maintained by its previous resident. We have been warm and snug inside. To the point that I thought I might run mad from the quiet and came out the moment even a hint of sunshine made itself known."

He smiled a little and some of the tension left his face. "I've also never enjoyed being trapped inside four walls. Give me a breeze in my face and blue sky above me. Oh, I see mud there on the path, let me help you."

She glanced ahead to where he indicated and found that there was a large mud puddle in the pathway. He held out a hand and she stared at it. He was wearing gloves, of course, because he had been riding, but this would be the first time he'd touched her since they kissed.

But there was no way to avoid his offer without treading through a nasty puddle so she placed her hand in his and tried to ignore the electric reaction that seemed to jolt through her entire body.

If he felt it, he gave no indication, only maneuvered her around the outer edges of the puddle. But the larger center was going to be more difficult. The hill above the path was slick with water and below was the little cliff into the Serpentine.

"Hmmm, perhaps we should just go back," she suggested.

"Or…" he said, and placed his boot in the center of the puddle. The water went over the sole and muddy sludge tarnished the fine leather.

"What are you doing?" she gasped. "Your boots."

"Can be cleaned," he said. "Now I would suggest you hike up

your skirt a little and then step on my boot to clear the puddle on the other side."

She stared at him. "Use you as a pathway?"

"Please," he said, and shifted, his face twisting rather comically. "And quickly, if you don't mind. I can feel the cold of the water and the wet will be next, no matter how fine the boots are."

"Oh dear," she muttered, and did as she'd been told, lifting her skirts to mid-calf and then stepping lightly on his foot to clear the puddle. She turned back and was surprised to find him offering the same kindness to Fanny.

Silas would have let her ruin her skirt and then screamed at her for it later. And he certainly wouldn't have given a damn about the safety of her maid.

Once they were both clear of the puddle, Callum returned to her side. He placed his wet foot on the edge of the grass and wiped some of the mud and muck from the leather.

"I shall pay for whatever cleaning or repair that requires," she said.

He glanced over at her, one eyebrow arched. "Don't be ridiculous. I'm fine and my boots will be fine. They're just things, Valaria." He shut his eyes. "Your Grace. I apologize for the over familiarity."

She drew in a long breath. "I suppose, when we are alone, you calling me by my first name is not so very distasteful...Callum."

She saw how much her saying his given name moved him. Saw it flicker over his face even as he tried to hide it. It was such a strange thing to see and recognize his desire.

Stranger still, she didn't recoil at the expression when she always had with Silas. Callum's expression only made her think of his kiss and that was not an unpleasant memory even if she'd tried to suppress it to no avail. It seemed her idea that she could make him meaningless to her was foolhardy.

She cleared her throat. "You said you run mad inside. Do you have regular pursuits that take you out of doors?"

He nodded. "Oh yes. The usual for gentlemen. I hunt and fish on my property in Blackvale during the summer and autumn. I enjoy snowshoeing when the weather turns foul enough. I like a good festival, Blackvale Village has the most remarkable apple festival. You really ought to see it some year."

Valaria caught her breath at how easy he was with her. Desire or not, he wasn't forcing it or himself on her. He chatted with her in nothing more than a friendly manner. It was very disarming. And charming. The man was charming.

"Of course, I also ride." He reached over and patted the big chestnut horse he was still guiding by the reins along the path.

She smiled and stepped back to stroke the horse's nose. Now that her initial reaction to the animal had passed, she was drawn to the gentle beast. "I would like to ride, as well, if it could be on this beauty. What is his name?"

"Fox," Callum said. "He is quick as one. Though he has a sad history. I bought him off a breeder who mistreated him."

She flinched and looked up into the soulful eyes of the animal. "But you survived it, didn't you, Fox?" she said softly, and smiled. "So you are twice as strong for it."

Callum was so quiet that she turned her face to look at him. Once again his intense focus was entirely on her, just as it had been when he first saw her.

"What is it?" she asked, almost afraid of the answer.

He cleared his throat. "I fear there was something about Silas that I didn't know. Should have known, perhaps, if it is true. It would be my failing. And it is none of my business, God knows. But...but I still feel compelled to ask you."

She stepped away from the horse and stared at him, heart throbbing so wildly her chest hurt from it. "Compelled to ask me what?" she whispered, glancing back at Fanny.

He opened and shut his mouth. "Did he mistreat you, Valaria? Did he do something so horrible beneath my nose and I was too blind to see it?"

His voice cracked as he asked and she staggered beneath the

weight of the question. There must have been something on her face, in the soft sound of pain she couldn't keep from her lips, that told him the answer because his entire countenance collapsed for a brief moment. Grief and guilt, pain and anger all at once.

She gathered herself. It would do no good to deny what he could already see, it seemed. Which meant she would have to address this with another tactic entirely. What exactly that was, she needed time to determine.

"I don't think the park is the place to discuss this."

He blinked and looked around. "Of course. I apologize, Your Grace. My home is but a short walk away. Might we go there, share tea and perhaps talk about this there?" He lifted a hand to his chest. "If you do not wish to do so, I understand. And I would never... never force you to do so. But I am...I am undone by this realization."

She could see that was true. This man who had loved her husband, a love Silas had never deserved, did seem truly crushed by the implication of these facts of him. She could only imagine what he might think if he knew the rest. But he couldn't. Not ever.

"I...I understand," she said softly. "My carriage is on the other side of the park. Perhaps I could return to it and then meet you at your home?"

"Yes," he said. "It is but a short distance on the circle path back. I'll take you there and then ride back on Fox. You can follow."

She agreed and they made their way back to her carriage with lighter conversation. Still, she couldn't help but think about what she might say to him as he helped first her into her carriage and then Fanny. He said goodbye, his gaze focused too intently on her as they rode off toward his house.

"It is not my place, I know, but I'm shocked you would not simply deny to that man that your late husband was the bastard he was," Fanny said, her tone sharp and worried.

Valaria looked at her maid. It was a good reminder that she

wasn't the only one in danger in these moments. She had others to protect, as well. "He saw the truth. If I had denied it, it would only have made him more suspicious. I can tell him half-truths now, control the narrative. And find…find some way to distract him so he doesn't dig further."

"He's already distracted when it comes to you," Fanny said.

Valaria sucked in a breath at the implication. "That's an impertinent thought, Fanny."

Her maid arched a brow. "Is it? He wants you. Anyone could see it written all over his face the way he watches you. You must know it, too."

Valaria flinched. "I…I do know it," she whispered, thinking of the warm weight of his lips on hers. Thinking of the electric jolt that hit her when he touched her or looked at her through that hooded glance.

"Then you know how dangerous that could be," Fanny insisted, a little desperation entering her voice.

Shutting her eyes, Valaria pondered that. Yes, being close to Callum was dangerous. She wasn't so foolish as to pretend it didn't open doors that perhaps were better shut. But when he was close to her, touching her, he didn't ask her about anything else, did he? He didn't press her about other topics best left unbroached.

Wasn't there power in that?

"But what if his desire could…could play into our favor?"

She hated herself for saying it. For thinking it. It sullied the kiss they'd shared. It made her a person that would use another's emotions or desires against them. Like Silas always had.

"I can't believe you would think that," Fanny breathed. "*Risk* that. After everything else."

Everything else. Yes, surely Valaria couldn't forget everything else. She shuddered.

"Well, hopefully it won't come to that," Valaria said as they stopped on his drive.

Now she would have to go inside and find some way to tell a man who looked at her like she was precious that a man he'd loved had thought her worthless. And she had no idea what that conversation would lead to. For better or for worse.

CHAPTER 9

Callum felt like he was going to vomit as he handed off his horse, explained the plan to his butler and then waited at the top of his stairs for Valaria's carriage to pull through his gate. She had not come out and said Silas had harmed her, but Callum could see the truth of it in the way her face had twisted with pain and horror when he asked the question. And he believed her, even before she told him one word of the explanation that he didn't deserve.

Why hadn't he seen it? Why had he been so blind? Was it willful on his part? After all, it had never affected him, Silas's cruelty. Didn't that make him complicit?

Callum smoothed his hands along the front of his waistcoat and struggled to contain his roiling emotions as he watched Valaria be helped from her carriage, then her maid, who was now stone-faced. He had to force himself to stay where he was, perched on the top step leading to his home. He wanted very much to go down to take Valaria's hand, himself, but considering what they were about to discuss, he doubted she wanted his touch.

And this wasn't about him and his thoughts on the matter at any rate. He couldn't make this about him and how he felt.

She moved toward him, her expression taut and nervous. "It is an even prettier prospect during the day," she said, a little breathlessly.

He inclined his head toward the house and allowed her to start off on such a benign topic if it pleased her. It lessened the tension at any rate. "I've always thought so. Please, come in." He pivoted toward Morris as she did so. "Please show Her Grace's maid to the servant area for her tea. Is ours awaiting us in the east parlor?"

"Yes, Your Grace. It should be ready now," the butler said.

"Good. Please don't allow disturbances," Callum said as he motioned Valaria down the hall to the back of his estate. They entered the parlor and she immediately moved to the window that looked over his garden.

"Oh, Callum," she breathed as she took in the winding paths and sparkling fountains and bright blooming flowers. "Your compliments on my own garden seem a little silly in comparison to this paradise."

He frowned. "I *like* your garden. This is massive and bright and lovely, of course. But it's too outlandish to keep myself. *You* can actually be a part of growing your own escape."

She turned toward him. "You could be too. Perhaps not the whole garden, no, but you can always claim a little corner of your own world, Callum."

His brow wrinkled at that thought. One he hadn't actually considered before. Sometimes it was so easy to be all or nothing in life. He didn't let his mind find halves very easily.

"May I get you tea?" he asked, motioning to the set.

"Perhaps shortly," she whispered, and her hands shook before she clenched them before herself. He could see how nervous she was. How she worried her lip, flexed her fingers, how her breath came a little shorter and she wouldn't quite meet his eyes.

Clearing his throat, he took a long step toward her, once again having to force himself not to touch her in comfort. "Valaria, you owe me nothing. No explanation. You don't have to cut yourself open and bleed for me if you don't want to do so. I shouldn't have pried in the park. I just..." He trailed off and shook his head.

Her gaze flitted over his face slowly. "You just what?"

"I want to know how blind and selfish I have been," he whispered. "How much I enabled the bad behavior of a person I called friend."

"You-you would blame yourself for something Silas did behind closed doors, specifically so that no one would see? *You* wouldn't see."

He drew in a long breath. "You sound like Theo. He says the actions of another are not my fault, as well."

"Then Lightmorrow is wiser than he pretends to be," Valaria said. "Let me make something clear to you, whatever Silas was... whatever he did..." Her voice broke slightly. "It wasn't your fault or your responsibility. I don't know you very well, but your reaction now tells me that had you known, you would have taken him to task if you'd understood."

"I would have ended my friendship with him, had I seen him be cruel to you," he said, and meant it.

She worried her lip. "He would have hated me for that," she whispered at last. "I think you were the only person he actually gave a damn about when it came down to it."

He bent his head. Once he would have liked that statement. Felt it reflected on their long friendship. But now Silas was tarnished in his mind and those words felt like daggers in his chest.

"Was he always that way to you?" He lifted his gaze to her. "*If* you wish to share some part of your story."

She swallowed hard. "He...he didn't want to marry me. It was all arranged, of course. I didn't want to marry him, either. But he was not unpleasant to look at and I had no choice, so I think I built some idea in my head that perhaps we could come to an accord. The very first night of our marriage, I realized it would never be."

He caught his breath. "On your wedding night?"

"He berated me and he..." She trailed off. "Well, he was very cruel."

Callum stiffened. Was she not sharing more than emotional cruelty? Had Silas gone so far as to physically harm this woman? Worse?

Callum's stomach turned at the thought.

"Over the years, his contempt for me only grew," she said. "He did flaunt his affairs in front of me, of course. You guessed correctly at that. Though I didn't mind so much. If he was off with another person, then at least he wasn't home tormenting me. But I could never please him. Never make him happy. And eventually I stopped trying."

"I was right there," Callum breathed. "God, I was right there and I never knew this. It is worth very little, but I'll say it again: I'm sorry, Valaria. Sorry I was blind to his shortcomings. Sorry I didn't stop him if I might have had the power."

She stared up at him, her expression almost confused. Then she lifted a hand and wiped away a tear he hadn't even realized had slid from his eyes. "It seems you suffer enough for this news. I don't think you have to be sorry."

He shook his head. "It's like a death all over again. His death. The death of what and who I thought he was."

She nodded as if she understood that. Then she took his hand in hers. A comfort for his pain, which made him a selfish prick of the highest order.

"I was miserable with him," she said softly, her blue-gray gaze holding his, drowning him in her. "But I'm free. And now you needn't feel guilty anymore about kissing me."

He couldn't help but snort out a scoff at that idea. "How so?"

She shrugged. "Because I kissed you back. And I did that because I wanted a little...goodness. Something sweet just for me. *That's* what you did for me that night, Callum. Even though I shouldn't admit that."

She leaned up at she said those words, her gaze becoming

hooded and heavy. The hand that didn't hold his brushed along his jawline and he felt her breath against his lips before she kissed him.

~

Valaria had suggested to Fanny the idea of exploiting Callum's desire for her. But when she pressed her lips to his, there was nothing about *control* that was any part of it. And perhaps she'd always known that. Perhaps control was an excuse so she could just...touch him again. Feel him want her the way no one else in the world had ever wanted her.

She'd told him the truth, or at least as much as it as she could. Seeing his genuine reaction to her pain, seeing his guilt over his part in it...she had wanted so much to lean up into him. To wrap this man's warmth around her and let it pierce the places where she had frozen during her loveless, horrible marriage.

Even though she shouldn't.

But for that tiny moment, she pushed aside the shoulds and the fears and the doubts and sank into his touch. His tongue slid past her lips, gentle at first, tracing and taunting. Then probing and promising. Heat spread through her at his touch, achy, wanton need that she had told herself she *couldn't* feel. But she felt it, oh how she felt it, in the steady embrace of this man.

And she would have done anything and everything to stay there. Would have sacrificed so much to never lose the quivering need that coursed through her. But she had no choice in that because he pulled away first.

He didn't remove her from his arms. No, he kept her there, pressed to his chest, staring down at her with a slightly dazed expression. Like he didn't know what to do with her now that he had her here.

"I-I still shouldn't," he finally murmured, his deep, rough voice barely carrying even though they were so tightly pressed against each other. "Whatever he was, it's wrong to want this. To want you, Valaria."

"Probably that's true," she agreed. "If anyone else knew it, they would judge me so harshly. And yet you do want me. And I want you. I wish it wasn't you, Callum. If I'm honest to my very soul, I will tell you that I wish it wasn't you that haunted me with these thoughts I shouldn't have."

His brow wrinkled. "Yes."

"But when you kissed me on the terrace last week, it woke something in me. Something I thought I could not have. A desire that I believed would never exist for me. So it is you, and it is me. We're here. And I…I don't want to walk away."

"Then what do you want?" he whispered, lowering his mouth back toward hers. She felt the brush of it to her lips and shivered with pleasure that seemed to pulse in every single sensitive part of her body.

"I want something that is *mine*, only mine, for even the briefest moment."

"God's teeth," he murmured as his lips found hers again. This time the pressure of him was less gentle. She felt a shift in him, a drive that called to her in a primal way. A focused way that was unlike anything she'd ever felt before.

He backed her toward the settee and they sank down on the cushions together. She was pressed against the arm of the couch, him leaning over her, his mouth seeking and driving and tasting her like he could do just that simple act forever.

But no kiss had ever been so complicated as this one. When he kissed her, it was like he was lighting every inch of her body on fire. Like he was somehow touching her everywhere, because she felt the tug of him everywhere. His kiss was in her veins, it made her fingertips tingle, it hardened her nipples and it made her stomach feel fluttery. It made her thighs shake and her toes curl and between her legs she felt the beginnings of a specific kind of pleasure she had only ever found with her own hand.

There was a moan in the air around them and she realized with a start that it had come from her. She was lifting against him, her hands clenching at his forearms like she was some cat arching in heat.

He lifted his head and looked down at her. She waited for the judgment. The censure for wanting like she clearly was. But instead he smiled, a very wicked expression on what she had only ever seen as a rather serious face. But right now he looked like a rake who would well-pleasure a woman.

Which was exactly what she wanted in this fog of need.

"I want to give you so much pleasure, Valaria. I don't want to take anything at all. Just give you so, so much pleasure. May I?"

She blinked, utterly confused at the idea of a man giving pleasure without demanding something in return. Did that exist? Her experience had been entirely the opposite, honestly.

"Yes," she whispered, almost without realizing she was doing it. "Please."

His pupils dilated when she said please and he claimed her lips again with a little moan. But before she could lose herself all over again, he dragged his mouth lower, down the side of her throat, across her cloth-covered collarbone, down over her breast. He cupped the opposite one, squeezing oh-so-gently, strumming a thumb over her nipple as she gasped out in unexpected pleasure.

He made another sound of desire that was muffled against the fabric of her dress. He continued to massage her suddenly very sensitive breasts as he slid from the settee to his knees on the floor before her. He let his mouth trace over the satin of her gown, across her hip as he slid her to the edge of the settee and wedged himself between her trembling knees.

There he stopped, sliding his hands down to settle on her thighs before him. "If you don't want me to do this, you can tell me no at any time. I want to make that clear before we begin. No will always mean no."

She stared down at him, this duke who was on his knees before her, watching her every move as if he could glean some truth about her from it. And he probably could. She could see that now in his eyes. See that he could pluck her secrets as easily as he plucked an apple from a tree in autumn.

That should have been enough to make her push away and run, but she couldn't. Not now when she was shaking with desire.

"Yes," she said instead, and placed her hands against his. She let her fingers glide across his knuckles, never moving her gaze from him, no matter how much she wanted to.

His breath hitched and suddenly the pressure of his fingers on her thighs increased. He pushed and her legs fell open, providing him a space to wedge his shoulders into.

He continued to watch her carefully as he slid his hands away from hers and down her to her knees, her calves, until he caught the hem of her skirt. With a deep breath, he began to lift the soft fabric, bunching it in his fist and lifting it to gather around her waist.

He was baring her, revealing her. It took everything in her not to push the dress back down, not to let him see. Not to be vulnerable with him. Vulnerability had never led to much good in her history.

"You are lovely," he whispered, almost like he could read her mind. He stroked the back of his hand against her stocking-clad knee and she sucked in a breath through her teeth at the shock of sensation.

When had that place become so sensitive?

She didn't have a chance to answer her own internal question because he cupped her inner thigh, stroking his thumb along the top, where her garter was tied.

"Callum," she murmured, captivated by the swish of his touch against the stocking, then her bare thigh.

"I want to take those off," he said, motioning toward her drawers.

Here they were at another place where she could say no. Where she could stop this madness and probably make enough of a fuss that this man never darkened her door again out of respect for her.

But she didn't take the opportunity. Instead she pushed her hands past the pile of black gown gathered at her stomach and untied the drawers. His gaze glittered as he watched her do that, watched her loop her fingers around the edge of the silky fabric and push. When they cleared her hips, he took them and tugged them down her legs the rest of the way.

And now she was truly exposed. Naked from the waist down as he stared at her with an almost worshipful expression. Why, she couldn't say. But he was intent in his focus and licked his lips like he was looking at a feast spread out before him.

He bent his head and stroked his cheek against the inside of her knee. He had shaved before coming to her, the touch was smooth and soft. When he turned his head into her and kissed the same spot, she moaned with unexpected pleasure.

What in the world was this man doing to her?

"You're already trembling," he whispered as he trailed his lips a little higher.

She was shocked to realize he was right. Her legs shook around him, her fingers clenching against the edge of the settee.

"I'm sorry," she gasped.

He glanced up at her and met her gaze evenly. He was all heat and promise, pleasure and danger and beauty all wrapped up in one.

"Oh no, I only meant that I intend to make you shake all the more before I'm finished. I'm going to make you twist and moan and beg and oh, yes, shake for me, Valaria. I'm going to do all of that right now."

CHAPTER 10

Before Valaria could respond to Callum's wicked promise of pleasures to come, he brushed his lips between her legs. He placed gentle pressure against her as she lifted into him with something between a gasp and a cry. Sensation spiraled through her as he used his thumbs to spread her open farther and then repeated the kiss, this time licking her.

"Oh God," she gasped, and her hand came down into the thick mass of his hair, fingers tangling in the soft locks, tugging him closer as he licked her again. "Please."

His gaze came up, dark and dangerous, even though he never stopped licking her. Over and over, long, languid strokes that woke every single nerve ending in that sensitive place between her legs. She found herself lifting into him, grinding to find even more pleasure.

He made soft sounds against her, like her desire increased his own. He never scolded her for taking part in what he was doing, he never withheld from her, only gave.

That gentleness, that lack of judgment, helped her relax. After a little while of teasing and desperate, glorious torment, he increased his focus on her clitoris. His fingers tightened against her thighs, as the rocking motion of their joined bodies deepened...the pleasure mounted. To her surprise, she felt the edge of release in her grasp, powerful sensation that would wash her away for a moment. She was torn between grinding herself to that edge and backing away to enjoy the feeling of his mouth a little longer.

He stole the choice from her though when he began to suck her clitoris. She jolted at the electric pleasure from the sucking, the flick of his tongue. And when he added a finger to her sheath, gliding inside of her gently and thrusting in time to his tongue, she was undone.

The edge came and she flew over it as waves of pleasure washed over her. She gripped his hair with both hands, bending against him, rocking and grinding for more as she gasped out his name in the quiet. All through it, he never stopped, giving more and more until she was weak. Spent. Nothing but a trembling mass of quivering and satisfied flesh.

Only then did he lift his head from her, withdraw his finger and casually licked it clean. She could scarcely move as she stared at him, his lips and chin slick from her release, his eyes bright with pleasure and oh-so-much desire that continued to call to her.

"That...was *remarkable*," he murmured.

She nodded, still unable to formulate coherent words. Even if she could, what did one say to a man who had just promised her a few moments in heaven and then delivered so much more than she'd hoped for? She'd never felt anything like it. Certainly not with Silas, not even at her own hand. What Callum had done was powerful and changing.

And in this heated, vulnerable moment, she realized one undeniable fact: she wanted more of it. More of him. At whatever cost. A terrifying thought. A tempting one. And yet she had no idea how to proceed with a man like this. How to ask for what she wanted. Or how to deny herself the same for self-preservation.

And so all she could do was stare at him, unspeaking, while her body still shook and she waited for him to give her…she didn't even know what in that moment. She didn't know anything except that her body felt alive in a new way. And he was the cause.

~

Callum remained on his knees between Valaria's spread legs, his heart throbbing and his cock aching. But all he could focus on was the slightly stunned expression on her face as she stared down at him. God, watching her in the aftermath of pleasure was almost as good as coming, himself. Almost.

She had let go. Utterly and completely as she rode the waves of pleasure, and it had been unlike anything he'd ever experienced before. Of course, it had also made a powerful truth painfully clear: how much constant pressure and tension she was under.

And now that he knew that, he had to think about it a little more. Explore it and the causes…perhaps figure out how he could help. Because he so desperately wanted to help her.

He smiled at her and slowly smoothed her skirts back down over her legs, covering her before he stood up.

She stared, eyes wide and completely confused. "You aren't going to—"

He swallowed. "I told you, Valaria, that was just for you."

She blinked up at him. "But you want…I can see you are…" She waved vaguely at his hard cock, plainly outlined against his trouser crotch.

"Oh yes," he grunted. "Very much. But I have control over myself. I can wait."

"Wait for what?" she asked, shaking her head.

A wave of wicked, tempting, wonderful things that he could do to and with this woman washed through his mind. He wanted to learn every inch of that body. He wanted to feel her come in a thousand different ways. He wanted to know every note of her flavor like she was wine. And he wanted to tangle his fingers through her hair after and feel her as relaxed when they were not actively fucking as she had been when she came a moment ago.

He wanted far more than he should ask for and...he was certain...far more than she was willing or able to give at present.

"I'm willing to wait for you," he said softly.

There was a flare of panic that first crossed her face at that statement. Powerful and brief before she hid it. A wall came down between them, the tension that was not of the sexual kind returned, and she got up. Was that to put them on more equal terms? He didn't know.

She moved away from him to the fireplace. There, she turned back and there was a falseness to her expression. One he recognized he'd seen before, many times. But now it was directed toward him.

"But why wait when I'm right here?"

He knew she was saying that to build a wall between them. To give him what she thought he wanted so that he wouldn't see what she wished to withhold. But the idea of what she would give nearly brought him to his knees.

"Christ," he muttered beneath his breath. "You are a temptation, Valaria. I cannot express to you how deeply I would like to cross this room, press you against any solid surface or piece of furniture and have my extremely wicked way with you until you're moaning my name like you did a moment ago."

Her eyes widened and he could see how much that description aroused her. He forced himself to continue, "However, today has been emotional. Both because of what we talked about regarding Silas and because of the unexpected nature of what happened a moment ago. And I don't want you doing anything more until you've had time to consider without those high emotions guiding every thought. To think when I'm not perched between your lovely thighs."

She shivered and her hands gripped at her sides.

He took a step toward her. "I don't want to be unclear. I want you. I want to be with you, even more now that I know your taste and how you flush when you come against me. What sounds you make in pleasure. I want to feel you rock against my cock as you shatter. I want to say your name when I lose control, myself."

Her breath was so short now that it bordered on nonexistent and she was trembling all over, much like she had when she came. Her pupils were dilated and she never took her wide, blue-gray stare from his.

"*That* is what I can offer you," he said, softer this time because he had almost closed the distance between them. "Something sweet, I think you called it. Something just for you. Without expectations or pressures. Under your terms, and your timetable. For as long as you want me, or as short."

"You're implying that I would have control of this," she said, and there was doubt in her tone.

He nodded. "You have all the control, Valaria. But I want you to go home and think about it. Take your time to decide. And when you're ready, let me know."

She lifted her chin, her nostrils flaring slightly. "And what if I told you this was all there could be? That we could never repeat what we just did?"

Her anxiety dripped from every part of that question. He tilted his head a little closer. "I would be very sorry to hear that. But I would accept it. And we would never have to speak of it again."

She stared at him, her expression softening as she explored every inch of his face. "I'll...I'll consider it, Callum," she said at last.

"Then let me escort you to your carriage," he offered, motioning her toward the door.

She blinked and then nodded, following him but not touching him, he noticed. As if he hadn't just worshipped between her legs not ten minutes before. He might have spoken to her more about her thoughts, but her maid appeared in the foyer a moment after they did.

He smiled at the young lady and noted that she seemed to have as much hesitation about him as Valaria did. There was a protectiveness in her stare even as she darted it away, as would be appropriate. It caused even more questions for him about Valaria and what she might have endured in the past.

Her carriage was brought around swiftly enough and Callum waved off the footmen who came to help. He assisted her maid in and then turned back to Valaria.

"Take your time," he said softly. "I'm here and I shall be here. Waiting for you."

She swallowed. "Yes, so you said earlier. And I…I will think about it, Callum. And what happened between us. I fear I shall think of nothing else."

With that, she took his hand and climbed into her carriage. He released her as soon as she was settled and closed them in, watching as the vehicle rumbled off onto the street before the house.

"I shall think of nothing else either," he murmured to himself, still tasting her on his tongue as he went back inside and tried to put some semblance of normalcy onto an afternoon that had all but changed everything.

~

"You are so pale, I fear you are going to faint even sitting on that bench," Fanny said as soon as the carriage rolled onto the street and headed back toward Kent's Row. "What in the world happened? What did he say?"

Valaria almost laughed. What had he said that she could share with any other person in her life? Should she say that he had made her come on his settee until she could hardly breathe? Or that he offered her even more pleasures without demand or cruelty? Or that when she looked into his eyes, she saw...well, things she did not wish to see. Felt things beyond desire that she didn't want to feel.

Fanny already disapproved enough.

"He just wanted to know more about my life with Silas," she said at last. "I was vague at best and he is so guilt stricken at the idea that his best friend might have been cruel and he didn't see it that he didn't press further."

"Well, he *should* feel that way," Fanny said, folding her arms. "Anyone who could be friends with such a man cannot be entirely good, can he?"

Valaria pondered the question. She might have thought the same until today. It was part of why she avoided all Silas's friends. But Callum...he was different.

"I...don't know why they were friends," she said softly. "Silas certainly did not share intimate details of his life with me. I think they were young when they met. Perhaps I'll ask him at some point."

She wanted to now. Felt increasing curiosity of how two such opposite men could be so close.

"You...you are going to spend more time with him?" Fanny asked, her face losing all color. "Your Grace...I...I fear this is a mistake. I know that isn't my place to say."

"It is," Valaria said. "I know it is. You are at risk from someone who might pry as much as I am. I haven't forgotten what you did for me, nor the risk you put yourself in by doing so. But I promise you, he isn't going to find out anything I don't want to share. Right now he has given me...I suppose I am in a position of power."

She said those words and actually felt them. That was exactly what he'd done. He'd asked for what he desired and then sent her on her way, making no attempt to push anything on her that she didn't want.

Which only made her want him more, truth be told. Perhaps that was his game.

"I just hope you'll be careful," Fanny said with a shiver. "A man can snatch power back so quickly one's head will spin."

"Indeed, I know that," Valaria whispered as the carriage rolled into the drive in front of her home. She glanced out the window and saw that the front door was open and standing on the top step leading in were Flora and Bernadette.

"Oh dear, I had forgotten we had planned for tea this afternoon," she gasped. That was what spending time with Callum did to her. Made her only focus on him.

She hopped from the carriage the moment it stopped and rushed toward her friends. "Goodness, you must think I'm the worst featherhead," she gasped.

Flora and Bernadette both laughed as they embraced her in turn. "Of course not," Bernadette said as they all moved inside together.

"Will you have tea readied for the parlor?" Valaria asked Higgins as they began to make their way to that very room.

"Of course, Your Graces," the butler said with a swift bow as he hustled away.

"I swear my new staff will all despise me, I've so been distracted of late. I'm certain I create a great deal of work for them," Valaria said as they all took their seats. Flora and Bernadette sat together on the settee, Valaria on a chair across from them.

"You are too hard on yourself," Flora said gently. "It sometimes feels you expect a perfection I do not think you would ask for from anyone else."

Valaria blinked as the truth of that statement sank in. And the root of it was equally clear to her. Her parents had expected perfection, for her never to make a peep or ask for too much. And they had married her off to a man who punished when great lofty heights had not been reached.

It was an almost instinctual thing to see failure in any flaw now. To await censure when she was not exactly as she "should" be.

"Perhaps that is true," she murmured. "I suppose it is something I do not have to force upon myself now that I am a widow of means and independence. I can make mistakes with impunity." She shuddered at those words, which now hung in the air around her. "Well, almost impunity."

Flora tilted her head. "What kinds of mistakes would you like to make?" she asked with a slight smile.

"Oh yes," Bernadette said, and her laughter was like music in the air. "I would love to plan some good old-fashioned mistakes that we can giggle over later. Make a scandal together."

Valaria shifted. A scandal was exactly what she wanted to avoid and what she could easily create if she took Callum up on his offer to become her lover. Oh yes, widows had far more leeway in how they managed their paramours, but not mere months into their "grief".

And yet…it was the mistake she most wanted to make.

"Dearest," Bernadette said, and Valaria jolted as she reached across the distance between them and caught her hand. "You are distracted and seem worried. I know it's…it's hard for you to trust new people, I think. That's understandable. But Flora and I consider you a friend. And perhaps if you talk to us, we could help you."

Valaria stared at these two women, with their kind eyes and easy kinship that had been such a balm on her soul in the short time she'd known them. She couldn't tell them everything, but couldn't she just tell them…tell them this?

She cleared her throat. "I admit, I fear you would judge me."

"We would *never*," Flora said with a firm determination that was hard to deny. "I promise you that if nothing else. You'll find no judgment here."

That was impossible to believe, of course. But she found herself drawing a deep breath regardless. "What do you think of a lady—hypothetically, of course—who took a lover while still in mourning?"

Both women drew back a fraction and exchanged a quick look. Valaria tensed immediately, but swiftly realized they were both simply surprised, not disapproving.

"I-I think it is none of anyone's business how a person grieves," Flora said carefully.

"Or doesn't grieve," Bernadette said, and met Valaria's gaze as if she understood better than Flora what the situation was.

"I-I do grieve what was," Valaria said softly. "And what never was." She hesitated. No, she would not go further than that. She was already in dangerous waters with Callum, she wasn't about to add these two to the mix. "But today something happened that made me feel..."

She trailed off and briefly thought of Callum between her legs, bright eyes watching as she shattered against his tongue. His fingers pressing into her thighs, his mouth so perfectly attuned to what she wanted. Needed.

"It made me feel alive for the first time in a very long time," she whispered. "And I don't want it to stop."

"Oh my," Bernadette said, and lightly fanned herself. "It sounds like something amazing. Why should you want it to stop?"

Flora leaned closer and her eyes were lit up as she smiled. "I'm going to be very personal. Who exactly was it who made you feel alive, eh?" She giggled, and Valaria found herself laughing along with her. She felt like a schoolgirl again and it was...nice.

"A lady ought not tell."

"It was Blackvale," Bernadette said, arching a brow. "I'd wager five pounds that it was Blackvale."

Valaria caught her breath and covered her suddenly hot cheeks with cold hands. "How did you guess?"

"Well, he is the only gentleman you have any contact with regularly," Flora said. "And it's obvious there is a connection of some kind between you, especially after our supper at his home the other night. He isn't the worst choice for a lover. He's rumored to be very good at it. Almost as good as his friend Lightmorrow. Though I suppose you wouldn't want to choose him."

"Of course she wouldn't," Bernadette said, a little too swiftly. "He wouldn't be a good fit for her."

"Hmmm," Flora said, and gave Valaria a meaningful look.

"Oh, I just don't know," Valaria breathed. "It's so tempting an idea. But there are dangers."

"There always are. But right now no one is looking at you. If you're discreet, it couldn't hurt." Bernadette smiled.

Flora shook her head. "Well, *almost* no one is looking. I forgot to pass along the message from the Duchess of Amberleigh."

Valaria jolted. Everyone knew the Duchess of Amberleigh. She was one of the most important women in Society. Even the patronesses of Almack's seemed afraid of her.

"What does she want with me?" she asked, voice shaking a little.

"Well, she lives two doors down from my home here on the Row," Flora explained. "And I bumped into her earlier this morning with her little dogs. She demanded I arrange a meeting between you. She always wants to meet the new arrivals on the Row."

"Could I beg off as being in mourning?" Valaria said hopefully.

"No," Bernadette said. "She doesn't give a fig for that. She is above the rules of mourning. You won't be able to avoid it. Honestly, it isn't terrible. She looks you up and down in judgment, but she isn't entirely unkind."

"No, she just sees into your soul," Flora said with a burst of laughter.

Valaria shifted. Wonderful, another person who could do that. She already had enough to manage with Callum.

"It's probably best to get it done with. I can tell her tea tomorrow. She'll demand we do it at her townhouse. But she has a wonderful cook and her scones are to die for, so it will be a positive tradeoff," Bernadette said.

Valaria sighed before she nodded. "There seems to be no escaping it."

But as she said the words and the others began talking about the duchess and her whims, Valaria had a powerful realization. She was no longer in a position where she *always* had to do things she couldn't escape. If she wished to stay up too late or read naughty books or have a wild affair with a handsome man…no one could stop her anymore.

So the trade *was* a positive one. And she could bear any duchess and her judgmental stares if she knew the rest of her life could be lived on her own terms and by her own whims.

She could do this. She could manage Callum, she could keep her secrets and maybe, just maybe, she could even have some happiness for once.

She deserved it. She deserved it all.

CHAPTER 11

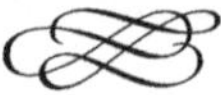

"It's like a museum," Valaria mused the next day as the she sat with Bernadette and Flora in the fine parlor of the Duchess of Amberleigh. "Gracious, that vase must be worth a small fortune."

"I cannot imagine," Flora whispered back. "And nothing is ever out of place here. Not even a book on a side table or a slightly turned miniature on the mantel."

"Nothing should be out of place," came a crisp voice from the door behind them.

All three stood and pivoted to face the Duchess of Amberleigh as she entered the room more like a queen. Valaria gave a curtsey and as she did so, she stared. She'd seen the duchess before, of course, but never so close. After all, there was a hierarchy even with the ranks of the titled, and this woman was at the very top.

And she knew it.

"Your Grace," Bernadette said, moving toward their hostess. "How kind of you to have us today. Your home is, as always, beautiful."

"Yes, it's such a pleasure to be here, Your Grace," Flora agreed with a wide smile for the duchess.

Her Grace glanced over them both, not quite dismissive, but certainly making her judgments. And then her gaze fell on Valaria.

"May I present the newest addition to the Row," Bernadette hastened to say. "The Duchess of Gooding."

"Your Grace," Valaria said, curtseying again even though she now felt like a bobbin in the water.

All of the Duchess of Amberleigh's attention swung to her and the woman looked down that long patrician nose at her, one eyebrow arched. "And there you are. You are quite pretty, aren't you?"

Valaria blinked and glanced at Bernadette and Flora briefly for some advice on how to respond to such a strange statement. "Er, thank you. I appreciate your kindness."

"Though the black does your pale features no favors, does it?" the duchess continued. "And you've circles under your eyes."

Valaria flinched. Those circles had come from tossing and turning all night, thinking about the afternoon with Callum and his statement that they could have more of that same passion. Thinking about the fact that she had invited him to her home later that very day, so they could discuss his offer further.

Though she still had no idea what she was going to do about it.

"How long do you have left in your mourning?" the duchess snapped, dragging Valaria from those very inappropriate thoughts that seemed to haunt her constantly now.

"Er, my husband died two and a half months ago," she said.

"Well, even half-black will help," the duchess said with a sigh as she moved to sit in the large, high-backed chair before the fire. She motioned the others to sit on the settee across from her and they managed to wedge in together. "Tunbridge, why don't you pour the tea?" she snapped, addressing the women the same way one might do a servant.

Bernadette rose up and nodded. "Of course, Your Grace. You take it with milk, no sugar, yes?"

"Indeed," the duchess said with a sharp look that she swung back to Valaria almost instantly. "It seems that youth is taking over Kent's Row."

Valaria hesitated. The duchess appeared to be waiting for her to respond, so she nodded. "Er, yes, I suppose so."

"There seem to be an alarming number of dead younger dukes," the duchess said, and then flitted her gaze to Flora. "Except for your husband, of course, Sidmouth. He was almost my age, wasn't he?"

Valaria cast a quick glance at Flora, who had always spoken kindly and warmly of her husband. Would this direct statement hurt her friend?

But Flora had an amused expression. "He was, indeed, Your Grace. I was his second wife, and very lucky to have had the time I did with him."

"Hmph," the duchess said, and glanced up at Bernadette as she handed over a cup of tea. "Well, I encourage you to marry a younger one next time."

Flora's smile became sadder. "I…I do not think another husband is on the horizon for me, Your Grace. My financial situation does not require it, and so I think I shall stay an independent dowager and take a page from your expansive book."

Bernadette gave Valaria tea next, and just as she took a sip, the dowager continued, "Take a lover, then, at least."

Valaria nearly spit her tea across the room and gulped the hot liquid instead to keep from doing so.

The duchess arched a brow at her. "Have I offended you, Gooding?"

"No, Your Grace," she said swiftly, and tried once more not to think of Callum. "I'm just surprised."

"Well, I'm not telling *you* to take a lover," the duchess said. "Not until you are at least in half-black. Otherwise it could be seen as uncouth. Discretion is the better part of valor in these situations. Shakespeare was right on that account." She turned her attention back to Flora as Bernadette gave her a cup and then retook her place on the settee. "Now, you always have excellent gossip, Sidmouth, do share!"

Flora laughed and then launched into a few stories about ladies and gentlemen of the Upper Ten Thousand. Since the Duchess of Amberleigh did not seem to think that Valaria had much to add, she was not pushed to participate. But she listened, and to her surprise she found she rather liked the sharp, observant dowager. One always knew where they stood with her, at the very least.

On the other hand, she wouldn't want to do anything to put herself on the bad side of this woman either. The Duchess of Amberleigh had power to elevate or destroy and she knew it. She *inhabited* it. Which meant if Valaria *did* decide to take up with Callum, she'd need to be extra careful about how she managed it. Oh yes, widows had more leeway, but they could easily be eaten up by Society if they weren't discreet.

Only Callum didn't make her feel discreet. He made her feel like opening her legs in a parlor.

"You have the strangest expression on your face, Gooding," the Duchess of Amberleigh said, and yanked Valaria back to the present.

She felt the heat of a blush in her cheeks and shook her head. "I apologize, Your Grace. My mind wandered."

"To what topic, one can only speculate," the duchess said with an arched brow in her direction. "But I suppose that is as good a place for us to part today as any." She pushed to her feet and it forced the rest of them to rise.

"Thank you for having us today, Your Grace," Valaria said. "I hope I didn't offend you."

"My dear, if you offend me, you will know it," the duchess said. "Now let me escort you all." She turned and exited the parlor in a perfumed cloud. The rest followed and they stepped out onto the front step and the bright sunshine together.

"It has turned out to be a fine day," the duchess said. "I shall have to take a turn about the park, I think." Her brow wrinkled as she looked down the Row toward Valaria's home. "And who is that arriving in your drive, Gooding?"

Valaria jerked her head toward her own home and gulped in a breath. "I…I believe that is the Duke of Blackvale, Your Grace. He was to call on me today at three. But it is two, so we must have had a misunderstanding on the time."

"Blackvale," the duchess mused. "I knew his father years ago. The son is far more handsome."

Once again, Valaria looked toward Flora and Bernadette for help in how to respond, but her friends looked as flummoxed as she felt. "He is…he is a handsome gentleman, yes, Your Grace. He was a very good friend to my late husband and I think he feels some…some obligation to take care of me now."

The duchess held her gaze a moment and then made a soft snort. "I see. Well, you ought not keep him. Good day, Your Graces."

Without another word, she pivoted on her heel and returned inside. When she was gone, the three of them looked at each other and then all began to giggle as they moved up the street toward their individual homes.

"Well, she is something," Valaria said as she kept glancing up the way toward her house. Callum was exiting his carriage now, his lean, tall figure unmistakable even from a distance. "Something, indeed."

They reached Bernadette's home first and there they stopped. Bernadette took her hand and squeezed gently. "Whatever you are about to do, Valaria…just be happy. Be free. Be careful."

Valaria looked at the two women, who both appeared anxious and pleased on her behalf. She nodded. "If I figure out what to do at all, I will be certain to be all those things. Good day, my friends."

She left them there together, watching her as she closed the last of the distance between her and Callum. The last distance between her and whatever would happen next.

~

Callum watched from the drive as Valaria came up Kent's Row, her gaze locked on his. She had called him to join her that afternoon and he had been pacing the floors of his home ever since, trying to glean her intentions from a few scrawled lines in a missive.

"Good day, Your Grace," she said breathlessly as she reached him. "I did not expect you for another hour. I apologize that I was not home and you had to wait for my approach."

He wrinkled his brow. "Another hour. Your letter told me to meet you at two." He removed the missive from his pocket and held it out.

She stared at it a moment, then back to him. "You—you have it with you?"

He nodded. "I have been carrying it since it arrived this morning. I suppose I forgot to remove it from my jacket."

She took it and read the lines she'd written, then shook her head. "I must have been distracted when I wrote the note. I apologize, it was my error. But do come in."

He followed her into the foyer and handed over his gloves to her waiting butler. She said a few soft words to him and then motioned for Callum to join her in the parlor.

"Tea will be here shortly," she said as she paced across the room and then looked at him evenly, her hands clenched before her. She worried one in the other.

"Where were you and your friends this afternoon?" he asked.

She stiffened at the question. "Is that any of your affair?"

He flinched at her quick and overly strong reaction. "It was small talk, Valaria, nothing else. Something to ease the tension, though that was a colossal failure since you are looking at me as though you are ready to fight. And you'd win, judging by the fire in your eyes."

She blinked and the wariness faded from her expression. "I… suppose I've spent so much of my life defending my position that I hardly know how to not do so. My apologies. I'm nervous, Callum."

He could see that truth, written all over her lovely face. Slowly he approached her, watching for her flinch, for her refusal in some twitch or expression. But she gave no indication and so he lifted a hand and gently cupped her chin. "I'm nervous too," he whispered.

"You? Again?" she gasped. "I'm still not certain how can that be?"

"When you want something, Valaria, and you are on the cusp of perhaps getting it, how could you be anything less than nervous?" he asked, stroking a thumb along the softness of her lower lip. God, but he wanted to kiss her. But he heard the servants coming up the hallway and so he stepped away instead and put a reasonable distance between them. "So, now that we understand each other, may I ask the question again about where you were?"

She nodded and cast a quick glance toward the servants who were laying out the service on the sideboard. "Bernadette, Flora and I were called to have tea with the Duchess of Amberleigh."

He couldn't help the face he pulled. "Oh Christ, she *does* live on the Row, doesn't she?"

"You look horrified," she said with a smile. "Is there something I should know?"

He scrubbed a hand through his hair. "Oh, it's nothing serious. She caught me and my one of my cousins sneaking punch and getting quite tipsy at a ball when I was a boy. The boxing she gave my ears still stings."

She giggled and he couldn't help but stare. Valaria was always lovely, but in this moment where she was genuinely amused, she was something far beyond that bland adjective. She was stunning.

"I am disappointed to report that the duchess did not mention your boyhood transgression when she noticed your arrival at my home," Valaria said. "However, she *did* inquire about who would be calling on me and made note of how handsome a gentleman you were." She shifted and the smile fell. "It is but a hint of the gossip that might follow us if we do as you suggested yesterday and continue our...*affiliation*."

She blushed as she said it, putting Callum to mind of how she'd done the same as she came against his tongue. Bloody hell, he wanted to see where that blush went beneath the neckline of her gown.

He backed toward the door and quietly shut it. "If we are going to broach that subject, perhaps privacy is best."

She nodded. "Probably true."

"Tell me your concerns. All of them," he encouraged.

She sighed. "I *think* I could control what is said from within my house. I don't have many servants and they are paid well, so they might not risk telling tales about a pathetic widow who took a lover."

"You aren't pathetic, Valaria. Far from it."

She ignored the interjection and continued, "But if we are seen together by those of Society, like the Duchess of Amberleigh, for example...I fear the scandal of such a thing might spread. And with it being so close to the date of Silas's death, I wonder if the speculation might be that you and I were engaged in an affair *before* his death."

He cleared his throat. Since learning that Silas was unkind to this woman, he had tormented himself with the idea of what he could have done to protect her. Of sweeping her away and rescuing her like some prince in a fairytale.

"I think you worry too much," he said gently. "After all, Silas was my friend. My checking on you should not be misconstrued."

"As what?" she asked with a shake of her head. "The truth? That you are bedding me?"

He shivered at that image of her wrapped in his sheets, their bodies rocking together as days bled into nights and weeks and months and years. He moved toward her again, just a little closer, but not too far. Still, she caught her breath and her pupils dilated.

God, but she was temptation embodied.

"Technically, Your Grace, I have not *bedded* you just yet." He tilted his head. "But if this is too much for you at this point, if you want me to leave—"

She stepped toward him. "No! I-I didn't say that, Callum." Her hand fluttered at her side, like she wanted to touch him but couldn't yet allow it. "I don't want you to go," she said slowly.

"No?" he whispered.

"I want…" Her throat felt thick, the words hard to conjure. "I *do* want what we talked about yesterday, though it might make me the most shocking wanton. I want to feel what I felt when you touched me. I want pleasure and I want it from you."

That admission was as erotic as her touch, as meaningful as any confession he'd ever heard. He closed the remaining distance between them and touched her cheek again. "We'll be careful," he promised.

She nodded, her lips slightly parted and her gaze bleary with obvious desire. "Then will you kiss me now?"

He didn't answer with words. He just bent his head and claimed her mouth.

CHAPTER 12

If Valaria had tried to convince herself that she had overstated the pleasure of Callum's mouth on hers, the moment he kissed her again, she realized it was quite the opposite. She'd heard friends describe a kiss as explosive, and now she understood. The pressure of his fingers against her jawline, the brush of his lips against her own, the taste of his tongue, it was all so perfect. As if he had been designed for her specific pleasure.

The kiss shifted, deepened as he made a soft sound of pleasure against her lips and slid his hand up and into her hair.

"What do you want?" he whispered against her mouth, the words muffled.

She gripped the lapels of his jacket and lifted into him, reaching for more and more before she answered, "You. I want you. All of you."

He pulled back a fraction, his eyes wide as he explored her face. Then he nodded. "Shall we retire to your bedroom? Because what I want to do will require far more than a flimsy chaise this time."

She could hardly breathe. Here was an opportunity to say no. But she didn't want to do that. She wanted exactly what he offered. So she stepped from his arms, took his hand and led him from the room. They moved up the stairs together, his thumb constantly moving against the webbing between her thumb and forefinger. And even that simple touch drove her wild, put her on edge.

When they reached her chamber, she hesitated. Once he came into this room, some memory of him would always remain here. That could be wonderful. It could be terrible.

But when he leaned in and pressed a kiss to the back of her neck, his hand settling possessively on her hip, she knew she wanted to risk it. She needed to do so, as much as she needed to breathe.

She opened the door and they stumbled in together. He reached behind himself and shut the door, then pivoted her against it, pinning her there as he kissed her again, this time wild and heated and driven in a way he hadn't allowed before. That touch and the promise it made burned through her like wildfire, making her arch against him as he cupped her backside and ground gently against her, letting her feel how hard he was already.

"Oh God," she whispered, burying her head against his neck, her nose tickled by the edge of his cravat.

He made a low chuckle, deep in his chest. A sound of confidence, of certainty that he was going to give her exactly what she needed. From another man it would have been irritating, but from him it inspired excitement, anticipation.

And a tinge of anxiety. She had built this up so high in her head —could he ever live up to it?

She was about to find out.

"Lock the door to my dressing room," she whispered. "I don't want anyone coming in."

He tilted her chin up toward his and kissed her gently as he reached around and locked the door to the hallway first. "A very good idea," he said.

He pulled away, the loss of his warmth making her shiver. She watched him saunter across the room, turn the key in the door to the dressing room. And now they had privacy. They had time.

He pivoted to face her, his light brown eyes roving over her with hunger, and then gentling. "You don't need to be nervous," he said.

"Need to be and cannot control being are two different things," she said with a shaky laugh. "It's been a while since I did this and never with a man who had so much…so much focus on me. Like he could see into every desire I've ever hidden."

His brow wrinkled. "I would love to fulfill every desire you've ever hidden. You deserve to be satisfied, pleasured, made weak with release." He motioned to the bed. "Please."

She glanced where he indicated and then slowly did as she had been told. She stopped at the edge of the mattress and faced him, only to find he had removed his jacket and was working now on the buttons of his waistcoat.

"What are you doing?" she gasped.

"Oh no," he said with a laugh. "If that is where we're starting, I have a great deal of work to do. My dear, when a man wants a woman and they have agreed to make love, nakedness is required."

She rolled her eyes, a little of her fear dissipated by his teasing. "I *know* that. I just didn't expect you strip first."

"There is nothing I would rather do than unwrap you from that pretty gown and lick every inch of your body. But you said you were nervous, so I hope that if I…" He paused to shed the waistcoat and began untying and unwrapping his cravat. "…am naked first, it will ease your mind a little."

The cravat fluttered to the floor and he stripped the buttons of his shirt swiftly before he tugged it over his head with one hand.

She stared. He was…well, she had never seen anything like this man. The lanky, lean body that made him cut such a striking figure in clothing was even more shockingly beautiful devoid of them. His broad shoulders led to a tapered waist and a lightly muscled stomach. His chest had a lovely V of hair that trailed off into the waist of his trousers like a path directing her to heaven.

"This does nothing to ease my mind," she choked out.

"Why?" he asked.

"Because all I can think about is touching you."

His eyes went wide. "Then come over here and do that."

Her legs shook as she moved to him. When she reached him, she waited for him to catch her in his arms and tug her into him, but he didn't. He just stood there, looking down at her with eyes bright with desire.

"Touch me if you want it, Valaria," he murmured. "I'm yours to use."

She blinked. Use him. She had often felt used in the two years of her marriage. A toy to be thrown away when it wasn't wanted. She didn't want to treat another person like that, but the idea that he was hers to play with was certainly a tempting one.

She placed the flat of her palm against his chest, felt the solid, heavy thud of his heart beneath. He sucked in a breath as she dragged her hand lower, across his ribcage, down to his stomach, her fingers playing just above the waistline of his trousers.

He made a low groan, a sound of both pleasure and frustration, and she smiled at the idea that she wielded such power over such a strong man. It was heady and it made her bolder, more wanton.

She lifted her gaze to him and held his stare as she slowly flattened her palm against the front of his trousers, across the outline of his cock beneath the thick fabric. His face twisted with pleasure, with need. She unfastened the buttons of his fall front slowly and lowered the flap. His cock freed, it curled against his pelvis, hard and ready to do such wicked things to her.

She wanted those wicked things.

"Touch it," he said, his voice strangled. "If you want it, touch it."

She nodded and caught him in hand. Shivered at the lovely meeting of soft skin and the hardness of his desire. She stroked him once, twice, and he dropped his head back.

"Fuck," he murmured. "My apologies, Your Grace."

"I've heard the word before, Callum." She shivered. "And I think I'd like to try just that now."

He jerked his gaze back to her with a gasp at her boldness. "Your wish is my command. Turn around."

She reluctantly released his cock and turned her back to him. His fingers dragged down her spine, tracing the line of buttons between her shoulders before he unfastened the first one.

"You blush when you come," he said softly. "Did you know that? The prettiest pink I've ever seen. It slashes across those beautiful cheeks of yours, it disappears beneath the neckline of your gown. And I want to see how far it goes. I want to watch it make a trail down your body as you writhe under me, over me, around me."

She reached back, catching his hip with one hand as she made a garbled moan at those wicked promises. "Please," she gasped.

"Oh, that's like music to my ears, Valaria," he whispered, kissing the side of her neck, first gently and then harder until she arched back against him. He pushed her gown forward, over her shoulders, over her breasts, drawing it down away from her arms, her hips until it pooled at her feet.

Despite the fact that she was wearing a chemise, she lifted her hands out of habit, covering herself as he turned her to face him.

"Don't hide," he said, so gently that it almost brought tears to her eyes. "I want to see you. All of you at last."

She drew a few long breaths, trying and failing to calm a racing heart. Then she let her hands fall away from herself and ducked her head as he looked at her.

"My God, you are beautiful," he murmured as he reached out to cup her shoulder. His fingers played along the thin strap of her chemise for a moment before he looped them beneath it and slowly glided downward.

She caught her breath when her chemise slid over her breast and he lifted his hand to the other side to reveal her from the waist up. His pupils were dilated to almost entirely black as he stared at her, his lips parted, his breath short.

"I am going to worship," he said as he slid the chemise the rest of the way down to join her dress at her feet. "this spectacular body, Valaria."

Had she ever been worshipped before? The answer came swiftly and brought unpleasant memories with it, which she shoved away. This was all that mattered. This man and this moment.

He caught her hips and kissed her as he slowly walked her backwards to the bed. He lifted her to the edge and backed away, unbuckling and removing her slippers, then carefully untying her garters and rolling her stockings away.

She was naked. He was naked. And they stared at each other, equally hungry at the prospect of what they could do to each other in this quiet room where no one would dare interfere.

He stepped forward, pushing his hips between her thighs, forcing her to open to give him space. But he didn't take. Not yet, even when she lifted to him. He cupped her breasts instead, filling his big hands with both of them, smoothing his thumbs over her light brown nipples, plucking the tips.

"Sensitive," he whispered when she gave a garbled moan in response. "Lovely."

He bent his head and kissed the inside curve of her breast, sucking a little trail to the nipple he'd been touching. He licked, then tugged it into his mouth as she drove her fingers into his thick hair with a soft cry of pleasure.

He responded by sucking harder and sliding his opposite hand down her side to cup her hip and drag her against him so they were pressed tightly together. He began to rock against her as he switched his mouth to her opposite nipple. He didn't claim her, but he ground so that she could feel him, could feel herself becoming more sensitive and ready. She let out needy moans in the quiet around them, she lifted into him shamelessly and surrendered to his touch.

His mouth drifted lower, over her stomach. She fell back on her elbows on the bed as he made his way down her hip, across to her sex for the second time in as many days.

"I've been dreaming of this," he whispered, his breath teasing her flesh.

She moaned again. "You did this yesterday."

His gaze came up, sharp and focused. "Oh, Valaria, I promise you I want to start with this every time I fuck you. I want to taste you all the time. I want to lick you until you writhe and come for me. And then take you while you still quiver with release. While it still drips down your thighs and my chin."

She twisted in response to his mouth burrowing between her legs. She reacted to his words, too. God, his words. Direct and wicked, heated and reverent. She'd never known how much power words could hold over a person. But she was weak to them and to him.

He knew it, it seemed. He took every advantage as he spread her legs wider and sucked her clitoris, swirling his tongue around her. He didn't tease this time or test. He was clearly driven for her orgasm and she was so close to the edge from everything else, that it seemed the fall was inevitable. She surrendered to it, grinding against his mouth, clenching her thighs around his shoulders as they began to shake.

The pleasure was there, increasing like a tidal wave, rising above her like a wall and she raced toward it, loving the build of it, the exquisite sensation of it growing. When the bubble burst, she wailed, arching nearly off the bed as she rode the waves of the pleasure. He tormented her through it, just as he had before, only this time as her cries softened, he didn't pull away. This time he dragged his mouth back up the path he had taken down and kissed her.

She tasted her release on his tongue. Sweet and salty. She devoured his lips, aware that he was positioning himself at her entrance. Aware of him stroking over her there and the crackle of heat that ricocheted at the movement.

And then he was pushing inside and she froze, mesmerized by the stretch of his cock in her. He took her gently, inch by inch, gripping her hips tightly as he gasped when he was fully seated.

"You feel so good," he grunted, his mouth finding hers again.

She clung to him as he began to take her. Not just thrusts, which was what her experience of sex had always been, but little hip swivels, his pelvis grinding against hers and triggering pleasure all over again. She rose to meet him, as desperate for this joining as he was, as needy for it as his moans made him seem to be.

He buried his mouth against her throat. "Come for me again," he whispered. "I want to feel you."

She lifted against him, chasing the high of release all over again. His ardor, his complete dedication to her pleasure, made it easy. She could already feel the ripples from her past orgasm increasing again, drawn back to the surface by his expert claiming. And as he ground harder, she came again, this time around him. And having his cock to grip against as she fell over that beautiful edge was nothing like she'd ever felt before.

He moaned once more, slowing his thrusts so she could match him, and she did. She centered her pleasure now, surrendering completely to the sensations, watching his face as she did so and feeling how much her pleasure pleased him.

"Fuck, Valaria, I need to…I need to come." His voice was wild, on the edge, reckless.

She nodded. "Please!"

She wanted to see it, wanted to feel his pleasure against her skin and know that she had inspired this man to fall at her feet like she had done for him. He thrust faster, his cock stroking through her as she raked her nails across his arms in some wild attempt for purchase in his storm. He moaned for her, his eyes closing and his tendons flexing as he came closer and closer to the same release she had found.

And as he found it, he pulled from her, stroking himself with a cry as he came. His release splashed against her skin and she rubbed it into the flesh, like she could take some part of him without risk, like she could save this moment in her body to revisit later.

He collapsed over her, his mouth claiming hers all over again, just as heated as when they had begun. Then gentler as he rolled away and tucked her against him, both sated and weak from each other.

And for the moment, she let that be what there was, without fear and worry. If only for a brief time.

CHAPTER 13

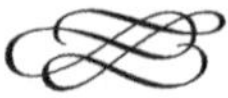

Valaria lost track of the time as they lay together in each other's arms. Neither of them slept, but there was a pleasant heaviness in every part of her body. A sated peace that she had never felt before.

In truth the entire experience was nothing like she'd ever felt before. Silas had taken her plenty of times. The experience varied from mildly pleasant to something she endured as a duty or as a way to keep the peace.

She looked up at Callum. His eyes were closed, his arms were tight around her, his extremely kissable lips were relaxed. He was different. In every way.

"And where does that lovely mind take you, Your Grace?" Callum asked without opening his eyes.

She lifted her head. "Why do you think my mind is taking me anywhere?"

He opened one eye and speared her with a playfully stern expression. "Because I can practically hear the wheels turning as you lay here. I felt you tense up. And I hate to see that happen after such a lovely time together. So what is it?"

There was no way she could tell him the truth: that she was

doing a comparison between the only two men who had ever been in her bed. She couldn't tell him any truths, really. That was the wall that would always remain between them, for both their sakes.

She sighed. "I suppose I was wondering what will happen now."

"Now that we've done this?" he asked.

He began to gently comb his fingers through her hair as he spoke, and she shivered at the sensation. Slowly, she rested her head back on his chest. It was such an odd thing to feel so entirely comfortable with a man and yet still on edge. But he did that.

"Yes," she murmured.

"We carry on," he said. "If you'd like to continue. We can do and be whatever you'd like."

She considered that a moment, then sat up, this time entirely, tucking the sheets around herself as she did so. "You are so blasé about this, Callum. Do you *want* to carry on?"

His eyes widened. "I'm surprised you have to ask that question. I think I made it very clear what a very good time I had this afternoon."

She shook her head. "You did. And what we shared was…was perfect. But I am not entirely certain where I stand and I want to understand that before I can know what I'd like to do. Do you want me? Or is it just a warm body in a bed that you desire and you're just as happy to find that elsewhere?"

"You!" he said, jolting to a seated position as well. "I want *you*."

In that moment, so close, so naked, so vulnerable, she saw something flicker across his face. Something…something that both intrigued and terrified her. But then it was gone, and perhaps she had imagined it in her longing to have a man care for her as much as Callum desired her.

"I have wanted you for a very long time," he continued.

She blinked. "You—you have?"

"It wasn't something I admitted, not out loud." He pursed his lips. "When I used to…watch you with him I told myself I was only interested because you were my friend's wife. That I liked you, but only with an appropriate level of acknowledgment. But I can admit now that I wanted you, even though I tried to hide it, even from myself. It helped that you didn't notice me."

"Oh yes, I did." She snorted without thinking and immediately wished she could take it back. She didn't want to be closer to this man who would see into her soul. She couldn't allow herself to be.

But oh, the way his eyes lit up when she said those words. They could make the world glow, they were so bright and captivating.

"You did?" he whispered as he settled back on her pillows once more. He seemed genuinely surprised, as well as delighted by this news. As if he didn't know he was beautiful and would catch the eye of any person with sense. As if he didn't know he could make a person want him in ways that were far too deep and far too dangerous.

Even now she extended a hand and drew it along his stomach, across his naked hip and watched as his cock reacted, as *he* reacted.

"Yes." She drew her thumb along the place where his thigh met his hip. "I thought most of Silas's friends were useless, but you...I couldn't help but notice you."

"You always avoided me," he said, his voice now rougher as her fingers slid along the curve of his hardening cock.

"So you wouldn't know," she whispered, staring at him, fascinated by what she could do to him. How she could make him react to her. "So *he* wouldn't know. He would have—"

She blinked as she heard herself and it was as if some spell was broken. She drew her hand back, lifted it to her chest and held it there like he'd burned her. What the hell was she thinking? Was she so addled by desire or pleasure or some other foolish connection to this man that she would almost say words that couldn't be taken back?

And he seemed to know, at some level, what those words would have been. His eyes were wide now, his jaw clenched tight. "Valaria," he said softly.

She cut him off by leaning up into him. By cupping his cheeks and kissing him. She felt his hesitation, but when she traced his lips with her tongue, that faded. His arms came around her waist as the sheets dropped away and he drew her into his lap. She straddled his waist and the kiss slowed. The purpose, to distract him, ceased to exist. Now it was just them.

And she was shocked to find that she wanted him all over again. A novel idea, and one she chose to explore. She rocked against him, feeling the hardness of him right there between her legs. He cupped her backside, tucking her closer, maneuvering her as she reached between them and aligned their bodies until she slid down over him in one wet, smooth thrust.

"Fucking hell," he murmured against her lips, and ground up as she met him. Their bodies moved together, almost as one. She gripped his shoulders, leaving half-moon shapes in his flesh with her nails. She felt the pressure of his fingers against her backside as he took her. Their breath merged, hot and short between kisses.

When she came, she sucked his tongue, jolting against him, milking him with her release. In response, he swore, a long stream of meaningless curses that ended only when she relaxed against him. He pushed her onto her back, kissing her harder as he took and took and finally groaned as he withdrew and came between them. And once again there was peace.

The kind she'd never hoped for. The kind that could cause as much trouble as it did harmony. She could only hope that she could get her emotions under control and quickly so that if this affair continued, it wouldn't drag her under and make everything worse in the long run.

CHAPTER 14

It had been three days since the first afternoon he made love to Valaria, and Callum couldn't concentrate. He sat at his desk in his study, staring out the window with unseeing eyes as he relived every heated moment of that day. And the day after. And the one after that. Because she kept crooking her finger...and he kept coming...in every sense of the word.

But was he entirely satisfied, even though their afternoons together were pure, sensual bliss? He had to admit...no. The sex, of course, was amazing. She was a responsive lover and the more comfortable she got with him, the more active she became in their mutual pleasure. She could look at him with those blue-gray eyes and he was almost undone immediately.

And when she touched him...even more so.

But beyond pleasure, she didn't allow anything else. In some ways the sex was how she built a wall between them. If he asked questions she didn't like, she always turned to seduction. And he certainly wasn't strong enough to deny her when she wrapped herself around him and drove him to the edge of oblivion.

"My God, he lives."

Callum glanced over to the study door as Theo entered, Morris at his heels. He waved the butler away and forced a smile as he rose to extend a hand to his friend.

"I didn't think that was in question," he said.

Theo raised both eyebrows. "I haven't seen you in half a week. You canceled fencing practice, you didn't show up to the club—you have been entirely absent, Callum. And it isn't like you."

Callum shrugged. "I had things to do."

"I'm sure." Theo hurtled himself into a chair across from the desk, crossed one foot over his knee and steepled his fingers against it. "You look like shit. You must be having a great deal of fun."

Callum laughed at the observation, despite how close it came to the mark of truth. He moved to the sideboard and poured them each a whisky. "How does that track? I look bad, so things must be good?"

Theo took his drink and watched Callum lean against the edge of the desk. "You don't look broody, so I don't think you are troubled."

Callum felt his nostrils flare a little. Theo pulled a face. "Oh, that's a *slightly* broody look. But I think you don't like my questions, it isn't some deep well of sorrow you've lost yourself down. You do, however, look tired. Like something is keeping you up at night. Someone, I think. And I would know. I'm the expert it such nocturnal activities."

Callum stared at his friend, speechless for a few seconds. "I don't even know how to respond to you."

"Of course, you don't, because you can't deny it. At least not in any way that will sound truthful." Theo took a sip of his drink. "So who is she?"

Callum hesitated. He'd never been one for much kissing and telling. Theo had met his mistresses over the years, of course, but even as much as his friend was a consummate rake, he was not a cad. They did not compare women or lewdly rank them as some of their set had over the years.

"She wouldn't like it," Callum said quietly.

Theo's eyes went wide and his mouth agape for a moment. Then he slugged the rest of his drink and set the glass down on the desk edge as he stood.

"Is it *Valaria?*" he asked.

The correct guess so threw Callum off that he sloshed his drink on the carpet as he burst out, "Fucking hell."

Theo shook his head. "Good God. I hardly know what to say."

"You'll say nothing," Callum said. "Widow or not, she's too early in her mourning period for this to be seen as a harmless indiscretion. She would be damaged if the truth came out, and I will not have that."

Theo tilted his head at Callum like he was speaking in tongues. "Settle yourself. I would never endanger the lady's reputation or your own. I hope you know me better than that."

Callum realized he was standing with both fists clenched at his sides and relaxed at this reminder. "I-I'm sorry. The whole thing is very new."

"And judging from your reaction, you need to talk about it," Theo said. "So drink that whisky and let me be a friendly, *discreet* ear."

"I don't know what I could say about it," Callum insisted, but he did drink his whisky in one glug and pulled a face at the fiery consequences.

"Well, start with what it is in the first place," Theo said.

Callum pondered the question, thought about the past few days in Valaria's bed. God's teeth, but she was something spectacular. He could scarcely think of anything else.

"An affair," he murmured. "It's just an affair."

"You don't sound very convincing about that fact...or pleased," Theo said.

Callum glanced at his friend. Theo was really far too observant —it was an unforgivable sin. "I should be pleased," he admitted. "We are having fun together. I have no complaints. And I should know there could be no future in it. She makes it clear she doesn't want more."

"But you do." It was a statement, not a question, and Theo was looking at him like he was daring Callum to deny it.

Only he couldn't. Because there it was, a fact he'd been trying so desperately to avoid. One he couldn't say out loud to any other person in this world except for the man standing before him.

"Yes," he said, his voice barely carrying in the quiet. "If I am honest, I would like more. I would at least like to know her more. To understand why she sometimes has...*fear* in her eyes. To ease that fear. To show her that she doesn't have to fear me."

Theo's mouth tightened. "Does that leave me to believe that I guessed correctly about the cruelty of her husband?"

Callum sucked in a harsh breath. "That isn't my secret to tell."

"I'll assume that's a yes." Theo shook his head. "Not that I ever believed otherwise. But you did. You cared for Silas, not that he deserved you. How do you feel now?"

Callum scrubbed a hand over his face. He'd been trying to avoid that question for days now. Trying not to let his feelings overwhelm when there were so many of them screaming in his head at once.

"I feel," he said slowly. "I feel like I don't know anything about the world anymore. Like nothing is entirely real. After all, if I can midjudge someone so close to me for so long, how can I trust anything anymore?"

"You misjudged him because you compared him to yourself. You believed that he would not do anything that you wouldn't do," Theo said, his tone remarkably gentle. "That was naïve, perhaps, which you normally aren't. But if you saw the best in him, that only means the best about you."

"Perhaps," Callum whispered. "I'd take naivety over purposefully blind any day." He sighed. "But now I must mourn what I thought he was, almost like he's dead all over again. And realize that Valaria's emotions on him are just as complicated and delicate. More so, because she endured so much."

"Then perhaps your time together will heal you both," Theo said. "Assuming she'll let you get past those walls of hers."

Callum nodded. If he could have nothing else, the idea that an affair with each other could help her heal even a little was intoxicating. How he wanted to gift her that, as well as pleasure to meter the pain for them both. "And how would you suggest I do that?"

"Show her that however long or short the future you could share would be, that you will protect her. That you will be exactly what you are: ten times the man Silas was. And that trusting you with either her body or something more...important...is something that shouldn't frighten her."

There was a thought, and one that Callum knew would haunt him. Share more than her body. Was that what he wanted? He couldn't think about that at present.

"I have no idea if what you suggest is possible. And I wouldn't think you'd approve, scoundrel that you are."

Theo laughed. "If you're going to moon over some woman, I'd rather see it be someone intriguing like Valaria, not a boring lady connected to fortune and title who drives you to an early grave. And if you think this woman could, at some point, make you happy, I suppose we should deduce that now so you'll know what your next steps could be."

"God, is it possible you are a good man in a bastard's disguise?" Callum teased.

Theo leaned closer. "If you ever tell anyone that, I swear I shall have your head."

Now Callum laughed, as well. "Well, if my secrets are safe with you, yours are safe with me."

"I'll drink to that," Theo said and held up his glass to Callum. But even as they playfully toasted and the subject turned to something far less fraught, Callum couldn't help but think of Valaria. And wonder what the future could bring with her if he could ever get past her walls.

~

"Oh, for God's sake," Valaria muttered as she read the invitation that had arrived in the midst of tea with Flora and Bernadette. "Why can the Duke of Lightmorrow not get it through his pretty skull that I am in mourning and cannot flit around London to parties?"

Bernadette got up from her place on the settee and rushed to her side, snatching the missive from her fingers. "Lightmorrow asked you to a party?" she asked as she scanned the pages with far too interested a gaze.

"No doubt he has invited you two, as well, as he says something about my friends," Valaria said, and paced across the room.

She was not in a good humor and she rather hated herself for it. She wanted to be light and fun for the sake of these women, but all she could think about was Callum. He had come to her every day for three days and then...poof. He had sent word yesterday that he could not join her and she hadn't heard from him at all today.

Was he finished with their affair? Had she bored him to tears and he was already off with some other woman? Oh, how she hated the tales she weaved while she lay in her bed, desperately trying to recreate the pleasures she shared with him and cursing her hand for its inadequacies.

"Did you hear me, Valaria?" It was Flora who spoke and Valaria forced herself to look at her friend, who was now holding the note. "You two are so distracted, neither one of you can read. The Duke of Lightmorrow is not having a *party*, but merely a gathering of friends. It's clearly just for the five of us, as it was that night when we went to Blackvale's London estate."

"You didn't mind that, Valaria," Bernadette said. "Certainly it would be nice to get out and have fun with friends."

"Yes," Flora said with a hard look. "*Friends*." When Bernadette blushed, she turned her attention back to Valaria. "You have been locked up in your house every day this week. You must want an airing out, as well."

Valaria was the one who blushed this time. Though she hadn't gone into detail, she knew her friends suspected her affair with Callum had gone from potential to reality. But if they had noted his arrival each day, no one had said anything about it.

"Er, I'm not sure I'm friends with Lightmorrow. Or Blackvale." But that didn't feel true. She did feel as though she and Callum *were* growing closer, despite all her attempts to keep him at arm's length. She…liked him. Despite herself, sometimes.

Flora snorted out a laugh as she crossed to Valaria and returned the missive to her. "Both of you are hopeless."

"What does that mean?" Bernadette asked, her tone as nervous as Valaria, herself, felt.

"It's obvious both of you like these men. More than like them. And yet you dance around the subject like two schoolgirls." Flora threw up her hands. "Am I the only reasonable person in the room?"

"Hardly," Bernadette muttered. "At any rate, it doesn't matter what or who I *like*, as you put it. Theo…the Duke of Lightmorrow… has known me for years. Decades, even. And he's never paid any more attention to me than he would a gnat. And why would he?"

"Oh, don't say that," Valaria said, pivoting toward Bernadette and grasping her hands. "You are worth five times that man. Fifty times. *He* would be lucky to have your attention."

Bernadette blushed. "I was a wallflower before my marriage and I will be a wallflower after, I fear. Luckily I have no need to go back out on the marriage mart and start all over again. So yes, I might admit that I find the man…I find him very attractive. But I will observe him like I do a painting in a gallery or a fine sculpture in a garden. He is out of my reach."

Flora rolled her eyes. "And what say you, Valaria? Do you have an equally ridiculous response to my charge?"

"What charge?" Valaria asked, though she knew exactly what Flora meant.

A bark of laughter was the response. "That you like the Duke of Blackvale. At least I hope you do, since you already confessed to wanting him and he's been showing up at your house over and over. I assume he has not taken up a position delivering the post."

Valaria bent her head. "Very well. You two already knew what I was considering with Callum. And yes…I have…we have begun an affair."

Bernadette squeezed her hand. "Oh, Valaria! How exciting!"

Valaria stared from one of them to the other. Once again, they both offered her nothing but support and friendship. There was no judgment, even if what she was doing *could* be judged by some in Society.

And for a moment she felt a swell of such sisterly love for them both, such deep friendship, that tears swelled to her eyes. How had she gotten so lucky to have met two people who would so swiftly bring her into their circle? Understand her?

"Oh no," Flora said, the teasing gone from her voice. She produced a handkerchief as if by magic and crossed the room to hand it over. "Don't tell me it's terrible. That would be waste of a very handsome gentleman."

Valaria laughed as she dabbed her eyes. "No, it's not terrible. Quite the opposite. I just…I have never felt such acceptance."

Of course, she knew it could disappear if these two women ever discovered her secret. Just as Callum would disappear. Which was why she had to be careful.

"Why wouldn't we accept you?" Bernadette asked, putting an arm around her. "You are a delight." She arched a brow toward Flora. "And now that you've made her cry, perhaps you would like to answer for yourself, Flora."

"What do I have to answer for?" Flora asked, tossing up her hands. "I'm not carrying on a secret affair or mooning after a handsome duke."

"And why not?" Valaria asked, jumping in on the teasing and

surprised by how comfortable it was to do so. "You're the prettiest of the lot of us—you could probably have any man you wanted."

For a moment, a shadow crossed Flora's face, a depth of sadness that Valaria understood in her deepest soul. "No. I loved someone, I married him. I shall never repeat that. I intend to be a blunt dowager like the Duchess of Amberleigh. I will look down my nose and terrify the debutantes. And cheer on my lovely friends, of course, as they live their rich and interesting lives."

She said it with such flair that Valaria almost believed that would be enough for Flora. But she still felt that sense of sadness beneath the surface. Flora was lying to herself that it would be enough.

And Valaria knew that because she did the same to herself every day. She'd lied to herself that she could endure the heartache Silas dished out. She'd lied to herself that she could accept shutting herself away from the world.

And she feared she was lying to herself when it came to Callum, as well. The barriers she had erected were clearly not strong enough if she missed his presence after just two days apart.

She stared at the invitation in her hand again and sighed. "I think it's clear we should all say yes, then. If only for Bernadette's sake, so she can ogle Lightmorrow."

Bernadette blushed to her hairline, but she looked pleased as she said, "Oh stop, you two."

They all laughed and then Flora kindly changed the subject. But as they talked, Valaria continued to slide her fingers over the invitation from Lightmorrow. And wonder exactly what it would look like to mingle with Callum in these circumstances.

CHAPTER 15

Callum had arrived far too early for Theo's gathering. His friend had punished him for it by making him sit in the parlor alone with his thoughts. Well, perhaps that was going too far. Theo had never been on time for anything in his thirty-two years, let alone early, so the fact that Callum had to wait alone was really on himself. He paced the room, staring at the clock on the mantel as he awaited the arrival of the ladies to this party.

Only when he heard sounds from the hallway did he freeze. There was Valaria's voice, rising above the rest. She laughed. God, that laugh. He so rarely heard it when she was so guarded with him, but it was beautiful.

The door to the parlor opened and the ladies streamed in, all chatting at once. Valaria noticed him first and came to a sudden halt two steps inside the room. She stared at him, eyes widening, lips parting like she had drawn in a sharp breath.

She wore a black gown, of course, a stark reminder of her mourning that made his stomach clench. Her hair was done simply in a chignon at the base of her utterly kissable neck, but she was still the most beautiful woman in that room. In any room in any place on earth.

"Your Grace," the Duchess of Sidmouth said, crossing the room with a hand outstretched. Her dark green eyes were trained on him. "How nice to see you again."

"Your Grace," he returned, taking the offered hand and briefly pressing his lips to her knuckles. "And Your Grace. And…er, Your Grace."

All of them laughed then, even Valaria, and it snapped some of the tension from between them.

"It's rather silly, isn't it?" the Duchess of Sidmouth said. "And so hard to track. But you know, it seems this little group of five is becoming…" She glanced back at Valaria and smiled knowingly. "… fast friends. Perhaps we could forgo all the Your Gracing and simply go by our given names if we are gathered."

Valaria was blushing and Callum arched a brow. It seemed she had been telling tales. Though he had no idea what that meant for their relationship that she would tell her friends something about it, but he couldn't believe it was bad. Especially since the other two duchesses were being friendly enough.

"Flora," the Duchess of Sidmouth said.

"Bernadette," the Duchess of Tunbridge added with a little blush of her own.

"Though I think our dear Lightmorrow calls you *Etta,*" Flora teased her gently.

"And *he* is the only one," Bernadette said, a little sharper though her eyes still danced with humor.

Flora motioned to Valaria. "And I think you already know what our lovely friend's given name is."

"I do," he admitted softly as he moved past the other two women to where Valaria still stood just inside the entrance to the parlor. "Valaria."

He drew out every syllable of her name, tasting each one on his tongue.

"Callum," she murmured, her pupils dilating.

He leaned over her hand to kiss and let his lips linger a moment too long. As he straightened, he whispered, "I do love hearing you say my name. Moaning is better, though."

Her mouth dropped open a fraction, but he didn't allow her to respond. He merely spun back to the rest with a wide smile. "Our dear host is running late, of course, so I will stand in his stead. What might I get you ladies to drink?"

Flora and Bernadette each gave him their request and he poured two sherries and one madeira. He took the wine to Valaria last. "I think this is your favorite, yes?"

She stared. "Y-Yes. How did you know that?"

"I darkened your halls too many times over the years not to know," he said. "And I remember everything."

"That sounds almost like a threat," Flora laughed. "It's unconscionable for a man to remember everything."

"Everything good then," he corrected himself.

"What is good?" came Theo's voice from behind them. The group turned as he entered the room, a wide smile on his face.

"*You* are late to your own party," Callum said, "and have missed a great deal. We are all going by our given names, but I refuse to share what they are with you because you are so terribly rude."

Theo snorted out a laugh. "I do like the idea of shedding all the Your Gracing. And I know all the names of these lovely ladies." He extended a hand. "Flora." Flora nodded. "Valaria." Valaria smiled. Then Theo stepped toward Bernadette. "And Etta. The best for last."

Bernadette ducked her head. "You are being ridiculous," she said, perhaps a little breathlessly.

Callum watched the exchange. Theo was always flirtatious—it was his nature—but the way he smiled at Bernadette was something different. Perhaps it was only because they'd apparently known each other as children, but Callum marked it regardless.

And also marked how briefly jealous he was at the ease with which Theo could interact with Bernadette. They could be open with each other. There was nothing stopping their teasing or flirting if they desired to do so.

As if to accentuate the difference in their relationship, Valaria sent him a quick glance and then stepped away to join the others across the room. It made the walls that she kept erecting even more obvious to him. Painful, even. And he wasn't certain he could overcome that.

But tonight was about trying, wasn't it? That was why Theo had suggested this entertainment. So that Callum could show Valaria how easy they could be together. How her walls were not required for this affair...or anything else that might follow.

So it seemed he'd best get to work.

Valaria had been surprised many times in her life, often not in a positive way. But this evening had proven to be one of the times she was astounded most. She'd prepare herself for a night of Callum's long looks and all the tension in the world. Instead it had been much the opposite. He had been entirely easy all night. He laughed and told jokes and engaged with her friends as they sat at Theo's long table, eating a magnificent supper.

And yes, Callum looked at her. But it was always with a slight smile or wink, as if they were sharing some little secret delight, not anything overwrought or dangerous.

It was impossible not to feel the effect of that down to her bones. To want to lean into it and to him, even though she still wasn't entirely certain where they stood. After all, he didn't pursue her. Aside from those little looks here and there and his teasing about her moaning his name earlier, he didn't behave as though they had any special connection at all. Nor had he expressed a reason for the distance that had come between them the last two days.

Not that he'd had a chance with the others around. She would have been humiliated if he'd brought that up, even if it seemed it was an open secret with everyone in the room.

Still, she was intrigued and flummoxed, all at once. A not entirely comfortable feeling as it sat in her chest like a rock.

"That was a wonderful meal, Theo," Bernadette said, drawing Valaria back to the table and the present moment. "The lamb was perfection."

"Well, Mrs. Ross recalled how you liked it," Theo said as he leaned back in his chair and watched Bernadette with a little smile.

Bernadette's eyes went wide. "Mrs. Ross? The same cook your family had all those years ago?"

Theo nodded and then seemed to recall there were others at his table. "As you know, my family and Etta's have neighboring estates and we've known each other an age. And yes, Mrs. Ross is the very same cook. She joined me in London after her dear husband passed about five years ago."

"Oh, he was a lovely man. Ran your father's estate, didn't he?" Bernadette asked.

"He did." Theo smiled. "She'll be pleased to know that you recall her"

"It is such a nice thing that you and Bernadette could become reacquainted," Callum said from the other end of the table.

"I don't know that we needed to be reacquainted. We always knew each other, didn't we, Etta? Though I suppose we didn't have much ability to speak in the last few years."

Valaria found herself looking at Callum as the conversation played out. She felt the topic in her bones. After all, she'd had many opportunities to talk to him and hadn't taken them. Now that she could be honest with herself, she realized it was because of the attraction that now dominated every single aspect of their relationship.

She sighed, a little too loudly, and Flora glanced her way, concern on her face. "Will we retire to the parlor for an entertainment?" she asked. "Bernadette, would you play for us?"

Bernadette's cheeks flamed. "Oh, I don't know."

"I wish you would," Theo said. "You always played beautifully. I have missed music in this house. Come, we'll go to the parlor, as Flora suggests."

They each got up. Theo moved toward Bernadette, of course, holding out an arm to escort her. Valaria glanced toward Callum, but before he could reach out to her and touch her for the first time since her entrance into the house, Flora moved in his direction.

"Your Grace, might I take a moment as we walk to speak to you?"

Callum glanced toward Valaria again, but nodded, as he had little other choice. "Of course, Flora. Please, let me take your arm."

"You don't mind, do you, Valaria?" Flora asked with a quick glance her way.

"Of course not," Valaria said. "One of us was bound to be the odd lady out. I am capable of following to the parlor."

Callum gave her one last look before he took Flora's arm and led her from the dining room behind Bernadette and Theo. She followed at a not-too-close distance so she wouldn't overhear whatever Flora had to say to him. Not that she wasn't curious. Especially since the pair did look very well together.

A flare of ridiculous jealousy seemed to tear through her. God, this was her friend. And the man might be her lover, but that was a temporary situation, obviously. They'd made no promises to each other. And yet when Flora leaned up a little to talk to him, Valaria had a brief desire to wedge herself between them. Like a petulant schoolgirl who had no control over herself.

And she *needed* to control herself.

She drew a deep breath and slowed her steps, creating even more distance between herself and the others. Off to the right was a door that was cracked. It seemed to lead to a study or library. She stepped away as the rest turned into the parlor up ahead and then slipped into the chamber to gather herself.

Because a lack of control was too dangerous. She knew that far too well.

"You said you wished to speak to me?" Callum asked, glancing down at the petite woman on his arm. Flora was lovely—no man could have denied that. He just thought Valaria was even lovelier.

"I admit I'm trying to get a measure of you," Flora said with a smile that was friendly. "Theo, I understand. But *you* are more difficult."

"If you understand Theo, you are far wiser than I, Your Grace," he said with a laugh he hoped might divert the subject.

Of course, it did not. "Well, he is a rake. But not the cruel kind, it seems. You are somewhat more layered. And I just want to..."

"Make certain I'm not some cad using your new friend?"

Flora's gaze lit up a fraction and she leaned toward him slightly. "I don't think you're a cad, exactly. And if you two are using *each other*, who am I to judge? But I think we all know that Valaria is still a bit...fragile."

He nodded. In truth, he liked that Valaria's friends would look out for her. She needed that. The more people who cared for and supported her, the better.

"I...like Valaria," he said softly. "And I want her to be comfortable at all times with whatever we do. Whatever she wants or doesn't want." They entered the parlor and he stopped, turning toward her as she released his arm. "I hope that helps."

She was watching him closely, examining his face. "It does. We don't know each other very well, Your Grace. But you seem a decent man. Valaria is difficult to get to know. She has walls, it seems."

"Yes."

"And I can only imagine the reasons she had to erect them." Flora shivered slightly as if the thought was distasteful. "But I think they are worth scaling."

"I agree," he said. He glanced to the door, expecting to see Valaria enter the room, but she hadn't. His brow wrinkled. She had not been so very far behind them.

Flora followed his gaze. "Why don't you go look for her? I will join the others."

"Thank you, Your Grace. Flora." He inclined his head. "I hope we will be fast friends."

She smiled in return and then pivoted toward Bernadette and Theo, who were at the pianoforte together.

"Play us a tune, Bernadette," Flora said with a laugh. "And I will sing terribly off key and make Theo pretend to enjoy the entertainment because underneath it all, he is a gentleman and cannot tell a lady that her singing is dreadful."

Theo let out a great snort of laughter that echoed as Callum slipped from the room back into the hallway. Valaria wasn't there, and he frowned. There was such a short distance between the dining hall and the parlor where Bernadette had now begun to play, delicate music drifting into the hall, along with Flora's boisterous voice as she sang.

Where could Valaria have gone?

He took a few steps when he saw that the door to Theo's library was slightly ajar and light spilled into the hallway from it. He pushed the door open and caught his breath.

Valaria stood before one of the tall bookcases, her back to the door, staring up at the shelves. For a moment, he considered leaving her to her thoughts, but she was too great a temptation.

He slid the door shut behind him and said, "The amazing part of this library is that Theo has actually read all the books. For a rake he has surprising depths."

She turned to look at him and he caught his breath. There were tears in her eyes and bright on her cheeks. He rushed toward her, hands outstretched. "Valaria, what is it?"

She shook her head. "It's nothing. Just a moment. You needn't worry yourself. I know you no longer desire to."

He stopped short of touching her. "I no longer desire to…to what? To worry about you?"

"To think of me at all, I suppose," she said. "So we needn't belabor the point. Go back to the others and I'll get myself together and return, as well."

"No, wait," he said. "What are you talking about, Valaria? Why would you think that I had no interest in you anymore?"

Her eyes went wide. "You haven't reached out to me in two days, Callum. And then you were…you were…" She huffed out a breath, her frustration clear.

He tilted his head. "I was what?"

"You were walking with Flora and you two looked so well together. So easy."

"Are you…were you *jealous*?" He could hardly believe that as he said it.

Her lips pursed. "No, of course not." She dropped her gaze. "I don't know. I don't want to be jealous. I have no right to be jealous. Or angry if you don't want me anymore. We never made any promises except for a bit of fun. You owe me nothing. I'm being a little fool and I hate myself for it."

He stared at her, hands clenched at her sides, shoulders trembling. For the first time since they'd begun this affair, he felt her lean toward him, but this was not the way he wished for it. He had never wanted to make her feel insecure or in pain.

Slowly, he moved toward the library door. He turned the key and then faced her. Her eyes were wide again and she looked at the door and then him.

"Callum?" she said softly.

"You are all I want," he said. "Do you understand that? You are all I want, Valaria. Constantly. Like a heartbeat that I can hear all the time. *That* is my desire for you."

Her lips parted and she took a step toward him. "Then why have you stayed away? Avoided me?" She huffed out a breath. "God, I sound so needy."

He shook his head. "No, you don't. I should have reached out. I *definitely* wasn't trying to avoid you. And I'm sorry I wasn't clearer when that was what you needed."

"It shouldn't be what I need," she whispered. "If this is just an affair."

Just an affair. Those words stung. But he ignored it as he crossed to her, cupped her cheek. It did feel like a lifetime since he'd touched her and he let out a ragged sigh as he did so.

"*Is* it just an affair, Valaria?" he whispered before he ducked his head and kissed her so she couldn't answer and destroy his dreams.

CHAPTER 16

Valaria wanted to keep control of her senses, but when Callum kissed her, it was impossible. She immediately lifted into him, gripping his lapels with both hands, working to mold herself to him as if that would be enough.

It wasn't enough. Nothing would ever be enough with this man, and it terrified her. But she pushed that away for now and surrendered herself to his touch.

His mouth was like fire on hers, a devouring pressure that lit a responding flame deep within her. She forgot everything else around her but him. His taste, the feel of his fingers gliding down her arm, catching her around her waist, the sound of him as he moaned a soft sound of pleasure against her lips.

She wanted him. All of him. And nothing else mattered.

He seemed to agree as he backed her toward the settee before the roaring fire. Together they sank down on the cushions, rocking against each other as the kiss grew more frenzied, as sensation took over entirely.

And oh, how she savored it. Savored his flavor as his tongue drove between her lips, savored the way his hands burned against her as he bunched her gown up and cupped her knee. Savored the tingle that spread through her entire body, taking over everything else in her mind and soul.

She pushed against him, straddling his lap as her gown gathered between them. This horrible black gown that said she was in mourning when she wasn't. But when he cupped her backside through the fabric and rocked her against him, she forgot that too.

"Please," she murmured, still chasing his tongue with hers.

He chuckled. "Who could deny that?"

His hand wedged between them and he unfastened his fall front. She lifted her skirts up more and pulled apart the slit in her drawers. It took a few seconds of aligning, but then he was coming home into her flexing sheath. He tilted his head back against the settee cushions with a rough groan as she fully seated him inside of her.

She couldn't help it. She began to rock over him, grinding for her pleasure. He didn't lean up to kiss her, but watched her through a hooded gaze.

"You think I forgot you?" he whispered, his tone nothing but rough seduction that made her arch harder and faster against him. "You are so wrong, Valaria. Every night I pulled myself off thinking of you. Thinking of burying myself deep inside of you just like this. Thinking of how tight you squeeze when you come and those soft sounds you make when you're so close to orgasm that it's written on every inch of your body."

She whimpered and gripped his shoulders tighter, sensation rising higher and higher, the orgasm right there where she could almost pluck it.

"I dreamed of your taste on my tongue," he continued. "I dreamed of your mouth wrapped around my cock and my fingers in your hair. There was never one moment when we were apart that I didn't want you."

She gasped. The pleasure was right there. So close.

He cupped the back of her neck, drawing her down, pressing her forehead to his. Their eyes locked and he whispered, "Come for me now."

It was an order, not a request, and she should have hated that, but instead her body responded of its own accord. Wave after wave of powerful pleasure rolled through her. She felt it in every nerve ending from her head to her toes.

"So good," he murmured, and drew her even closer. He kissed her as the tremors began to fade and lifted harder into her. She gripped him, still haunted by the remnants of pleasure, and pulled away to watch him as he had watched her.

There was nothing like his face as he moved toward release. His expression was taut, his mouth parted as he gasped for breath beneath her.

And when the moment came, he gently moved her aside, caught his cock and stroked. Her hand trembled as she reached out and let her fingers tangle with his. His eyes went wide and he gulped out pleasure. Together they moved their hands over him, using the wetness of her release to ease the way. He lifted into her hand and then he came with a strangled cry.

For a short while after it was over, they simply sat there together, staring at each other in the firelight. Then he reached into his breast pocket and withdrew a handkerchief. He took her hand and gently wiped the evidence of his release from her fingers.

"Have I proved I missed you?" he whispered.

She shook her head with a little laugh. "I suppose you did. Callum—"

She didn't get to say anything else. Before she could, there was a rattle at the door. They both turned toward it, watching as the knob turned but could not open because it was locked.

Valaria leapt to her feet, heart pounding, as she pushed her skirt back down. "Get dressed," she hissed.

Callum arched a brow, getting up slower and tucking himself back in, buttoning the fall front of his trousers without haste. "Calm yourself," he said gently. "Whoever it was has gone now. It was probably a servant."

"A servant who will now know that someone was in this room

with the door locked," she whispered. "What if they note that you and I are missing from the party? What if it is the Duke of Lightmorrow who came looking for us? What if—"

Callum reached out and took her hand, and she hated that a sense of peace came over her when he did. She couldn't afford such sentimentality, not with this man. Clearly she was compromised when it came to him and that was how one ended up in Newgate or worse.

She yanked her hand away. He stared at her, brow wrinkled in confusion.

"Valaria," he said, even more gently. "No servant is going to note who is at or not at the party. Even if they did, I imagine you'll find no more discreet staff than Theo's. And the same goes for the man, himself. No one at this gathering would think to harm you. You know that, don't you?"

She stared at him, so handsome, so gentle when she needed him to be. There was a flutter in her chest and it wasn't of mere desire. No, it was much worse. Something far more terrifying. She pushed it away with all her might and turned away from him.

"Reckless," she said. "I have been so reckless from the moment I agreed to this affair with you. In my position? With all I have to lose?"

He moved toward her and she took a step back on instinct. He stopped immediately, his light brown eyes searching her face, and she feared they saw some of the truth she was so desperately trying to hide.

"I won't let you lose," he promised.

She shook her head. "You can't promise that."

He was quiet a moment, his head bent. "This is not the time to discuss this," he said at last. "I think it will require more care and time than what we have to give to it tonight. May I call on you tomorrow?"

She caught her breath. If he came into her space, she knew what would happen. And if he didn't like what she said, she also knew she would be trapped until he could be convinced to leave.

"I'll call on you," she said softly.

"Very well."

She moved past him. "We should return. I'll go first. Will you wait a few moments, please? Perhaps you're right that everyone will have already guessed what we were doing, but I'd like it not to be entirely obvious."

She didn't wait for his response, just slipped from the room. And hoped that she could find some way to regain control of herself before she was alone with him again.

Callum sat in Theo's study long after Valaria and her friends had departed for the night. He had a whisky clenched in his hand, but he had not sipped it. He just stared into the fire and thought about…well, he thought about everything.

Theo entered the room and Callum glanced up at his friend. For a moment Theo hesitated, then closed the door. "What the hell happened, Callum?"

He sighed. "Nothing good. No, that's not true. Everything good. And then nothing good."

"It seems so." Theo poured his own drink and then came to sit in the chair next to Callum's. His friend pondered him closely. "The night was going well. There was laughter and music and I thought we were giving the duchess a glimpse at what a future could look like. But then you two snuck off together, and when you returned, the funeral pallor came crashing down."

"She's going to end things with me," Callum said, and nearly choked on the words.

Theo's eyes went wide. "What? How do you know?"

"Because she clearly intended to do so tonight," he said. "Until I convinced her we needed more time to discuss it. But tomorrow she'll come to me and she will tell me this was a mistake. And she's stubborn enough that I fear there will be no talking her out of it."

His friend was quiet a long moment before he downed half his drink. "And that's a problem because you're in love with her."

Callum shifted. And there it was. The thing he had begun to realize and tried to pretend wasn't true. Spelled out by Theo, of all people, who didn't even like to say the word. "You see that, do you?"

Theo nodded. "Yes. Even I can see it, and you know I'm not entirely certain such an emotion exists. But if it does, it is in your eyes."

"I suppose," Callum said softly. "That I was always in love with her in some way. From the moment Silas introduced us, I started falling in love with her. And I hid it, even from myself, because he was one of my closest friends. But he's dead now. And it turns out he was a bastard in every word and deed. And the moment I'm with her, I can't deny what it does to me. The moment I'm not with her, I can't stop thinking about her. The closer I get, the further I fall."

"Oof, that sounds like a terrible malady," Theo said, but there was no teasing to his voice.

"And yet I suffer it willingly," Callum replied, setting his still untouched drink aside. "The pain is worth the pleasure any moment I'm near her. So what do I do, Theo? What do I do with that if she cannot allow me close? If she will walk away rather than risk any part of herself."

"I don't know," Theo said slowly. "I have never been of a mind that a person was worth suffering for. Perhaps that is a failing." His expression fell a little, then he shook his head. "What can I do for you?"

"Nothing, I fear," Callum said. "In the end, only Valaria can decide what she is willing to receive. What she is willing to risk. It's obvious from her panic that she will guard herself, even to her own detriment. And I can't take away her choice. I think Silas did that more than enough already."

"You love her enough to let her go."

Callum flinched. "If I love her, then I must, if she won't accept whatever I offer."

"I'm sorry," Theo said. "For what it's worth. And I hope you'll come here after you talk to her if things don't go your way and we can drink until it all fades."

Callum smiled, though it was pained. "My friend, if things don't go my way tomorrow, I'm not sure there's enough alcohol in this country to make it fade. But I will turn to you, I promise. I'll need to."

"Then let's drink to the best outcome for you both," Theo said, and lifted his glass. Callum swept his own back up and they clinked them together. But as he took a slow sip, he tried not to think too hard about what might happen tomorrow.

And how he could lose what he recognized was everything to him.

CHAPTER 17

Valaria's hands shook as she looked at herself in her mirror mounted above the fireplace in her parlor the next day. She hated what she saw. She was pale and made paler by the stark black of her mourning gown. Her eyes looked haunted, there were circles under them that showed she hadn't slept at all the night before. She looked haggard.

She felt haggard. It was like all her armor had been stripped away. When she went to Callum's, he would see that.

"Bollocks," she muttered.

"That doesn't sound promising."

She turned toward the door and found that Bernadette was standing there, a bonnet in her hand.

"Good afternoon," Valaria said, trying to make her voice light. "I didn't expect you."

"I didn't let you know I was going to call," Bernadette said as she entered the room and held up the hat. "I'm returning this. Thank you so much for loaning it to me."

Valaria wrinkled her brow. "I loaned it to you a week ago. Were you coming to check on me?"

Bernadette blushed as she set the bonnet down on a nearby table. "I *was* coming to check on you. You were so quiet when you returned to the parlor last night and all the way home in the carriage. I've been worried about you, Valaria."

"I suppose you should be," Valaria admitted on a sigh. "I know I've been odd. I wish I could explain it."

"Does it have to do with…with Callum?" Bernadette asked softly, pink filling her cheeks.

Valaria sank into a chair by the fire with a long sigh. "I suppose I'd be a fool to pretend that he didn't have something to do with it."

"Are you going to call on him today?"

"How did you know that?"

Bernadette smiled. "Your hair looks stunning and it has very fancy pins in it. You can only wear your black gowns, but you can make your hair pretty. I assume you and Fanny went through half a dozen iterations to get to this very style."

Valaria lifted a hand to her hair. "Fanny was not pleased."

Bernadette wrinkled her brow. "No?"

Valaria shook her head. She couldn't explain that part to Bernadette either. So she focused on the part she could. "I…I think I must end things with Callum today," she whispered.

Bernadette straightened. "Oh, Valaria. That is sad news. I watched you with him last night and you two seem well matched."

Valaria shut her eyes. "Yes."

"Couldn't you work it out? Obviously it's complicated with you not quite three months into your mourning, but discretion is possible and widows have more freedom. Perhaps we could talk it through and—"

"There are things you don't know," Valaria interrupted, and lifted her gaze to Bernadette's. "You and Flora don't know. *He* doesn't know. Things I can't tell you, both for my sake and for yours."

Bernadette held her gaze. "I'm sure that's true." She reached out to catch Valaria's hand. "And you owe none of us your secrets. But perhaps if *he* knew, then he could help. He cares for you."

Valaria caught her breath. She feared that was true and that was something she could and would lose. "He wouldn't care if he knew what I withheld," she whispered. "So it is better for everyone, him and me, to end it now before it only gets ugly. Before everything in my life shatters because of it."

Her breath hitched on a sob as she pushed to her feet. "Thank you for returning the bonnet. I do appreciate it. I'm to meet him in half an hour, though, and my carriage will be ready in a few moments."

Bernadette tilted her head. "Valaria, you mustn't go like this. He'll understand if you are late. Stay and talk to me. I'll call for Flora. We can discuss it and—"

"No," Valaria whispered. "I must go now. I must go before I'm too weak to do what I must do." She made for the door. "See me out?"

After a long pause, Bernadette sighed heavily. "Yes. Of course."

Her friend linked arms with her and together they made their way down the hall and down the stairs into the foyer. As Valaria's carriage was brought around, Bernadette surprised her by tugging her into a tight hug.

"We are more than our pasts," she whispered. "You deserve a future filled with happiness and pleasure and laughter. Please don't forget that."

Valaria squeezed her eyes shut and felt a tear slide free. She wiped it on the back of her hand as she tugged away. "You might think differently if you knew the truth. Thank you, though. I appreciate your friendship so deeply."

She didn't wait for Bernadette to reply, to try to convince her yet again to stay, or to consider a life she could never have. She just got into her carriage and off it went, carrying her to a moment she dreaded.

Carrying her to the end of the affair with a man she felt more for than she could allow herself to admit.

"The Duchess of Gooding is here, Your Grace," Morris said.

Callum had been standing at the picture window in his study, looking out at the garden below, and now he turned, heart throbbing. "I'll see her here," he said.

"Yes, sir." Morris didn't move, but worried his hands before him.

Callum tilted his head. "What is it?"

"I-I believe the lady has been crying, Your Grace," the butler said slowly. "Her maid was loathe to leave her, as well."

Callum clenched his jaw at that idea, though it had to give him hope. She was just as conflicted about this as he was, and perhaps he could convince her not to do something rash.

"Thank you, Morris. Bring her here and then no disturbances."

Morris bowed away and Callum smoothed the line of his jacket with both hands as he stared at the door and awaited he moment Valaria would walk through. When she did, he caught his breath. He didn't even hear Morris say her name, hardly noticed as the butler reached into the room and pulled the door shut behind himself.

"Good afternoon," Callum managed to squeak out.

She nodded. "Callum."

They stood like that, eyes locked on each other for a long moment, and then he shook his head and moved toward her. "May I get you a drink? I've sherry here. Or I could ask for tea to be brought."

"No, thank you, I'm fine," she said.

He hesitated and searched her face. She *had* been crying, Morris was right about that. Her eyes were red and a little puffy.

Slowly, he extended a hand and traced the line of her chin. "What can I do?"

She made a small, sharp intake of breath as she stared up at him. Her bottom lip quivered, but then she turned away and paced to his window where she looked out at his garden for a moment, just as he had been doing when she arrived. It seemed they brooded the same way and he almost laughed at the irony of that.

"It is not your job to *do* anything, Callum," she said at last.

He wanted so much to deny that, but he could see how close to the edge she was. He didn't want to push her over. To force her to make a move that they might both regret.

It was obvious that crying made her feel vulnerable around him. And the answer for that was to give her some vulnerability, himself. Something he had never been comfortable with.

But comfort didn't matter in the face of losing someone he loved.

Slowly he moved to the seats by the fire and took one, gripping the armrests. "Did Silas ever tell you how we became friends?"

She remained staring out the window and did not look at him. "N-No. Silas didn't speak to me about much. Certainly rarely about you."

Callum refuse to ponder the reasons for that and instead continued, "He saved my life."

At that she did pivot, her mouth dropped open and her eyes wide. "What?"

He nodded slowly and forced himself to think of that day. It was not something he liked doing. "We were thirteen. You may not think it to look at me now, but I was a scrawny child. Skinny as a rail and small for my age."

She shook her head. "It is hard to picture you as anything but what you are now."

"Oh, well, I have portraits in the gallery in my home in Blackvale if you need proof, Your Grace," he said, and briefly pictured her in his ancestral home. In his life in the country, in his bed there.

She shifted as if she, too, was thinking of those things. "I will trust your word," she said softly. "But how does Silas come into the tale?"

"I was often bullied by the other boys at school, or ignored. I preferred the ignoring." He sighed. "And Silas was, I admit, one of those bullies."

Her cheek twitched and she dropped her gaze. Once again, he questioned what her experience with his late friend had been.

"I was standing on the bridge over a river one day in the early spring. It was cold, so cold. This group of boys, including Silas, came up and they started tormenting me. I was trying to ignore it and that only seemed to enrage some of them."

"Silas?" she said softly.

"No, he was in the background mostly. One of them got angry enough that he picked me up and dangled me over the bridge. Well, apparently I was heavier than he anticipated, because he dropped me. I fell into that cold water and the current was racing."

"Oh no!" Valaria gasped. "How terrifying."

He felt his breath becoming heavier at the memory. "It was. I kept going under, the flow was so strong. I swallowed so much water. But I somehow managed to paddle over to an old bunch of tree roots that stuck out into the stream. I was clinging there, crying out for help and knowing that none would come."

"What had happened to the boys who did this to you?" she asked.

"Run off the moment it was clear what they'd done." He shivered. "I knew they weren't going to fetch help or they might have to admit their part in what had happened. I became more and more certain that I would die there. My arms were getting tired holding on and the current would eventually win and I would drown."

"That is horrific," she whispered. She sat in the chair next to his and reached out to cover his hand. "What happened? How were you saved?"

"Suddenly I looked up and Silas was there on the banks of the river, staring at me. We locked eyes, and then he grabbed a stick and held it out to me. He was screaming at me to grab on."

"He...he came back for you?" She shook her head.

"Yes. Apparently he had been the only one to stay long enough to watch me struggle and realized the same thing I had: that I would die. I grabbed the stick, he hauled me to shore and saved my life."

She blinked. "I see."

"Now, he told me he just didn't want to get into trouble." Another ripple went through her face. "But after that, he took me on as a mascot of sorts. The rest of the boys stopped picking on me as much. And then I grew into my body and became much better at fencing and boxing. Eventually we were friends." He shifted. "I suppose...I suppose the fact that he saved me perhaps colored my view of him over the years."

"Did he ever mention it to you?" she asked. "Remind you that he'd done it?"

"Yes," he said. "He often teased me about my owing him a boon because he saved my life."

She nodded. "That sounds like Silas. He might have pretended to be playful, but I'm sure he meant it when he said you owed him."

He caught his breath. This was the closest she'd ever come to opening up about Silas with him of her own volition. And he wanted to know more about her past with his friend. He wanted to understand everything about her and what had made her who she was.

"Did he do the same to you?" he asked gently.

Her nostrils flared slightly and she lifted her chin. He could see the answer she wouldn't give written all over her face in pain and hate. But then she pushed it away and her expression became serene again. Blank. She slowly removed her hand from his and set it in her lap.

"I'm so glad you were saved, Callum. The world would be a much dimmer place without you." She darted her gaze from his. "But I came here to do something and I should do it."

"What you *think* you need to do," he said.

She shook her head. "No, I know it. And you do, too, if you think about it long and hard enough. We need to end this affair."

He flinched at the words he'd known were coming and yet had hoped to stave off. "Valaria, please—" he began.

She ignored the interruption as if he hadn't even spoken and her words fell out in a rush, "I made a rash decision to jump into this… this *thing* with you because of a great many things. And while it was very enjoyable, it was also rash and foolish to do. There are far too many risks. And…and since it was a lark, I think the risks are not worth it."

"A lark," he repeated, and it was like she'd reached into his chest and squeezed his heart. "You don't mean that. I might not be certain of a great many things, but whatever is between us is much more than a lark."

Once again her lips trembled, but she lifted her chin in defiance. "How could it be? You and I barely know each other, we have no bond, we have very little history. This is pure attraction, Callum, nothing more. So it follows that there should be nothing to walking away from it, especially to a man of your experience."

He recoiled at that assessment. "A man of my experience?" he repeated. "Please don't disregard who I am and what I feel so easily, Valaria. Not to make that the reason you would walk away. I have been with other women, yes, but if you think for one moment that what I felt for them, what I wanted from them was anything compared to what it's like the moment I…" He hesitated. To tell her his heart now was risking a great deal. But if he didn't, he risked even more. "The moment I see you across a room. The moment I touch you. There is no one in this world like you, Valaria, not for me."

She pushed to her feet and staggered back, like those words were weapons. He saw the terror in her eyes.

"Don't try to manipulate me," she gasped out. "Not you."

He also stood and his voice elevated. "I'm not. Goddamn it, Valaria, don't you understand that I love you?"

He moved toward her as he said those words and to his shock, his horror, she turned, cowering slightly, her hands lifted as if to keep him from striking her.

He immediately stopped, dropped his hands to his sides to show her he was no threat. She slowly straightened and their eyes locked. A world of understanding flowed between them and his heart broke as the thing he had suspected but never asked became clear. Silas had not only been verbally cruel to her.

And that explained everything.

"I would never hurt you," he whispered.

Her hands were shaking. "You can't promise me that, Callum." She backed away, still wary, still guarded, never responding to his declaration that he loved her, only the physical fear he had put into her. "I'm sorry. Goodbye."

Only at the door did she pivot before she raced into the hall and away from him. He wanted to follow her, but after watching her reaction, he knew that was the wrong thing to do. She had clearly spent a great many years, too many, being physically controlled and harmed. He would not be the next man to make her feel that threat.

He would not force her into something, even if he knew that they could be happy if she could see her way past that fear.

Slowly, he sank back into the chair before the fire. He covered his eyes with one hand and let the devastation wash over him. Because that's all one could do when one had lost the love of one's life.

Valaria threw herself into the carriage and sucked in a few heaving breaths as she waited for Fanny to step in behind her. She wanted to maintain some modicum of control in front of her servant. Fanny might know all her secrets, but that didn't mean Valaria wished to be weak in front of her. No, she wanted to save her breakdown for when she was alone, when no one would see the vulnerability. But there was no way to do it. The emotions rolled up in her and overtook like a tidal wave on a helpless beach.

Callum had said he loved her. Those words rang in her ears and through her soul like a church bell declaring some joyful Hosanna. No man had ever loved her. Not her father, not her brothers, certainly not her husband.

But *this* man, with all his gentleness and passion, with his decency and intelligence, he *loved* her. Or he thought he did. But his story of how Silas had saved him, while it explained some of Callum's blind allegiance to her late husband over the years…it also made her realize exactly what would happen if the truth of what she'd done, who she was, came out.

Callum wouldn't love her anymore. He would despise her, just as everyone would despise her. Just as she often despised herself.

She slumped against the seat and began to cry then. Fanny's eyes went wide before she lurched to Valaria's side of the carriage and gathered her to her chest. "What is it, Your Grace?"

"I ended it," she managed between gasping sobs that seemed to come from her gut. "I ended it with him."

Fanny's arms tightened around her and she began to smooth her hair gently. "Oh, Your Grace."

The pity was heavy in Fanny's voice and it stabbed through Valaria's upset. She could not be so weak. Slowly, she was able to manage her sobs and sat up.

"I was a fool to think I could have such a pretty thing for myself. Not after what I did. You were right, it was too risky. But surely he will hate me now." She shivered as she thought of Callum's abject horror when she had recoiled from him in the parlor. "And he'll forget."

Fanny's expression softened. "I am sorry."

"I-I can't be sorry. I must be strong," Valaria whispered, more to herself than to her servant.

Fanny frowned at that declaration, but she produced a handkerchief. Valaria cleaned herself up carefully and then stared out the carriage window as the vehicle turned them back toward home. By the time she got there, she would have to find a way to put the mask back on again. She had let it slip a little with Callum, but she couldn't do that ever again.

CHAPTER 18

In the week since Valaria had rejected him and fled his home, Callum didn't know how many times he'd started a letter to her. His fireplace had burned up so many pages of words that he hoped would touch her heart. He never sent them because he kept recalling that moment when she'd looked like she feared him. His heart broke every time he relived it and it stayed his hand.

He couldn't push or force her after what he now knew to be true. He couldn't deny her a say in her own life. It was obvious she'd already experienced such behavior, and far worse, from her husband. So Callum had to practice patience. Show her that he would not push her to do anything. Not ever.

And accept the fact that she might *never* come back into his life. That he might have lost her forever.

Pain ripped through him at the thought, but he had felt so much pain recently that he was able to ignore it. He had to carry on his life somehow.

Which was why he had accepted an invitation to the garden party of some marchioness or countess—he couldn't even remember which one. He felt the eyes of other ladies on him as he stood to the side of the group. They were on the hunt and he was eligible prey. Usually he didn't mind the game, but none of it meant anything to him now. Lovely as they may be, none of those women were Valaria. No one else ever could be.

"Blackvale."

Callum froze and slowly turned to find the Duchess of Amberleigh approaching, her eyes bright and focused entirely on him. He forced a smile as she reached him. "Your Grace," he said with a small bow.

She smirked. "Your gaze looks rather terrified, young man."

He snorted at the idea that he was a young man and shook his head. "Terrified? Of course not."

"That is a disappointment," the duchess said as she took up a place beside him to look over the party. "One does work hard to maintain one's reputation."

His eyes boggled as he glanced at her. "Well, then I shall not disappoint you. I suppose I cannot deny that you have been a source of awe, if not fear, for most of my life."

"Good. And have your ears recovered from that boxing?"

He lifted a hand and touched one of those said ears with a smile at the memory she brought up. Him, a boy of fourteen, sneaking into a party, trying to secret out a drink and see what it felt like. And then her, looming above him, a hawk swooping in on a baby rabbit.

"Barely," he admitted. "I certainly never snuck punch again until I came to my majority."

"Somehow I doubt that," she said with a little snort. "But you have grown into a rather handsome man, haven't you?"

"Thank you, Your Grace," he said, tilting his head.

"Hmmm." She was examining him more closely now. He wondered at the reason, as well as the outcome of her sharp thoughts. "You do not come by Kent's Row anymore."

It was a statement of fact, not a question and she arched a brow as if daring him to deny he had been visiting regularly before. He supposed he should have expected that his calls would be noted by a woman like her.

He cleared his throat. "No, Your Grace."

Her gaze narrowed. "You do not like the hospitality there any longer?"

"I-I do not think it is offered to me anymore," he said softly. "And I must respect that, mustn't I?"

"Hmmm." She faced him more fully. "You know, I never thought much of the Duke of Gooding. He was a hateful child and grew into something not much better, it seemed to me. But you two were somehow friends, I believe."

Callum bowed his head. "I have begun to reconsider my friendship with the man, actually."

"Because of *her*."

Well, now the duchess had hit the subject directly instead of dancing around it. He drew a long breath. He supposed he could feign ignorance about what she meant and find an excuse to end the conversation, but he didn't. He shrugged instead.

She seemed to take that as an answer even if he didn't really give one. "Why don't you come around tomorrow for tea?" she suggested. "I would enjoy your company. And perhaps you'll even see some friends, ones you are clearly missing."

He hung his head a moment and then managed to shake it. "I do appreciate the offer, but would not feel comfortable doing so."

"And why not?" She was sharper now, demanding the truth. But when he looked at her, he saw no cruelty in her expression. There never had been, as intimidating as she could be. In truth, he had seen this woman be a champion more often than a devil. She liked to help those who were hurt and weary, even if she would have denied it with a sniff and an upturned nose like everything was a little beneath her.

He cleared his throat. "If the friends were not informed that I would be there, I would not wish to surprise them. The person in question has made it clear they…they do not wish to see me."

"Leave it to me," the duchess said with a wave of her hand.

Callum sighed. The idea that he would see Valaria again was so utterly bewitching. He could not say no to it. Even if she refused to speak to him or treated him like a stranger, at least he would have a moment where he would breathe the same air, fill himself with the sense of her.

He needed that so desperately.

"Very well, Your Grace," he said. "I will be happy to join you."

"Excellent." The duchess pivoted away. "Good evening, Blackvale."

Callum watched her go, a poof of intimidation and spark, and couldn't help but smile. He had never believed in the fairy godmothers of children's tales, but if the Duchess of Amberleigh could give him a moment's peace, he wasn't about to turn her down.

When the Duchess of Amberleigh had sent a request asking Valaria for a neighborhood tea that morning, she had almost refused. She had been refusing all invitations, even the ones from Bernadette and Flora, since her last encounter with Callum.

It was simply that she could not seem to put the mask she'd been wearing for months back into place now that he was gone. And she feared what friend or foe alike might see if she made her true self known.

In the end, even though the Duchess of Amberleigh had worded the missive as an invitation, it was clear it was more like a demand. And Valaria had known it would cost more to refuse than to acquiesce.

And so she found herself in the duchess's parlor, Flora and Bernadette off to one side of the room with one of the duchess's other guests, the Marchioness of Merrywood.

Valaria had been locked in reluctant conversation with the

Countess of Pittsgreen for the longest quarter hour of her life. She had never liked the older woman. She was stylish and sleek, a sight to behold. And she was as sharp a wit as her contemporary, the Duchess of Amberleigh, but while the duchess had softness to the edges of her, there was a cruelty to the countess. She could destroy with her power… and she liked doing it from time to time to remind people of that fact.

She also loved gossip. She'd been dancing around trying to pry the details of Silas's death from Valaria for the entire conversation, all while pretending sympathy and parity for her loss.

Of course, Valaria had been avoiding questions about Silas's last moments for months. She could dodge them now without even paying much attention. Which was what she was doing when the duchess's butler stepped into the chamber and announced, "The Duke of Blackvale."

Conversation ceased immediately, not that Valaria would have heard it even if it continued. All the blood rushed to her ears, drowning out everything but the sound of her own heartbeat as she watched Callum step into the parlor.

"Oh," she whispered. She couldn't help it. She was thunderstruck by him—that had not faded in a week apart, no matter how she'd hoped that would be true.

He was unbearably handsome in his afternoon formal attire. His jacket was a hunter green and perfectly accentuated his fawn breeches, which fit tightly against firm thighs. He was freshly shaven, his harsh jaw cutting a line across the expertly tied cravat.

And when he turned his light brown gaze across the room and settled it on her, her heart almost stopped beating.

"Why in the world would the Duchess of Amberleigh only invite one man to this gathering?" Lady Pittsgreen snapped. "That one is *always* up to something."

Valaria blinked, her captivated reaction wiped away by the comment. What *was* the purpose of Callum's being here? *Was* the Duchess of Amberleigh up to something? Had he manipulated the situation in order to see her? Or perhaps come to try to convince her to change her mind about the end of their affair?

Irritation lifted in her chest and she glanced at the countess with a forced smile. "Who can say why anyone in particular is invited to these things? Will you excuse me? I see an old friend I must acknowledge."

The countess looked annoyed that she had not extracted the information she'd been fishing for before Valaria removed herself. Still, Lady Pittsgreen waved her off. "I certainly hope we'll meet again, Your Grace," she said. "I'll wheedle your secrets out of you eventually."

Valaria forced a smile before she stepped away. She could hardly breathe as she made her way around the perimeter of the room. Her gaze was locked on Callum and his locked on her, even as he now spoke to the Duchess of Amberleigh and Flora. She gave him a little shake of her head and then nudged her chin toward the door. Hopefully he would understand her meaning and follow her at a reasonable distance. She obviously had things she needed to discuss with him and they could not be said in this public gathering.

With her hands shaking, she made her way down the hall and into the closest parlor. She stopped in the doorway and stood watching down the hall, waiting for him. And, to his credit, he did follow. A few moments later, he stepped from where the party was gathered and looked down the hallway toward her. His eyes went wide when he found her and he strode in her direction.

Her heart stuttered when he neared, and she sucked in a deep breath and then pivoted away into the room. As he entered, she closed the door behind him and folded her arms.

"Did you know I would be here?" she snapped without any other preamble.

He faced her, his expression pained for a moment. "Yes," he admitted softly. "And I was told by the duchess that she would tell you she had invited me, as well. But I can see from your expression that she did not do so."

She wrinkled her brow. "Why...why would the duchess equate us? Did you tell her something about our...our affair?"

He tilted his head. "I would never be so crude. But she is your neighbor, Valaria, and a sharp-eyed one at that. She did note that I had been calling on you regularly and then stopped."

Valaria's heart sank. "Oh God. Do you think she would tell anyone? Or that others noticed?"

He pursed his lips as if the question displeased him. "The Duchess of Amberleigh may be a great many things, but she seems to like you. She seems to like me. Enough that she orchestrated this meeting without telling you. And I will have to have words with her later about that. I would not have violated your privacy, Valaria. You made your desires clear." His expression fell. "I-I will go."

She caught her breath. "Wait."

She said it without meaning to. Except she did mean to. She didn't want him to leave.

"Just wait," she repeated, and moved toward him, drinking him in.

God, how she had missed him. Missed everything about him, from his handsome face to the way he stood, to the scent of him, to just the way he made a room feel safer when he was in it.

Even though he was the most dangerous thing in any room. At least for her.

He stared down at her, hope and hesitation sparkling in his eyes. "Wait for what, Valaria?" His voice grew rougher. "Wait for *you*? I will do that until the day I die if you ask me to. Even if it breaks my heart to not see you. And also to see you and know I can't touch you. I missed you so desperately."

She shut her eyes. When he said those words in that hungry, harsh tone, it was a physical touch to her body. To her soul. And everything she felt but couldn't allow rose up in her. Made her want to say things and do things she shouldn't.

And yet he was undeniable.

The brush of his fingertips across her jawline made her open her eyes. He had eased a little closer, and now she felt his warmth wrap about her like a cloak, a comfort in the icy chill that her life had become.

"Callum," she whispered.

His fingers trembled, but he didn't remove them. He nodded slowly. "Valaria."

He drew out her name slowly, a rough caress that reminded her of the way he moaned her name when he came. Every barrier that she had tried to build was crushed then, and she lifted up on her tiptoes, wrapped her arms around his neck, and kissed him.

He didn't hesitate to return the kiss, making a low, hungry sound in his throat as he devoured her with a focused passion she had been dreaming of every night. She lifted closer to him as his hands began to rove down her back, along her side. He caught her knee and lifted it against his hip, rocking against her as she parted her lips from his with a harsh sigh of pleasure. She could feel him now, hard against her, as needy for her as she was for him.

If they had nothing else, there was always this. She feared she would never forget it. It would live just below the surface forever, a volcano ready to explode with the most benign spark.

"Tell me you didn't want me," he whispered against her ear, his breath hot there. "Tell me you don't want me now and I'll let you go."

She gripped the rough fabric of his jacket. She should tell him that lie and extract herself from the dangers of this moment. But she couldn't. She was too weak, he was too tempting.

"Just kiss me again," she murmured against his jawline. "Please."

He cupped her chin and tilted it up, his eyes locking with hers before he dropped his mouth and did just that. Everything slowed in that moment. Yes, there was desperation in this reunion, that didn't change. But now he savored her, tasting her, teasing her, his mouth a promise of all the wicked and wonderful things he could do to her if she just let go.

And she wanted to. She would have. She knew that in her heart as much as she knew her own name.

But there was no chance to be so reckless, because before she could surrender to what he had to offer, the door behind them opened. She shoved away from him and pivoted, but it was too late. There in the doorway, eyes lit up with pleasure, was Lady Pittsgreen, and she was smiling so broadly and cruelly that Valaria flinched.

"Well, well," the countess said, folding her arms. "What an unexpected vision."

CHAPTER 19

The look on Valaria's face as she stared at the intruder who would destroy her world was unlike anything Callum had ever seen before. It would haunt him until the day he died, he knew that. All the color left her cheeks and she looked...defeated. Utterly broken, as if she could see the path to the worst future laid out before her and there was nothing she could do to turn away from what would happen now.

"Lady Pittsgreen," Callum said. "We did not see you there."

She arched a brow toward him. "I assume you did not. You were her husband's best friend, were you not? What a scandal this will be, on every level."

Valaria sucked in a breath. "And that is what you were looking for, isn't it, my lady? What you are *always* looking for."

There was that defeat in her voice, too, even as she raised her chin and put an expression of cool detachment on her face. He could see what a mask it was, feel how deeply this humiliation cut her.

And hated himself for being part of it.

"How dare you, you little—"

"That is enough, Evelyn."

They all looked toward the door as the Duchess of Amberleigh entered the room. She glanced toward Callum and Valaria with an arched brow and then turned her full attention toward the countess, who was smoothing her hands along the front of her gown with a scowl.

"Don't tell me what is enough, Your Grace. You have no idea what I walked in here to find. These two using your parlor for an assignation."

Valaria made a soft sound and stepped away from him, hot redness entering her cheeks as she darted her gaze from the duchess and the countess.

"If that is true, there is certainly no harm in it," the duchess said mildly. "Plenty of widows have had affairs."

"With their husband's supposed best friend? Not three months into her mourning for a husband who died under, shall we say, mysterious circumstances?"

"What do you mean by that?" Valaria burst out, lunging forward. Callum stared at her wild eyes, the way her hands shook at her sides.

"A strong man like that falling off a horse in his own stable?" The countess snorted.

"You might want to have a care, Evelyn," the Duchess of Amberleigh said softly. "Everyone has their secrets, don't they? And you would not want yours to come out any more than I think the Duchess of Gooding would want hers. Now I suggest you go. I will call on you tomorrow to discuss this further, and if I hear you have spread any scurrilous rumors in the meantime, I will be *very* put out."

Lady Pittsgreen glanced at Callum and Valaria again, then back at the Duchess of Amberleigh. Her expression fell. "Fine."

She turned on her heel and marched from the room, leaving Callum and Valaria alone with the duchess. She turned toward them, spearing them in turn with an even stare. "Was what she said true? Were you two engaged in an assignation in my parlor?"

Valaria swallowed hard. "Y-yes. Or nearly so." She immediately moved toward the door. "I am certain you wish to remove me from your home, as well. I apologize for the humiliation that I have brought to your doorstep."

Callum stared as the duchess dipped her head back with a laugh. "I am eighty-two years old, Valaria. It takes a great deal more than this to humiliate me, I assure you." The duchess looked between them again. "When you two were meeting privately in your own homes, you could have subverted a scandal. But I won't be able to keep that wretched woman from spreading some version of this tale, and likely with worse details than were true."

Callum shook his head. "It is my fault. I should have had more control over myself."

"We were both at fault," Valaria whispered. "And now we will both pay. There will be some who do not accept me back into good Society after this. I suppose I deserve that."

Callum arched a brow. She was pretending disappointment, but he knew her well enough to see what she withheld. She was relieved at the idea that she would not have to go out into the world again. It was all very confusing.

"Unless you make this into a great love story," the duchess said softly. "After all, the handsome friend of your late husband offering comfort and having it turn into love and marriage would be something whispered about for the ages."

Callum darted a look toward Valaria and found her staring, mouth agape. She did not look pleased with the option, even though he realized it was likely the only one. He would have to marry her. Well, not have to—he would never be forced into such a thing. He loved her.

But *she* would have to marry him.

And he could see that the very idea terrified her. But now he wondered why. They were compatible sexually, they had a great deal in common as far as their likes and views of the world. And he was trying to prove, and would continue to prove, that she could trust him. And yet she looked like the very idea was akin to being marched off a cliff to rocks below.

What *was* she so afraid of?

"Valaria, she is correct," he managed to choke out.

She pivoted toward him. "Don't you start! With all due respect, the duchess is entirely *in*correct. Lady Pittsgreen will spread her tales and I will have months left of my mourning period. By the time I return to Society, if I even chose to do so, they will forget.

"Unless she doesn't allow them to forget," the duchess said. "And my dear, it is not only your reputation at stake. Perhaps you can forfeit a life in public, but Blackvale here will also suffer. Especially if she implies he moved in an untoward fashion and took advantage of you in your grief. Perhaps even before your husband was in the grave."

"But he didn't take advantage!" Valaria burst out. She faced him. "You never took advantage."

"A fact that will not play with the masses quite as well," the duchess pointed out. "And while the affairs of rakes may be ignored in many circumstances, this one could damage him."

Valaria's expression became stricken and Callum's heart hurt. This was not what he'd ever wanted for her. What he'd ever wanted an affair with him to do to her.

"May I have a moment with Valaria?" he asked without looking away from her.

The duchess nodded. "Of course. I shall return to the party and ensure that no one is the wiser. Though I would suggest that you return separately when you do come back." She leaned in and squeezed Valaria's hand. "I do like you, my dear. Don't be a fool."

With that she exited the room. Callum followed her to the door and shut it, this time locking it. "No further interruptions," he said softly.

She nodded but didn't move toward him. She just stood in the middle of the room, her hands clasped before her. She looked so small in that moment. Like she'd shrunk in her humiliation and guilt and shame.

"I'm sorry," he whispered.

She glanced up. "She is right. You are the one who will be hurt by this. I should be the one who is sorry."

He shook his head as he moved toward her. She stiffened, but didn't withdraw when he took her hands in his. He stroked his thumbs across her knuckles gently and stared down into those remarkable blue-gray eyes.

"This isn't what I wanted," he began. She drew in a sharp breath and he hastened to continue, "I want to be with you, Valaria. I have never given much thought to marriage beyond a duty that I must perform, but when the duchess suggested it was the best option to mitigate the scandal, I knew that was exactly the future I desired. With you. But I didn't want to force you into a position where you had no choice. I have realized over the past few weeks that it's a position you've been in far too many times."

Her breath exited in a shaky exhalation. "I had the choice to kiss you in a place where we could be caught. I knew the risks, the reckless nature of surrendering, and I did it anyway."

He touched her face. "Why?"

She blinked. "Because I can't resist you. I…I…"

She hesitated and he held his breath. Perhaps she would tell him that she cared for him. Perhaps she would give him part of that lovely heart that she guarded so jealously. But she turned her face instead.

"If you wish to marry me when my mourning is over, I will do it," she whispered. "For your sake. But if you change your mind before the next nine months are over, I won't be angry with you. I won't ever judge you for that."

Slowly he cupped her cheek and turned her face back toward his. He smiled at her, gently, carefully. "I won't change my mind," he whispered, and bent his head to kiss her.

She let him, lifting against him, although this time with much less abandon. When their mouths had merged for what felt like far too short a time, she stepped away and he allowed it.

"Will you tell anyone?" she asked.

He nodded. "Theo. And if it's brought up to me because of Lady Pittsgreen, I will do as the Duchess of Amberleigh suggests and spin a very romantic tale of how comfort turned to affection." He drew a short breath. "And it will be true, Valaria. What I say will be true. I said this to you before and I say it again, without expectation of you returning the sentiment: I love you. And I will do everything in my power throughout the remainder of your official mourning period to show you that we can make a happy life together." He moved to the door and opened it. "You return first. I'll wait a few moments and follow."

She nodded shakily and headed for the door. There she paused and looked back at him. "I'll do my best, Callum."

"Your best will always be enough for me."

She didn't look convinced, but left the room. He watched her go, his heart soaring with the realization that he had a future with her now. And sinking because, yet again, she had not responded to his declaration of love.

He feared she might never be able to, because whatever secrets she kept inside were the kind that would stand between them, even when nothing else did.

~

Valaria shifted as she and Fanny walked back from the Duchess of Amberleigh's later that afternoon. How in the world she had managed to survive the remainder of the gathering, she would never know. It was all a blur, punctuated by moments when she looked across the room and found Callum there, both a settling influence and also a disruptive one.

She would marry him. There was no other choice. And she had

so many conflicting emotions in her chest, she could scarce parse them out. But chief amongst them was absolute terror.

"You have the strangest expression, Your Grace," Fanny said as they reached the house. "Is there anything I can do?"

Valaria sighed. She would have to reveal what had happened to her maid eventually. Now was as good a time as ever. "Come into the parlor," she said while they entered the house and she smiled at Higgins.

Fanny did as she had been instructed and Valaria paced across the room, worrying her hands before her as she tried to find a way to reveal the truth.

It seemed being forthright was the only way that came to mind.

"I...I have agreed to marry the Duke of Blackvale."

Fanny pivoted and rushed to the door. She slammed it shut and faced Valaria again. "You cannot do that, Your Grace. You cannot!"

Valaria bent her head. "I understand your fears—"

"Do you? Could you?" Fanny interrupted. "We *both* were involved with what happened to your husband that night. We *both* played a part. And there is no way that the Duke of Blackvale won't figure it out eventually, either by seducing the truth out of you or putting the pieces together himself, especially if you are married. And where will that leave us? You'll be protected, won't you? His name will protect you, at the very least to subvert a scandal. But a servant like me?"

Valaria moved toward her. "I would never allow you to be accused."

"You say that, but in that moment when you could protect yourself? You have no idea what you would do. Or what he would do, this man who was Gooding's closest friend. You cannot guarantee my protection if you become Duchess of Blackvale."

"Fanny," Valaria began, but before she could finish, Higgins knocked on the door.

"The Duchesses Tunbridge and Sidmouth have arrived, Your Grace," he said through the door.

Valaria glanced toward the barrier. "Show them in after a moment," she called out. As they heard Higgins shuffle away, she took Fanny's hands. "I do understand your feelings, but there is no stopping the inevitable now. I was foolish enough that it cannot be avoided."

Fanny's nostrils flared. "Oh, Your Grace," she muttered.

Valaria pursed her lips at the censure. One she surely deserved. "I-I'm sorry. And you may not believe me, but I will do all in my power to protect you."

Fanny *didn't* look like she believed that. She lifted her chin, clearly holding back a great deal because of her position. "I hope that is true. May I be excused?"

Valaria hesitated a moment. She wanted to say so much more, but she could see her maid was upset. She deserved those feelings. And perhaps after a little while, she would calm down enough to continue the conversation. "Of course."

Fanny stepped away and exited the room just as Flora and Bernadette entered. Both women glanced toward her, but then refocused on Valaria. It seemed she would be sharing her "good" news with everyone all at once today. And she could only hope her friends would react better than Fanny had.

"We were so worried," Flora began as she moved to embrace her.

"You looked positively sick this afternoon at the Duchess of Amberleigh's gathering and you have not been yourself for days," Bernadette said. "Oh, please, Valaria, won't you trust us? Tell us what is going on and how we can be of help."

Valaria shut her eyes and let out a ragged sigh before she motioned to the settee, where she took a place, her friends on either side of her. And then she told them what had happened at the party earlier in the day. And what would happen because of her reckless abandon when it came to Callum.

"Married!" Flora and Bernadette declared together when her story was over.

Every time she heard that word, it felt like a bell ringing in her head. Joyful and warning all at once. A cacophony that blanked out all other thought and sound and breath.

"Yes," she said, bending her head. "What else is there to do? The duchess was correct that Lady Pittsgreen could hurt Callum's reputation by telling her sordid tale of finding us together. And at least if we marry, it will look as though it is an undeniable love that brought us together."

"As opposed to..." Flora encouraged gently.

Valaria shook her head as she got up and paced away. "It was only supposed to be an affair," she said. "It never would have come to this if we hadn't been so irresponsible." She glanced at them. "What you two must think of me now."

Bernadette snorted less than delicately. "What I think is that you deserve happiness and it is clear that you are drawn to Callum. That he could make you happy if you allowed him."

There it was. The thought she always chased away whenever she dared to have it. That Callum could make her happy. That she *was* happy when she was around him, perhaps for the first time in years...decades.

"He...he told me he loves me," she whispered. "Twice."

Flora caught her breath, and she and Bernadette swiftly exchanged a look. "It is clear that is true," she said. "On every line of his face."

Valaria nodded slowly.

"What did you say to him?" Bernadette encouraged.

"Nothing," she admitted on a shaky breath. "Both times I simply pretended he hadn't said it. That those words couldn't exist."

Flora covered her hand. "Why? Is it just the timing? Or the fact that he was such a close friend to your late husband?"

Valaria worried her lip. She couldn't tell the truth to these women who had become such dear and powerful friends to her. For Fanny's sake, as much as her own. But she needed their counsel, even if they didn't truly understand her motives. "It is impossible to fully open my heart to…to anyone I care for if I am lying to them." She hesitated. "Isn't it?"

Bernadette's expression softened. "Are you lying or keeping secrets?" she asked gently. "They are not the same thing. Your secrets may be your own."

"What if they are both?" Valaria asked. "How in the world could I ever be happy with him, be happy with anyone, let him love me…if I am a liar?"

Flora considered the question a moment. "My late husband was many years older than I was," she said at last. "And though many thought it an odd match, or a mercenary one, the truth was that we loved each other. And in that love, we found safety to be ourselves and to tell our secrets. Callum *does* love you, of that I am certain. And your secrets…or your lies…would be safe with him, I think."

"At least you would know for certain if you confessed whatever you are so afraid of to him," Bernadette said. "He seems a gentle person."

"He is that," Valaria whispered as memory after memory of just that tenderness came through her mind. "But what if he hates me? What if this changes how he sees me?"

"Then we'll work something else out," Flora said without hesitation. "We will make sure there is another path for you that doesn't involve a man who can't accept you for everything you are."

"Indeed," Bernadette said. "We're not so helpless as we might have been before our marriages. Our widowhoods give us money, independence, freedom. We won't let you lose those things."

Valaria stared at the door Fanny had gone through before. "Would you…would you protect Fanny if it came to that?"

Flora drew back a fraction. "Good God, Valaria. These must be dangerous secrets, indeed, for you to ask that."

Valaria didn't answer, and after the silence hung for what felt like a lifetime, Bernadette took her hand. "I promise you, we would protect Fanny if it came to that."

Valaria stared at her two friends and tears filled her eyes. "You two have become so precious to me in such a short time."

From either side, the women hugged her, and for a moment they were nothing more than a blubbering mass. But at last they all laughed, wiping tears and trying to pull themselves back together.

"If we are not here for each other, then nothing else in life is worth anything," Flora said.

Valaria nodded. She had not always believed that, or thought it possible, but now those words felt very true. And for the first time she felt brave enough to attempt to make Callum understand her hesitations.

Now she just had to figure out how to tell him before her bravery fled.

CHAPTER 20

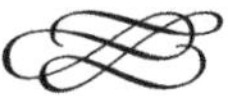

Callum was not expecting visitors when the bell rang after supper that night. He lifted his head from the letter he was writing in the study and listened. It was likely Theo, which was fortuitous, since he was writing his friend to arrange a meeting so he could confess his future marriage.

But it wasn't Theo's voice that floated down the hallway toward him a moment later.

"…apologies…so late…in?"

The broken words were in a feminine voice and one he recognized instantly.

"Valaria." He pushed his chair back with a screech and hustled around the desk to the hallway. He made his way toward the foyer and met her and his butler halfway.

Both she and Morris looked startled by his appearance, but the butler rallied admirably. "The Duchess of Gooding, Your Grace," he said.

Callum looked at Morris. "That will be all, thank you."

Morris nodded and slipped away, leaving Callum to stare at her in the dimly lit hallway. She was so beautiful standing there, light from the foyer outlining her. Her hair was pulled up in a simple chignon, her blue-gray eyes were focused on him and her cheeks were pink. He realized she was also wearing color, a dark blue gown that skimmed over her body in the most bewitching way.

"You—you're wearing color," he whispered.

She nodded and smoothed the gown. "For you. Just for you. Callum—"

He didn't allow her to finish, but crossed the distance between them in a long step. He swept her into his arms, tight against his chest, and kissed her.

She didn't resist, but made the same soft sound in her throat that she had earlier in the day before they were caught in the parlor. A needy, hungry sound of pleasure and desire.

And oh, how he wanted to give her everything she needed, wanted. Everything he couldn't live without in that moment.

"Come upstairs with me," he whispered against her lips.

She hesitated and pulled back, staring up at him. He could see she had a thousand things to say. Probably as many arguments to make against what had already been decided. But in that moment, he couldn't hear them.

All he wanted to hear was her sigh out his name as she shattered around him. All he wanted to see was her body rocking against his. The rest could be resolved later. They had all the time in the world for the rest.

"Let me make it good for you, Valaria," he murmured, turning her, backing her toward the back stair that went almost directly to his bedchamber above. "Let me make you forget every other thing but how it feels when I take you, when you ride me, when you come against my tongue and my fingers and my cock."

She shivered, her pupils dilating wide and dark. "It's impossible to deny you," she said. "I wish I could hate you for that."

He smiled as he led her up the stairs, down the hall, into his room. As he shut the door, he pivoted her, pressing her back against the barrier as she gasped out his name in the quiet.

"God, yes," he murmured, burying his mouth against her shoulder. "There is nothing that drives me wilder than when you whisper my name like that. When you shout my name. When you whimper my name as your legs shake. I have never loved those two syllables more than when they fall from your lips."

He began to drag his mouth down, dropping to his knees. He pushed her skirt up, revealing her pretty stitched stockings as he gathered the fabric around her hips.

"Take this," he ordered, handing the pile to her.

Her hands shook as she did so and she stared down at him, mouth opening and shutting. "I wanted to talk to you—" she began.

"And I wanted to lick you," he said, and spread her legs wider. He slid his hands up her thighs, under the edge of her drawers. He caught the opening in the fabric between her legs and tugged, ripping the delicate satin so that it fluttered to the ground at her feet.

"Callum!" she gasped.

He smiled up at her. "Keep saying it, Valaria. Never stop saying it."

She made an almost feral sound at the back of her throat, and while she continued to cling to her skirts with one hand, she tangled the other in his hair and drew him up against her.

"Make me say it," she murmured.

His cock twitched at that order and he pressed his palms more firmly against her thighs. She widened her stance and he lifted into her, drawing in the scene of her desire before stroked his tongue along her entrance.

She tasted salty-sweet and he wanted to drown in that flavor, to always taste her on his tongue until the moment he drew his last breath. She whimpered as she writhed against him and he looked up the length of her body to watch her reaction.

She had closed her eyes, dropped head back against the door, and she was grinding against him, seeking the pleasure he wanted so much to give her.

So he didn't deny her, or himself, for even a moment longer.

~

Callum shifted beneath her, arching one leg over his shoulder, spreading her wider for more access. The feel of his tongue dancing across her, teasing her clitoris, God, how she had missed this. Missed him when he pleasured her…but also in all the other ways.

And she was a coward for not telling him what she had to say before she allowed this, but she pushed those thoughts away and focused instead on the sensation of his mouth. He was so good at this, so good at making her feel alive. She never wanted it to stop.

He sucked her clitoris now, the wet sound of it like music in the air around them. She ground against him, crying out when he slid one hand from her hip and pressed two fingers into her sheath. She gripped against him, grinding for her pleasure. He gave it in spades, building her toward the orgasm as her legs began to shake.

When it hit, she buckled, but he kept her upright, continuing to torment, to please as she wailed out his name, as she cursed, as she shuddered. And only when she went limp did he rise up, pressing his fingers to her lips so she could suck the evidence of her orgasm from his fingers.

"More," she found herself whispering, demanding because he always made her feel safe to do so.

He swept her into his arms, carrying her to his bed. He set her next to it and turned her, pressing her hands to the high edge as he flicked the buttons along the back of her dress open. He shoved the dress and chemise down. She kicked from her torn drawers and now all that was left were her stockings and her slippers.

"My God, what you do to me," he grunted, stepping back, removing the heat of himself from her back. She whimpered and looked back over her shoulder to find that he had shed his jacket and was untangling his cravat from his neck.

"I want to see what I do to you," she whispered as she faced him, leaning on the edge of the bed. "Show me."

His eyes went wide, pupils dilating with even more desire. He unbuttoned his shirt and tugged it over his head, then lowered the placket of his trousers and pushed them away too.

His hard cock curled up, so tempting. She shivered as she moved toward him, pressing herself to his now-naked body and reaching down to take him in hand. He hissed out pleasure as she stroked him. She watched that reaction, loving the power he allowed her when he showed her that she moved him.

She wanted more of it. More of him. She wanted to make him just as needy and filled with pleasure as he always made her. She leaned in and kissed his shoulder, lower to his pectoral, swirling her tongue around the nipple there. He grunted her name, almost primitive as his hands dug into her hair and scattered the pins down on the floor.

She kept kissing lower, repeating his earlier action by dropping to her knees before him.

"You don't have to—" he began.

She stared up at him as she brushed her cheek to his cock. "I want to."

Then she drew him inside her mouth. It had been a long time since she did this. With Silas she'd never much liked the act. Of course, she had stopped wanting Silas mere months into their marriage. But this man she wanted, needed, craved, and so having him between her lips, taking him into her throat so he jolted with pleasure...

That was magical.

She stroked over him, rolling her tongue around his length, sucking him as she worked him as deep as she could. She could feel him edging toward release and she found herself craving the moment that she could steal this man's control.

But he didn't allow it, at least not this time. He caught her elbows and she was dragged away from her work as he kissed her.

"Not this time," he panted against her lips. "I need to feel you too much."

With that, he pivoted her so her back was against him. He curved his body around hers, pinning her hands to the bed with his. She lifted her backside, offering herself shamelessly. And he took that offer without hesitation.

He aligned his cock to her entrance and then he was sliding home. They moaned together, grinding in time as he began to thrust. She worked a hand between her thighs and began to circle her clitoris with her fingers, gripping his cock with every stroke as he worked her, once again, toward release.

When she came, his mouth closed around her shoulder. She rocked back against him, riding the unceasing waves of pleasure that seemed to roll through every nerve ending in her body.

"Christ," he grunted, pulling from her body to spill against her back with a long cry.

He collapsed against her, pinning her to the bed for a moment as he kissed her shoulders, the back of her neck. She reveled in the weight of him, the brush of his body against hers. She felt…safe.

Even though she wasn't. Not really. She hadn't told him what she'd actually come here to share. And she had to.

Slowly he shifted off of her and climbed onto the bed. He patted the place beside him. She eyed it, feeling the rush of temptation. "I don't know, Callum," she began.

He reached out and caught her hand, his light brown eyes locking with hers. "Please, Valaria. Come into the bed with me. We're getting married—we have months and months to come where you can tell me all the reasons you have for hesitation. Right now I'd like to just…hold you. Be with you. Have you stay with me today, tonight."

Her lips parted. "You want me to stay with you?"

He nodded. "Yes."

She swallowed hard. She'd resisted this man, not physically, but in her heart, because of her fears. But he was offering her something now that was so precious. So lovely.

Her hands shaking, she climbed into the bed beside him,

cuddling her head into his shoulder. He wrapped his arms around her, their bodies pressed together as he dropped his lips to her temple.

"This is all I want, Valaria," he whispered. "This is what I can give you. For the rest of our lives."

She looked up at him. He looked so serious, so gentle, and so in love with her. He truly did love her. And that swelled up in her with a power unlike anything she'd ever felt before. She didn't want it to end. Not right now. So she could tell him her secret later. Later she could confess everything and see how it would change them. If it would.

She rested a hand on his chest, measuring the steady thud of his heartbeat against her fingers. "I'll stay," she said softly.

He smiled down at her. "I'll send word for your maid to join you, so she can help you tomorrow morning," he said.

She flinched at the mention of Fanny. God but she would only be angrier thanks to this. Still, there was no denying where this was going, was there? And one day her maid would understand.

Valaria reached up and cupped his cheek, drawing his mouth toward hers. "Later," she whispered before she kissed him.

And then she pushed all thoughts aside and drowned in him all over again.

CHAPTER 21

Callum was feeling cautiously optimistic. Valaria had stayed the night with him...then another...and then a third. And now she sat at his breakfast table, reading his paper, looking so lovely and natural there that it made his heart ache.

This was the future they could share. *Would* share once her mourning was officially over and they could be wed. The future they would share now, quietly together, privately bound in their hearts, even if they could not be in the eyes of the law.

And he would have been only optimistic and not cautious if he didn't still feel the remnants of her hesitation. Oh yes, she curled herself into him, spent the long nights in his bed exploring passion, becoming more attuned to him, just as he did with her. She spent longer afternoons reading with him or talking about everything and nothing all at once.

They were becoming closer with every passing hour, but she was still holding back. Sometimes she started to tell him something, but stopped herself. He saw her fear. He saw her pain.

And he could only hope that the longer they were together, the more he could prove that he was trustworthy and true. That she could give him her heart, her soul, her secrets, without fear of recrimination or whatever abuse she'd suffered at the hands of Silas.

"You suddenly look very serious, Your Grace," she said without looking up from the paper.

"You can tell that with your nose buried in the news?" he teased. "You are so aware of me?"

Now she did glance up. "You know I am aware of you. Always," she said. "You make it impossible not to be, the way you fill every room you're ever in."

He chuckled. "How boorish of me."

She smiled in return. "Very discourteous, I agree." She tilted her head and her smile faded. "Is something troubling you?" she asked.

He shook his head. "How could anything trouble me when we've had such a perfect few days together?"

She worried her lip. "It has been wonderful," she admitted softly. "I hate to see it end."

"Does it have to?"

She glanced up at him. "I cannot stay here forever, Callum. Not yet, at any rate. I must go back to Kent's Row and at least maintain some semblance of my prior life. Flora and Bernadette will expect to see me later today at the very least. Fanny brought me the invitation to join them for tea when she went home last night to fetch my dress for today."

"And so you will run away," he said. "Will you come back?"

She shifted. "You make it impossible not to." She reached across the table and covered her hand with his. "Why don't you come with me today? I could request that the duchesses join me at my home instead of at Flora's. We could invite Theo. It would be a very happy fivesome."

He smiled at the fact that she wasn't entirely pushing him away. "I would love that. Yes."

"Wonderful! Let's finish eating and I'll write a little note to the ladies and to Theo about the change of plans. I'm certain they will be just as pleased with that as anything else. Then Fanny can gather my things and we can return to Kent's Row together."

He stared at her, this woman who had lit up his world so entirely. And he wished with all his heart that he could do the same for her someday.

"You could write your note to the duchesses and *I* could invite Theo," he suggested. "And then with our chores done, we could go back up to my chamber."

She arched a brow. "And what would we do in your chamber, Your Grace?" she teased.

He locked his gaze with hers. "Well, I could find at least five or six different ways to distract you from all your plans one more time."

A smile fluttered across her face and she nodded. "An excellent notion. Let's do just that." She cleared her throat. "But…but after the tea with our friends, before you return home, or decide to distract me as you do again…I do want to talk to you about something. Something serious."

He nodded slowly, even though his heart lurched at that statement. "Yes. If you're ready to do so, I would love to hear whatever you would say."

Her breath left her lips on a shaky sigh. "I hope that will be true," she said. She shook her head and got up. "I'll go write my message and meet you in the bedroom shortly."

She leaned down to kiss his temple and then slipped from the room. He watched her go, his heart throbbing, and hoped… prayed…that whatever would happen today would make them stronger, not tear them apart.

Valaria's head spun as Callum's carriage ferried them onto her drive back at Kent's Row. It had only been a few days since she was last home, but it felt like a lifetime now. She felt…*different*.

The time in his home, in his arms, had felt like a moment stolen from time, a place where she could picture a future she'd never dared to hope for and forget everything she feared.

But now those fears came back. Those worries about what Callum would say when he knew the truth about her and what she'd done.

The carriage stopped and her servants rushed forward, helping her down. She moved toward the door with Callum at her heels. In that moment, she realized that it was entirely obvious where she had been during her time away, and what she'd been doing. Heat filled her cheeks and she shook her head as she reached Higgins.

"Welcome home, Your Grace," he said kindly, not a hint of judgment in his dark eyes. "And Your Grace." He acknowledged Callum with a slight nod.

"Thank you, Higgins," Valaria said, lifting her chin with as much pride as she could manage. "I assume there are a great many messages and things to discuss."

"Yes, Your Grace," he agreed, and began to take gloves and hats, handing them to a footman who was standing by. "Mr. Stout came by to discuss the painting of the parlor. They will begin Tuesday next, as long as that is agreeable to you."

Valaria blinked. She'd all but forgotten her desire to renovate that room. "Of course," she said with a quick glance toward Callum. "If we host friends during that time, we can easily use the terrace room. It gets lovely sunlight in the afternoon around teatime."

"Quite, Your Grace," Higgins said. "I'll send him the confirmation this afternoon and let you know if there are any other issues to resolve. You also received several letters, which I'll bring to you momentarily."

"Thank you, Higgins," Valaria said. "I assume the parlor for our little gathering of friends?"

"Yes, Your Grace. Tea has already been laid out."

"Very good." Valaria glanced over her shoulder to see that Theo's carriage was beginning to turn onto the drive. "It looks as though our friends are arriving. His Grace and I will move to the parlor so you may announce them."

"Yes, Your Grace." Higgins nodded.

Valaria turned to say something to Callum and found that he was watching her, a little smile turning up his lips and his arm outstretched in offering to her.

"May I?" he asked.

She nodded and slid her hand into the crook of his elbow. A little shock of awareness worked through her at the touch. Amazing how he could still do that despite the fact that an hour ago she had been writhing above him, lost in pure pleasure. But there didn't seem to be enough of this man.

"Our rush is my fault," he said softly as they entered the room. "I distracted you from returning sooner."

She released him and smiled up at him. "I don't think you heard me complaining."

"Keening," he teased. "But not complaining."

She sighed. "And now we are gone from that fantasyland. Back to reality."

"But reality does not have to be so bad, does it?" he asked.

She worried her lip. Let him say that later today, after she'd confessed her darkest secrets. She shrugged. "It depends on the reality, I suppose."

Before he could respond, Higgins led Theo to them. "His Grace, the Duke of Lightmorrow." As Theo entered the room, Higgins followed. "And the correspondence, Your Grace."

He handed over a small stack of missives, which Valaria took as Theo greeted Callum. Once Higgins had gone, she smiled at the other duke. "Forgive me, Theo, I only just arrived home."

He smiled. "Sort away, Your Grace. I am perfectly capable of pouring not only my own tea, but his. And yours." He glanced toward the door. "I assume the other two ladies will join us shortly?"

"They should be here momentarily," Valaria confirmed as she started flipping through the notes. There was one from a distant aunt, a note from Bernadette, something from the Duchess of Amberleigh that likely could not be ignored for too long.

As she was sliding the next note in the stack to the top of the pile, Higgins reappeared with Bernadette and Flora on his heels. Valaria turned toward them, moving to press a kiss to first Bernadette's cheek, then Flora's. When the ladies stepped away toward the gentlemen and the room became a happy, loud place of greeting and jokes, some of the letters in Valaria's hands slipped to the floor.

She laughed as she gathered them up and then paused. Here was one she hadn't seen yet, written in a difficult to read hand with no return address above the direction to her home.

Her heart began to throb with a sense of dread and anticipation as she glanced at her friends. They were still talking. Slowly, she broke the wax seal, which was plain and in no way identifiable.

I know what you did to your husband. How much are you willing to pay to ensure no one else finds out?

She stared at the words. So few and yet so powerful and her hands began to shake. Nausea roared up in her, along with tears that flooded her eyes.

"Valaria, what is it?"

She started and found that Callum was moving toward her, his face lined with concern. She shook her head, shoving the letter down to her side. The room had gone quiet now, everyone was looking at her.

"Nothing," she lied, but she could hardly catch her breath. "It's nothing."

"It's not nothing," he said. "What did that letter say? Why is it so upsetting?"

He reached for the page and she gripped it tighter. "Don't," she whispered. "Please don't."

He hesitated, stopping without taking it, but he was still taut with concern as he stared at her. She let her gaze move to the rest of the room and saw all their questions, as well. Saw that her friends, like him, wouldn't let her lie her way out of this. They would think that forcing her hand would help, not knowing what they would unleash. But it was inevitable now. Not something she could hide.

Perhaps the true fantasy was her foolish belief she ever could. The moment she let any of these wonderful people into her circle, her heart, the truth was bound to sully it all. She glanced back at Callum and their eyes met. She held there, memorizing this last moment before he would find out the truth. Before everything in her world came crashing in. How she had treasured these few scant weeks when she had been considered a friend. When she had been loved.

"Valaria," he said gently, and reached for the paper again.

This time she let him, because there was no use playing keep-away. Callum read the two lines, his expression becoming confused and even more deeply concerned.

"What does it say?" Flora asked gently.

Valaria forced herself to look at the other three. She had not wished to do this with an audience, but it seemed there would be no hiding the truth from anyone anymore. Not if someone else, someone with a terrible agenda, already knew it.

"It…it says that the author of the letter, whoever they are, knows what I did to my husband," she whispered. "They know…they know that I murdered him."

CHAPTER 22

Valaria couldn't tear her eyes away from Callum, from his confused expression, from his dawning realization about what she meant. That she was being truthful. And then it was just...*horror* on his face. And when she dared to look at the others, the same was on their faces, as well. But the room remained silent, as if no one knew what to do, what to say.

Until Theo moved forward. His usual playful expression was now serious as he gently squeezed her hand. "I think you must explain, Valaria. Explain, and I hope we can help you."

There was such kindness in this man's eyes. Such gentleness she'd never seen before. And it gave her some of the strength she lacked.

Slowly she looked at Callum again. *He* was the one she owed the explanation. And he was the one whose response to her words she cared most about.

"I-I think you have all guessed that my marriage was a deeply unhappy one," she said, hating that her voice broke when she wanted to be strong.

"He was harsh to you," Callum said, his voice shaking. "Cruel.

And I've guessed, though I didn't push, that he was also…physically abusive."

Valaria's breath hitched. "Yes," she admitted. "Once we were married, he moved swiftly from verbal cruelty to physical. Pushing, then slapping, then backhanding, then with a closed fist."

Flora lifted a hand to her mouth. "Oh, Valaria."

"I'm so sorry, dearest," Bernadette breathed, tears filling her eyes. "I'm so, so sorry."

Their kindness, at least thus far, buoyed her, and she drew another shaky breath to continue. "He always reminded me that I had nowhere to go. That I had no escape."

"What about your family?" Theo asked gently.

She shook her head. "I was a commodity to my father and brothers. My value was in my match. Once I had fulfilled that obligation, they had little use for me. I once tried to tell my father and he brushed me off. Told me I should be a better wife if I wanted a better husband."

Callum made a harsh sound in the back of his throat and his face reddened, but he did not speak.

And so she continued, "I tried so very hard to please Silas. To never invoke his anger. To stay out of his way. And sometimes it worked. He had his lovers, of course. I know you thought that was the source of my anger toward him, Callum, but I was always pleased when he had a steady mistress. They took the focus from me in many ways."

"Things must have…escalated," Flora said.

Valaria's legs felt unsteady and she clutched the back of the closest chair to remain upright. Images of that horrible night bombarded her, images she had tried to forget in the past few months as she healed and hoped for a better future.

One that was very likely lost now.

"H-he came home, very drunk, after a night of carousing and gaming and…and losing."

Callum straightened. "The night he died?" he whispered.

She nodded. "Were you with him?"

"I was." His tone was strangled now.

"When he came into the bedroom, I was almost asleep. He..." She turned her face. "He attacked me without any warning, dragging me from the bed. And when I resisted, he began to hurt me." Tears were streaming down her face now, but she didn't wipe them away. She just focused on the words, focused on the truth.

"I told him to stop. I told him that if he didn't stop, I would tell his friends what he was. I would tell everyone what he was, scandal be damned." She shivered. "He stood over me with the most horrible look in his eyes. And I saw that he would...he wanted to..." She swallowed hard. "He wanted to kill me."

"Oh, Valaria," Bernadette sobbed.

"He dragged me down the stairs by the hair, reminding me all the way that he could end me without anyone even noticing or caring. And then—"

She cut herself off. This was the point when Fanny had entered the fray that night, chasing after them as Silas hauled her from the house, out into the rain, down toward the stable.

But she had promised Fanny that she would be protected. So she shook her head and continued without adding that moment to the already horrific tale.

"He dragged me toward the stable, and then he was distracted by..." She hesitated. "Something. I grabbed a hammer from the wall and I swung it as he headed for me again. I hit him in the forehead." She choked on the words. "He was so enraged. I hit him again and he fell."

"He died," Theo whispered.

She heard those words and nausea rose up in her. She fought to keep it down, fought to regain control before she said, "Y-Yes. He... he died. And I panicked. I knew what would happen if I was found out. I knew what it would bring down on me and...on me. He had this wild horse, this animal he was so excited to break."

"Firebrand," Callum breathed.

She nodded. "So I rolled him into the stall with Firebrand so it would look like he'd drunkenly come into the horse's space and been trampled. And I went inside and snuck up the back stair and went back to bed and...and waited."

"And no one knew? No one saw?" Bernadette asked.

"I thought no one knew," Valaria whispered. "But..."

She held up the note that had started her confession. The one that left her feeling wrung out, but also...relieved. She had born this for so long and even though her world would collapse now, at least she was no longer living in a lie.

"Someone knew," Theo said. "And waited until now to reveal themselves to you."

"I don't know why or what they might want." She threw up her hands, feeling the surrender of it all. "I have enough money to keep myself comfortable, but I am by no means rich in my widowhood."

"But *I* am," Callum said softly. "And Lady Pittsgreen caught us together and has likely begun the whispers about us. The fact that we will marry when your mourning period is over is already being spoken of, I'm sure."

"And suddenly blackmail has value," Valaria whispered, bending her head. "Oh Callum. I'm so sorry."

He said nothing, but looked at the others. "I would like a moment alone with Valaria. Please."

Valaria stared at him, heart throbbing so loudly she was certain everyone in the room could hear it. She glanced toward her friends and saw that Flora and Bernadette were waiting for her to verify that she wished to be alone with Callum. And she adored them for it, even if she feared what they now thought of her.

"It's fine," she said softly.

Flora sighed and turned toward Bernadette and Theo. "Come. It's a fine day and I think we could all use some air."

She moved toward the parlor door with the other two behind her. As she passed Valaria, she gently touched her hand, and Valaria could almost feel her friend's strength and love pour into her.

Bernadette kissed her cheek and she felt the same. Even Theo held her stare for a moment, that warmth and kindness he had shown earlier still bright on his handsome face. He also squeezed Callum's arm as he left the room, shutting the door behind them.

Shutting her in alone with Callum. A man who loved her…or had loved her. A man who had also loved the man she killed. And she had no idea what he would do or say…what she would lose… now that her secret was out.

~

After he was left alone with Valaria, Callum stood silent for what felt like an eternity as he tried to wrap his mind around the words she had just said. Those horrible words, and her terrible, broken expression as she said them. It made no sense. And yet it made all the sense in the world at the same time. Her confession explained everything.

"I understand if you want to end this engagement, if you can call it that," Valaria said at last. "I will take the blame for it if you do. I should because all this is my fault."

"That is what you think?" he said. "That I believe what happened is your fault?"

"I killed him," she whispered, and that choked sound returned to her voice and stabbed him through the heart. "How can it be anyone's fault but mine?"

He moved toward her, slowly now, gently because he never wanted to give her a reason to fear him. The very idea she'd ever had to fear anyone still felt like poison in his veins. She stiffened, but didn't draw away as he took her hands.

"It's Silas's fault," he said, slowly and succinctly. "Look at me, Valaria. Look into my eyes and hear what I'm saying to you. Everything that happened that night is Silas's fault."

Her lower lip began to tremble and she bent her head, leaning forward to rest against his chest. He folded his arms around her, reveling in the warmth of her, the fact that she was alive and here with him after all she'd endured.

That she almost hadn't been was so devastating he could scarcely grasp it.

"I know you loved him," she whispered. "I know losing him was very difficult for you. And if you hate me for taking him, I understand."

He cupped her chin and tilted her face toward his. He met her eyes and held, hating the hesitation he found there. The terror. God, he hoped that one day he would prove to her that he was not Silas. That he was someone she could depend upon, someone who would always be on her side.

"I cared about the man I thought he was," he said. "The man he never was. I *hate* who he truly was. Hate him down to the core of me."

Her lips parted. "Callum."

"It is true. If I had known what he was doing to you, I would have killed him myself to protect you, Valaria. I'm sorry you were so alone in facing that monster. And I am so happy that you defended yourself that horrible night. That you *lived*." His voice broke as the emotions rushed up in him. He tucked her back into his arms and held her closer. "That you are here. It's all that matters."

She wept then, softly but with enough strength that he wondered if she had never fully allowed herself to do so before. That if today was the first time she'd really faced what she'd endured and what she'd been forced to do.

He gently smoothed his hand over her hair, allowing her this moment where she could be safe in his arms. But he released her when she pulled away.

"You must have questions," she said, moving to the settee.

He followed and took a place beside her. He drew in a long breath. "You've said so much today, I wouldn't press for details unless you wished to give more of them."

Her brow wrinkled and she stared at him. "You are truly unlike any man I've ever known."

"Considering the caliber of man who has darkened your door, I will take that as a compliment."

"It's meant as one." She sighed. "And you cannot know how much your acceptance about this means to me. I don't know if you will feel differently as this sinks in—"

"I won't," he assured her, and meant it.

"But the consequences, Callum," she said. "It was bad enough when no one else knew, but now it seems someone did. We—I was so careful that night, I thought. But the note makes it clear that someone knows. I cannot imagine what they will want to keep their silence."

He flinched and held out a hand. She passed the offending missive over to him and he examined it. The handwriting was shaky and awkward, almost childlike. But the paper the note was written on was very fine and heavy. Curious.

He read the two sentences again, analyzing every swirl of the letters and turn of the phrases. "Thus far they have not asked for anything. It seems they only want you to know they know. To torment you a bit."

She shivered. "Silas would approve, I think. But they do mention what I'd be willing to pay to keep the secret. So they are not finished with me, I don't think."

"Well, the first step will be determining who wrote this note," he said.

"How will I do that?" she asked.

He tilted his head. "We. *We* will do that."

"Oh. You would...you would drag yourself into my ruination."

He shook his head. "Yes. Always. Every time, Valaria. That is what one does when one loves someone. One day you'll know that without having to ask me to remind you. But if you need me to, I *will* remind you every day."

Her expression softened. "You...you could still love me after this?"

"I do love you, Valaria," he declared, and held his breath as he prayed she would return that sentiment. For a moment he thought she might. She clung to his hand, her blue-gray eyes locked with his. But then she broke away and bent her head.

"What do you need from me?"

He sighed. "I suppose we'll start with a list of any person who might have a reason or ability to blackmail you. Servants who were on the property that night, neighbors who could have seen what happened in the stable. And we'll go from there. Theo will help, I know. And your friends will be there at your side. Because no one judges you, Valaria. You know that, don't you?"

"I could see it on their faces, their wonderful, kind faces," she agreed. "But I admit, I find it hard to believe. How could you not judge me? How could they not see me differently knowing what I did?"

"They will see you differently," he said softly. "They will see you as an even stronger, braver woman who saved her own life. Who faced something horrific and overcame it because she has steel at her core."

She blinked. "Is that how you see me?"

"That and so much more." He leaned in then, praying she would allow him to kiss her. She hesitated for a moment, but then lifted her mouth to his. He kissed her gently, sweetly, because this caress was not about desire or passion or claiming, but about connection. It was about love.

He wanted her to feel his love so completely that she couldn't deny it, even when she questioned herself.

He sighed as they parted, and traced the curve of her cheek with his fingertips. "I do have one question."

She nodded. "Anything. You've earned it."

"Would you have...would you have told me the truth if I hadn't seen that letter today?"

Her hesitation, the way she broke eye contact from him, told him everything he needed to know before she even spoke a word. She worried her hands in her lap, staring at her fingers as they flexed together and apart over and over.

"No," she whispered. He sucked in a breath and she did dart her gaze to his then. Watching for his reaction. For his anger, he could see. She sighed. "I need to be honest with you, Callum. Even if it upsets you. I would have taken this secret to the grave with me if I'd been able to do so."

He pursed his lips. The answer was to be expected. But it still cut. He wanted her to be able to trust him. She didn't yet. She might not ever fully be able to do so. And yet he was bound to try to earn that trust. Earn that heart she guarded so closely.

"I'm sorry you were forced into this confidence with all of us thanks to some blackguard who would threaten you," he said. "And I vow to you that I will find him. I will stop him. By whatever means necessary. Because I also vow to protect you, Valaria. Protect you with all I am and all I wish to be. You don't have to accept that now, to understand it. Not after everything you've been through. But I *will* do it."

She looked confused by that vow, then her cheeks filled with pink heat. "We should…we should get the others."

He knew she was right, even though he wanted to remain alone with her, sheltered in the quiet together where nothing else could reach them. But he rose to his feet and helped her to hers. Then he kissed her once more and pressed his forehead to hers.

"Whatever you need, Valaria, I will give it to you. I promise you."

And he hoped it could keep that promise. Hoped she could accept it and him. And that he could protect her from whoever threatened her and the future they could build together.

CHAPTER 23

Valaria's head spun as their fivesome sat at the dining room table half an hour later. Neither the duchesses nor Theo had shown her anything less than kindness and friendship since they were reunited as a group. And their offers to help her, to help Callum, had been genuine and immediate.

Which was why Bernadette was now writing a list of any person who might have uncovered Valaria's secret. It covered exactly who Callum had suggested: servants and neighbors who could have seen what she'd done. It wasn't very long, but it was a start.

"What about your maid?" Flora asked. "Fanny, isn't it?"

Valaria jolted. "Fanny is not involved in this."

Callum wrinkled his brow as he gazed at her from down the table, as focused on her as he had been the entire afternoon. That regard was so powerful and so terrifying all at once. Right now he accepted her, forgave her, and it meant the world.

But would that hold? Would he come to hate her for what she'd done? For the threats her presence brought to his life and financial well-being? She couldn't imagine he would turn so cruel as Silas had over the years...but losing his affection would sting in a different way.

"You cannot say that for certain," he said gently. "Fanny has intimate knowledge that no other servant does. We must at least consider her."

Valaria shifted. Telling her own secrets was one thing, potentially exposing Fanny to harm was quite another. "I refuse to believe that," she insisted. "At least let us pursue other avenues before we bother Fanny with questions."

Callum didn't look certain, but he held up his hands as if in surrender. "As you wish, Valaria. We'll push her down the list."

He nodded toward Bernadette, and she added Fanny's name to the collection with a sigh. "You have a good start," she said. "But what will you do with the information so as to not raise suspicions?"

Valaria swallowed past the lump in her throat that formed there when she thought of this next part. "I wonder that myself," she croaked out. "Three months after his death, having the servants and neighbors questioned by Silas's former best friend will be odd, at best. The new duke might not even allow you access to his staff."

"Silas's cousin is wretched," Callum conceded. "But I think I'll have some leverage considering he pushed a grieving widow from her comfortable home during the height of her mourning." When Valaria pulled a face, he nodded. "I know, I know. A ridiculous lie considering what we all know. But Franklin always cared what people thought of him. I'm going to imply that in your haste to evacuate, something of value was misplaced. And see if he'll let me in as an emissary in your place to gently question those under his control who are on our list."

"I'm sure he'll know about you and me by now," Valaria said, her cheeks growing hot as fire. "I shudder to think what he'll say about that."

Callum shifted. "I promise you, I won't do anything to draw any more negative attention toward you than has already occurred." He pushed from the table. "I *will* return home now, though. I have a letter to write to the man to arrange the meeting."

Theo got to his feet, as well. "Let me join you. Perhaps I can be of some service in this."

"I'd appreciate it," Callum said.

Valaria sighed as she and the other ladies accompanied the men to the foyer. As Higgins rushed off to call for the carriages, she slipped to Callum's side and stared up at him, unable to find words.

She'd expected things to change between them when he knew her secret. And they had. But not the way she had feared. If anything, she felt closer to the man. Dangerously closer.

"Will you…come back?" she whispered, needing him in that moment more than she had ever needed any other person. And she wasn't strong enough to deny it, deny him.

His expression softened. "Would you like me to?"

She pondered that question and knew the answer immediately. She wanted him with her, to comfort her. To help her forget. To offer him comfort, as well, if he needed it. She nodded. "Tonight?"

"Yes." His hand quivered at his side, as if he wanted to touch her. But he didn't. Instead, he executed a quick nod and then left her home with Theo on his heels.

As the carriages rode away, two knights somehow charged with protecting her, Valaria turned back to her friends. She found them each with tears in their eyes and let out a ragged breath.

"I'm sorry I didn't tell you," she whispered.

"Oh, dearest," Bernadette said, and then enveloped her in a tight hug. "Come. Let's finish our tea."

"Finish," Valaria said on a shaky laugh as they all returned to the parlor. "We hadn't really begun."

"I'll fix that," Flora said, and rushed to the sideboard to prepare three cups.

After everyone had their refreshment and they had all settled back on the settee, Valaria between them, she sighed. "You must have so many questions."

"Not a one," Flora said, taking her hand. "Except what can we do?"

"How can you all be so kind?" Valaria whispered. "You two, Theo…Callum."

"Because we *care* for you," Bernadette said. "And Callum…well, Callum loves you."

"Yes." Valaria let out a shaky breath. "Callum does love me. He proves that regularly now, and makes my resolve so shaky."

"Perhaps in this case, a solid resolve is rather unforgiveable," Flora said. When both the others looked at her, she shrugged. "I believe I am the only one of the three of us who loved her husband, yes?"

"I…wanted to love him," Bernadette said weakly.

"Hardly a sterling sentiment, dear," Flora said with a laugh. "I will tell you that love is a complicated thing. And a simple thing. And a wonderful, terrible thing."

Valaria flinched. "You are not selling me on the concept. It sounds dreadful. So much to risk, so much potential for pain."

"Of course. The risk is very high," Flora agreed. "And the payout is even higher. I would not have traded those years with my Stuart, not for all the gold in all the world. And when he died…" She hesitated and swallowed hard. "When I lost him, it changed me. It changed my world. Since none of us knows the future, or how quickly a loss may come, I would hate to see you turn away love, Valaria. Especially with such a remarkable man."

Valaria bent her head. "Callum is that. Tender and passionate, kind and confident, intelligent and witty. Almost the perfect man that I dreamed of as a girl before…well, before everything."

"And the fact that he is handsome as anything and rich as Midas doesn't hurt either," Bernadette giggled.

Valaria was shocked that she could still smile considering what her afternoon had entailed. "Yes, those things, too."

"All of that is fine and good." Flora said, holding her gaze evenly. "Amazing qualities all. And the fact that he worships the ground you walk upon is also of vital importance. But the most significant thing is whether or not you love him. Do you?"

Valaria drew a few long breaths. She had been avoiding that very question since the moment Callum had shown up at her door weeks ago. Perhaps even longer than that. And yet the answer rose up in her like a tidal wave and overwhelmed everything else in her world.

"Yes," she whispered. "I do love him."

Bernadette let out a little squeal. "Then nothing else matters, does it?"

"I think the fact that I'm being blackmailed and if the truth comes out we shall all be ruined might matter," Valaria said. "No matter what he says to the contrary."

"You'll get through this," Flora said, squeezing her hands. "He won't have it any other way. But you'll have to let him in, Valaria. You'll have to open yourself up to the pain, knowing that the joy will be more than equal to the task. Certainly today he's proven that he can be trusted."

"Yes," Valaria whispered. "He's certainly done that in spades. And I know you're right. I just don't know if I'm strong enough."

"You are," Bernadette assured her. "But I can see you're overwhelmed after such a horrible day. Why don't we drink tea and gossip like usual and pretend that everything is normal? As long as you know that any time you need to talk about this, day or night, we're here."

Valaria looked from one woman to the other, these two who had been strangers until recently, and who she now loved as powerfully as she might have loved her own blood sisters. "I am so lucky to have you both."

And she knew she was. She just hoped that Flora was right and that she would survive the storm that had crashed upon her shores. And find a way to tell Callum just what was in her heart.

~

Callum entered his study with Theo on his heels. He went immediately to the sideboard and poured them each a tall glass of whisky, one of which he handed over to his friend. Theo took it, but set it on the edge of the desk without drinking as he watched Callum settle into his chair.

"You must have a great deal to say," Callum said, hearing how rough his voice was. "So go ahead."

Theo tilted his head. "I have nothing to say. I do have a question."

Callum drank the whisky in one long slug. "Ask away."

"Are you well?"

Theo's voice was so gentle that Callum jerked his gaze up and found only support in Theo's expression.

"This was a horrible day," Theo continued. "What she went through…what she was forced to do…hearing it was difficult for me, and I don't love her. I cannot imagine the pain it caused you. Especially since the damage to her was perpetrated by someone you cared for. So I ask again, my old friend, are you well?"

"No," Callum admitted softly and his voice cracked with the emotional weight of what had happened. "I am anything but well. I am…undone. I am lost. I am heartbroken for her. I hate him and I hate myself for not knowing what he was and intervening."

"But you didn't, so you couldn't," Theo said firmly. "But what you can do now is protect her. And that will be enough."

"I hope so," Callum said, shrugging because it didn't feel like it was enough. Not by a long shot. "What do you think of her list?"

Theo held out a hand and Callum turned over the list of names Bernadette had neatly laid out not an hour before. A slight smile tilted Theo's lips briefly as he let his gaze slide over the words.

"Etta's handwriting is perfect," he explained when Callum arched a brow at him. "Mine is terrible."

"You don't have to tell me," Callum muttered.

"As for the content, I would say your culprit is very likely on this list. The most obvious answer is someone who was in the house that night. Hiding from the violence, but quietly aware of it and its consequences. So if you can get that toady new duke to allow you access, you'll likely find your culprit."

"Yes." Callum let out a long breath before he opened his drawer and carefully removed a stack of fine stationery, a quill and his wax sealing kit. "Then I should begin." He laid a sheet before him and as his fingers brushed the fine paper, he paused. "That's odd."

"What is odd?" Theo asked as he finally took his own drink and sipped it.

Callum dug into his pocket and withdrew the note from the blackmailer. He spread the sheet open and laid it next to his own paper. "The weight is the same," he murmured. "The feeling is the same, even the color is the same."

"It's paper," Theo said, but he leaned across the desk to examine the similarities, himself. "How could you be certain it's the same?"

"I had this paper specially ordered," Callum explained. "It soaks longer so the color is a bit darker than the usual paper. It's a touch heavier."

"You are fastidious," Theo muttered. "So you believe it is the same paper. Isn't it possible that the author of the letter had access to the same stock?"

"I don't think so. As you said, I'm fastidious when it comes to these things. What I write on is rare, indeed, and expensive. I cannot imagine a servant in the new Duke of Gooding's home finding it there. Silas would not have had it and Franklin is, let me put it kindly…I doubt he spends much time on any literate pursuits."

Now Theo's brow wrinkled. "So why would he invest in fancy paper? Then perhaps the culprit came from a different house. One of the neighbors."

"Perhaps." Callum stared at the pages. "Or perhaps there is a simpler explanation. The author of the blackmail letter got the paper from this very desk."

"What are you talking about? Someone in your household staff?

How would they know about what had happened between Silas and Valaria?"

"They wouldn't," he said, rising. "But there was one person in the household who might. Valaria's maid."

"Franny, or Fanny, isn't it?"

Callum nodded and his stomach sank. "Valaria has been so defensive of the young woman. If it is true that it is her own close confidante and friend who is doing this…it's yet another betrayal. Yet another heartbreak for her."

Theo shook his head. "Yes. So what will you do?"

"I'm returning to her tonight," he explained. Theo arched a brow in response and Callum rolled his eyes. "Don't get all prim and proper on me now, you notorious rake. Yes, I'm going to call on the woman I love, the woman I will marry, to comfort her after what has to have been one of the worst days of her life."

"And you'll reveal these suspicions?" Theo asked.

Callum nodded. "I'll get more information about the delivery of the letter. And question Fanny."

"What about Franklin?"

"I'll hold off on contacting him. If I can resolve this without raising further questions, then that's what I'll do." He scrubbed a hand over his face. "I both hope I'm correct and that this terrible thing can be stopped before it truly starts, and pray I'm wrong so I won't be the cause of yet another pain in Valaria's life."

Theo stood and clapped a hand on his shoulder. "My friend, if there's one thing I know, it's that you aren't the cause of her pain. I watch you together, I see how protective you are—if you can overcome her barriers, you two could actually be happy."

Callum arched a brow. "Are you getting soft in your advancing years?"

Theo snorted. "It seems I am. Unconscionable." His expression gentled. "Can I help?"

"No, you're helping just by refusing to say I told you so about

Silas. And about the fact that I…that I always cared a great deal more for Valaria than perhaps I wanted to admit."

"I take no pleasure in the former and a great deal in the latter," Theo said as he pushed to his feet. "And now I'll go so you can have a moment to prepare yourself for how you will broach this delicate subject with Valaria. If you need me, send word."

"I will," Callum said, smiling with distraction as his friend left the room. But once he was alone, he picked up the two letters and looked at the paper again, his stomach turning with the thoughts he had in his head.

And the ways the truth could cut as deeply as a lie.

CHAPTER 24

Valaria sat at her dressing table, watching as Fanny put the finishing touches on her hair. She had dressed tonight in black, of course, but her best black gown. One that didn't make her feel too terribly maudlin.

"You look lovely, as always, Your Grace," Fanny said softly. "Are you expecting your friends after supper?"

Valaria shifted. Fanny had made her feelings clear so many times that Valaria had hesitated to reveal the truth of what had happened earlier in the day. But her maid deserved to know. And to understand that Valaria had and would continue to protect her.

"I'm expecting Callum," she replied.

Fanny had begun to replace the combs and brushes in Valaria's dressing table, but now her hands faltered and some pins scattered across the top. She faced Valaria.

"He is coming back here tonight?" she asked slowly.

Valaria nodded. "Yes. And before he returns I must tell you that he…he knows the truth about what happened with Silas that night."

Now all the color left her maid's face and Fanny staggered away, crashing into the corner of the table in her haste. Valaria lunged to her feet and held out a hand to steady the maid, but Fanny jerked away.

"He knows?" she repeated, her breath harsh and hard in the quiet of the room. "What does he know? How?"

"I told him," Valaria said. "I told him and I told the duchesses and the Duke of Lightmorrow."

Fanny was silent for what felt like an eternity, but then she shook her head. "How could you? Better yet, *why* would you?"

Valaria bent her head. "Something has happened. Someone has written me a letter claiming they know what happened that night. Determined to blackmail me about it."

Fanny's nostrils flared slightly. "And your response was to invite even more strangers into what happened? How foolish of you."

Valaria caught her breath. Fanny must be frightened, indeed, to be so forward. And she had earned that reaction, so Valaria tempered her own. "I had no choice," she said. "If someone else knows what happened, then finding allies was my only option. And I…I trust them all. I never expected to do so, but I do."

"A lot of good that will do me, your trust in your powerful friends," Fanny snapped, and slapped a hand down on the table. "You don't exactly have a history of good judgment."

Valaria turned her face from the barb, expertly placed and stinging, even though she did understand where it came from. "You and I are close, Fanny, and I will never be able to repay you for your help the night Silas died. But you are crossing a line."

For a moment, Fanny was quiet, and then she bowed her head. The heat went out of her and was replaced by a pale horror. "I am sorry, Your Grace. I should not have been so bold, but you must understand what this means. They will come for me long before they come for you if there is punishment to be meted out."

"No!" Valaria got up and moved toward her, catching her hands gently. "I didn't tell anyone about your part. And I won't. Not ever. If there is a consequence for my actions, then only I will pay it."

Fanny's expression softened. "You didn't tell them?"

"I told you I would not betray you and I *won't*. Never! If something does come of this, if Callum cannot protect me and I am ruined or arrested for what I did, then I swear to you I will also ensure that you are well taken care of. Part of bringing others into this situation was so that I could ask them for their assistance for not just me, but for you. I know they'll make certain that you have a new position that will pay you and treat you well. I owe you that and so much more, my dearest friend."

"Your Grace—" Fanny began, her eyes welling with tears.

But before they could continue the conversation, there was a light knock on the chamber door and Higgins voice came from the hall. "His Grace has arrived, Your Grace."

"Thank you, I'll join him straight away," Valaria called out. She squeezed Fanny's hands. "We'll talk about this more later, I promise. I'll go to him now."

Fanny jerked out a nod and said nothing else as Valaria left the room. Her tangled emotions eased a little as she went to the stairs and down them to where Callum waited. No person had ever brought her peace and yet he did. And she supposed that was part of the love she felt for him. He was her comfort in a storm.

She only hoped that these storms wouldn't wreck him, as they would likely wreck her, on rocky shores.

When Valaria entered the parlor, all thoughts briefly left Callum's mind. All he could do was stare at her with her brown hair done up so that it accentuated the angles of her face, her blue-gray eyes warm as they fell on him. God, but she was beautiful, both inside and out.

And he wanted to protect her, not hurt her, even if he feared he was about to do just that.

"Good evening," he said as she moved to him.

To his surprise, she wrapped her arms around his neck and

hugged him. He folded his arms around her, and for a moment, they just stood like that, in this embrace that was as intimate and meaningful as any time he'd made love to her or kissed her until they both forgot their own names.

At last she tugged away, her cheeks brightening with a blush. "Good evening, Callum."

He smiled. "You know, if you're going to greet me like that when I come here, I may leave just to have that welcome."

She laughed, though he recognized the hollowness of the sound. How long had she been wearing a mask, protecting herself, protecting others from the horrible truth of what she'd endured? And now he would have to reveal yet another potential betrayal.

He hated it. So he touched her face and put it off a little longer. "Come, let me get you a drink. I assume we have some time before supper?"

"Yes," she said. "Though I believe you are depriving me of my duties as hostess, Your Grace."

She sat despite that statement and he smiled as he moved to the sideboard and poured them each a glass of madeira. "I like taking care of you."

She took the glass. "I'm beginning to see that is true. It seems to give you great pleasure to do so."

He sat beside her, resting an arm along the back of the settee as he memorized every line and angle of her face. "It does."

"I have never known a man like you," she whispered.

"Is that a compliment or a curse?" he asked softly.

She leaned in, resting a hand on his thigh as she brushed her lips to his. "A compliment of the highest regard, I promise you."

There was nothing in the world he would rather do than follow up on that kiss. To take her upstairs and make love to her and forget that he had information that would hurt her all over again.

But he owed her the truth. He owed her protection, even if it caused pain. She'd lived too many lies for too long already.

So he drew in a long breath. "How are you after what happened this afternoon?"

She shrugged. "I'm as well as can be expected. You were all so kind, so accepting. I had never dreamed I would be believed and supported like that. So it helps. I am nervous about what Franklin will say when he receives your letter asking to speak to his servants. You have not already heard back from him, have you?"

He shifted. And there was the opening he needed. "Er, no. But that is because I did not write him the letter as expected."

Her brow wrinkled. "Oh. I see. Was there a reason you didn't?"

He nodded slowly, holding her gaze. "Yes. But before I give you more details, would you mind if I asked Higgins a few questions? With you in the room, of course."

She appeared confused, but he was relieved when she nodded. "Certainly, if you think it would help." She got up and rang the bell at the door. A moment later, the butler appeared and she motioned into the room. "His Grace has a few questions for you, Higgins."

"Certainly, sir," the servant said, turning his attention on Callum. "How may I assist?"

Callum drew a deep breath and removed the blackmail note from his pocket. He had refolded it and held it out to the butler. "This may not be a question you can answer, but do you recall when this letter arrived for Her Grace? It was while she was away."

Higgins took the letter. He didn't open the pages, but turned them, examining the address carefully, running his fingers over the pages. "I do not, Your Grace, I apologize." His brow wrinkled.

"You look concerned by that," Callum said. "Why is that?"

"Well, sir, I am usually the one to answer the door and receive all messages. Even on the rare occasion I'm not available, I'm always immediately informed by staff so that I may personally add correspondence to the tray. I manage that portion of the household quite closely."

"And you recall every letter that arrives?" Valaria asked.

"I do try, Your Grace." He stared at the letter again. "You said this was in the pile of correspondence from when you were away?"

She nodded. "Yes. Mixed in the with the rest when I opened them earlier today."

Higgins shook his head. "Well, I did not receive it, Your Grace. So I'm not certain how it was added to the pile." He frowned. "I will inquire with the staff."

"Certainly you may do that," Callum said. "And if you hear anything of note, please report it back."

"I shall. Is that all, Your Graces?"

Valaria glanced toward Callum and he inclined his head. "Yes. For now. Thank you, Higgins."

When the butler had gone, Callum returned to the settee and Valaria did the same. She stared at him. "I assume there was a purpose to that."

He drew a shaky breath, hating what he must say next. "I do not think Higgins will find a servant who accidentally forgot to report a delivery of the letter. Because I don't think it was delivered by an outsider."

She was silent for what felt like an eternity, with the color draining from her cheeks, eyes widening with terror and confusion. "Wh-what do you mean?"

He sighed and removed the sheet of vellum from his pocket, then handed it and the original letter to her. She held them, one in each hand and continued to look confused. "Is this supposed to mean something to me?"

"Feel the paper," he suggested softly. "Feel the similarities."

She did so and shook her head. "And?"

"The blank sheet is from a special set from my own desk, Valaria. I believe whoever wrote that note did so from my household."

"One of your servants?" she gasped. "But how, why?"

"No, not one of my servants," he said, and caught her trembling hand. "But someone who had access because she was in my home… with you."

Her expression crumbled. "No."

"Fanny," he said softly.

"No!" she repeated, and tugged her hand away. "Fanny would *never* do that to me."

"If she wrote the letter at my desk, with my stationery and pen, then returned to the house to collect things for you, she could have slipped the letter in with the rest of the correspondence."

Valaria looked sick as she stared at the letter, but Callum could tell that what he was saying was sinking in. That she understood it could be true. Probably was true. "Which is why Higgins doesn't know its origin."

He touched her hand lightly. "Is Fanny available to speak to?"

Tears were in her eyes as she looked at him again. She nodded. "Y-Yes. I could ring for her."

She got up as if to do that but before she could reach the bell, the door opened and the maid, herself, entered the room.

"You don't need to ring," the young woman said, her voice trembling. "I'm here. And…and he's right, Your Grace. I did write the letter."

The world felt like it was tilting and Valaria reached for the back of the closest chair to keep herself from falling over. Then Callum was at her back, holding her up by her elbow, his presence comforting and warm behind her.

She stared at Fanny, searching the face of a woman who was far more than a servant to her. "But why?" she asked, hating how her voice trembled and barely carried when she wanted to be strong. Firm. "Why would you do that, Fanny?"

"Money," Callum said, his voice rough with a protective anger that seemed to vibrate in the air around them.

"No!" Fanny burst out immediately. "Not money."

"I find that hard to believe considering it's a letter of blackmail," Callum snapped.

Valaria turned toward him and looked up at him. "Let her speak. Please."

She could see how he wanted to hurtle between them and use himself as a shield. But he didn't. He inclined his head, respecting her request, and grew silent.

"Tell me," Valaria said softly, returning her attention to Fanny. "Tell me why."

Fanny let out a low sob and then shook her head. "Because I…I wanted to tear you two apart."

CHAPTER 25

Valaria stared at Fanny, her shock and hurt and confusion sitting like a ball in her chest that made her heart ache so deeply. "Tear us apart?"

Fanny nodded. "I knew you were hesitant about His Grace," she whispered, tears beginning to stream down her cheeks. "But it was also clear that things were escalating between you. That you wanted what he offered and if you took it…if you took it then there would be so much danger to us both."

Valaria flinched. Fanny had been saying that same thing to her for weeks now. Trying to convince her to walk away from this man who loved her. "What was the purpose of blackmailing me, then? Especially after you knew Callum and I were engaged."

"You've always been so guarded, especially about this." Tears were streaming down Fanny's cheeks now, her eyes bright with them and her hands trembling at her sides. "I thought that if you believed the secret would come out, that someone was threatening you with it, that you might push him away. End things with him so that he wouldn't know what you did. What…what *we* did."

Valaria heard Callum's sharp intake of breath and he moved forward half a step. "You helped Valaria that night."

Fanny ducked her head. "Yes," she whispered. "In the end it will come out anyway. Her Grace will confess everything to you because of her heart. So it might as well be now."

"Oh, Fanny," Valaria breathed.

"Tell him," Fanny said, sinking into the closest chair and covering her face with her hands.

Valaria turned toward him and shook her head. "Fanny followed us when Silas was dragging me to the stable," she whispered. "At great risk to herself, she tried to intervene, to save me. It distracted Silas. He was about to strike her and that…that was when I hit him. Killed him."

Fanny didn't remove her head from her hands, so her voice was muffled as she said, "Together we covered up the crime, and vowed never to tell another living soul."

"Until she told us," Callum said. "Told me."

"You'll have me transported to protect her, I know," Fanny sobbed. "People like me are always the ones that get trampled on by people like you."

Valaria watched Callum, but there was no hint of any negative emotion on his face as he slowly moved to where Fanny sat. He pulled up a chair close to hers and gently reached out to lower her hands from where they caged her face. The maid looked at him, waiting for the punishment that men like him had doled out over the years.

But Valaria knew *this* man. And she knew he would never do such a thing. She knew it with a strength that was almost as overpowering as the love that rose up in her in that moment where he stared at her servant, her friend, and showed the same kind of acceptance and gentleness that he had always shown her.

"You saved the woman I love," he said gently. "You were brave in the face of something I can only imagine was terrifying. And I would never do anything to harm you, Fanny. Just as I would never do anything to harm Valaria. This secret…it will go to the grave with me."

Fanny caught her breath and stared at him. Valaria saw the same doubt in her expression as she had felt in her own every time Callum offered kindness and gentleness to her. But she also saw… hope. "You would do that?"

"Of course," Callum said. "I vow it on my own life."

"And what of the others?" Fanny asked. "Your friends. Her friends?"

"They would never tell anyone," Valaria said, and she knew it was true. Understood it herself for the first time. "They will protect us both and likely only be relieved that there is no true threat."

Callum still held Fanny's gaze evenly. "There *is* no true threat, is there, Fanny?"

"No," the maid whispered. "I would *never* harm the duchess."

"I believe that is true." Callum patted her hand. "So then there is nothing to fear. From you. From me."

Fanny stared at him for a long moment and then glanced at Valaria. And it was clear her friend had come to see just a glimpse of what she knew this man to be. There was a softening to Fanny's features. A relief. "I'm so sorry, Your Grace."

"I understand," Valaria said. "I understand your fear and that sometimes we do desperate things to protect ourselves and those we care for. But it's over now. And we have nothing to fear ever again."

Fanny let out a little sob and Valaria saw just how damaging the pressure of the last few months had been on her maid. How much weight Fanny had been holding. As much as she had been, herself.

She squeezed Fanny's hand. "I forgive you, Fanny. And I hope you can forgive me for not providing you with more reassurance."

Fanny nodded and wiped her tears. "Of course."

Callum moved to Valaria's side as she stepped away from Fanny. She felt the warmth of his hand at the small of her back. Comforting, powerful, and she leaned into it and into him.

"I'll leave you two," Fanny said as she smoothed her gown and wiped her face once more.

"I won't need you tonight," Valaria said. "Just rest now."

Fanny bent her head, her exhaustion as plain as Valaria's own. She left the room and Valaria faced Callum.

"Come to my chamber," she said softly. "Forget supper."

He nodded and took her hand, leading her from the room and up the stairs. They entered her chamber and she expected him to pounce, to kiss her, to seduce her as she so desperately wanted after this dreadful day. But instead, he simply cupped her face.

"She truly believed you would break with me rather than have the truth come out," he said softly.

"She had reason to believe that," Valaria admitted. "Thanks to what I endured, I had closed myself off for so long. My first instinct was to hide everything from you. To keep you from finding out."

"And then I did," he said.

She nodded and stared up at him. At this wonderful man who loved her so deeply. And who she loved just as powerfully. The fear she'd had about that emotion seemed to bleed away. It left behind only...joy. Certainty. And a deep desire to confess her heart as she had confessed her past.

"Fanny didn't understand...perhaps *I* didn't understand...that when I came to Kent's Row I found a family, a far better one than the one I was born into. Sisters in the duchesses, a brother in Theo." She shifted as she prepared to make the most terrifying confession of her life. "And...and *you*."

He caught his breath and she saw how deeply her words moved him. "Valaria."

"You are the love of my life," she continued, and found strength with every word that fell from her lips. "The whole of my heart. The person I can trust with my secrets and my body and my soul. And I know that this beginning was not..." She laughed a little. "Optimal. But if you still wish to make me your wife, I want us to be happy. To love each other. To make a future that is so beautiful and bright that it blinds even the sun."

He blinked down at her, seemingly stunned by this, by her. "You love me?" he asked.

She nodded. "I do."

His breath grew shaky and she was surprised that tears leapt into his bright eyes. "Then I am the luckiest man in this world or any other. And I cannot wait to make you mine."

"I'm already yours," she whispered, and drew him closer, leaning up for a kiss that felt like a lifetime in the making.

A kiss that sealed them as much as the way he backed her toward her bed and proved to her, over and over and long into the night, that he was hers, too.

Forever.

EPILOGUE

Nine months later

"Her Grace, the Duchess of Blackvale," Valaria breathed close to Callum's ear as they spun around the dancefloor at their wedding exactly one day after her mourning period had ended.

Not that they had been acting as anything but man and wife for all the months before that. They had been going back and forth between each other's homes almost every night. And yes, there had been a stir at the beginning, thanks to the whispers caused by Lady Pittsgreen, but Valaria's friends had eased that. Flora and Bernadette, along with the Duchess of Amberleigh, had spread a very different story. The truth: that Callum had comforted her in her worst moments. That they had fallen deeply in love. That it was the height of romance and a triumph of the heart over grief and pain.

And Society had, as promised, eaten it up. An invitation to the day's festivities had been one of the most sought after of the Season.

"That is music to my ears," Callum said, drawing her from her thoughts. "Say it again."

"Your wife," she repeated. "In body now, as well as soul."

"A body I happen to adore," he said.

She laughed, lighter now than she had ever been. Thanks to him. This wonderful man who had been everything she ever needed. Who would always be that. He had lifted the weight of the world from her shoulders and eased not only her fears, but Fanny's, as well. Her maid had come to adore him as he proved his honesty and protectiveness over the months. Even now Fanny beamed from across the room, all fear erased from her countenance.

Fanny had earned that, and Valaria was so happy to see her at ease again.

Which meant now she only worried about her friends. She scanned the ballroom looking for them. Flora stood on one side of the room, but she was not alone. Her last few months had been interesting, to say the least, and her new happiness was reflected on her face.

She found Bernadette stood on the other side of the floor, standing beside Theo. In the months since Valaria's engagement, Theo had come around more and more often. And his renewed friendship with Bernadette had grown. Bernadette refused to speak of it, of course, dismissed any question about how she felt when it came to the handsome duke.

But now the two were engaged in deep conversation, one that did not look entirely happy.

Valaria shook her head. "I only hope my two friends will soon be as happy as I am."

Callum tucked a finger beneath her chin and tilted it up so that suddenly all there was was him. And as always, the fears fell away as he smiled at her. That was the gift of his heart and his love. He just made everything in her life better.

"They *will* be happy," he assured her. "Though happy as we are could be a stretch. No one in the world could quite reach these heights."

"No," she agreed as she clung to him tighter and let him spin her around the floor. "No one in the world."

ENJOY AN EXCERPT OF NOT ANOTHER DUKE

BOOK 2 OF THE KENT'S ROW DUCHESSES

Fall 1815

Roarke Desmond made a slow count of ten in his head and schooled his expression so that his utter disgust with his surroundings would not be clear. It was something he had been doing for most of his life when he was forced to visit his three hateful cousins, so he was very good at it. After all, he had no other choice.

"Do you remember little Gregory Parson?" his cousin Thomas was asking now, drawing Roarke back into the conversation.

Roarke inclined his head. "Er, yes. I think so. He lived out near your father's estate in Sidmouth, did he not?"

"*My* estate in Sidmouth," Thomas snapped, and Roarke clenched his jaw.

His eldest cousin had been impossible to take for his entire life. Thomas was always lording his elevated position over Roarke and anyone else he deemed less than worthy. Roarke had hoped he might grow out of such immature nastiness, but Thomas's entitled posturing had only increased in the three years since Roarke's uncle Stuart had died and his oldest cousin had become duke.

There was almost no bearing him now.

"Of course," Roarke soothed with a stifled sigh. "Your estate. What about him?"

"Do you know that Gertrude saw him scuttling about *Cheapside* the other day?" Thomas pivoted his head and speared his younger sister with a glare. "Tell him."

Gertrude had been staring into her tea, apparently as bored by all this as Roarke was, but now she lifted her gaze and gave a smile. It seemed cruelty was a trait all his cousins shared. "I did. He owns a shop there—can you imagine?"

Roarke drew in a long breath and once again schooled his tone. "It's a very successful mercery, if I recall. They import and sell the finest fabrics for furnishings. He and his wife run the shop."

All three of his cousins pulled a face, clearly unimpressed by the success of their old neighbor's business. But of course, so many of their rank were like that.

"Well, that's quite a fall from his upbringing," his third cousin, Philip, snorted as he chewed a biscuit from the tea set on the sideboard, little flecks of food flying from his mouth as he did so. "Then again, I suppose you know about that, don't you, cousin?"

The three of them laughed, as if this were good-natured ribbing, not cruel taunting. Roarke shifted in his seat. It wasn't as if he could deny the charge. He had certainly fallen far further than the man they were discussing. Although his connection to their family was on their mother's side, rather than their duke father, Roarke had still been raised with a level of privilege and expectation.

Both of which had been ruined over the last two years. His father had started it. Francis Desmond had been a kind man, a good man, but he was a dreamer. Sometimes that led him to be too trusting or too certain of an investment. He had whittled down every bit of money he had available to him by the time of his death in a carriage accident.

Roarke had done little better. His mother had been left behind and was not well. She needed constant care—some days she didn't even know who he was. Desperate, he'd followed in his father's footsteps, trying to catch up, trying to make enough that he could take care of his responsibilities. To keep her comfortable.

He had failed. Almost as spectacularly as his father had. Which was why he had to come here and listen to his snobby cousins gossip about people they knew and be generally unpleasant. He was, for all intents and purposes, a dependent person now. If he wanted their continued financial support, this was the only way.

His stomach turned at the thought and he set his own teacup down. "What are your plans now that the Season is coming to an end?" he asked, hoping this would change the subject from one vapid subject to another more palatable one.

"I would say I was happy to be returning to the country estate," Thomas groaned, and rolled his eyes at his siblings. "But I feel as though we are always working there to undo the damage that dreadful woman did before our dear father's death."

Roarke wrinkled his brow. "Are you talking about the dowager? Your stepmother?"

Gertrude slammed her cup down on the sideboard and let out a little pained cry. "My God, but I hate that she gets to claim any title that has to do with my father. Hateful, wretched thing. She married my father at his lowest point and did everything she could to turn him against us."

"She used her grubby hands and smutty charms to grab everything she could," Philip agreed, and Roarke recoiled. He was shocked his cousin would use such plain language with Gertrude in the room. She was a lady, after all, and an unmarried one at that. It was unseemly.

He shook his head. "I know she was a good deal younger than your father—"

"Younger than me," Gertrude said. "By two years. So what does that tell you?"

Roarke didn't respond. He had some thoughts about what that said, most of which were a bit more judgmental of his uncle than the young lady he had wed. After all, women had fewer choices when it came to their fate. And from what he knew of the lady, she had come from a good family, one that would see a union with a duke, old or young, as a triumph for her.

And though he hadn't spent much time with his uncle after the death of his aunt, his father's sister, the few times he'd bumped into him at a club or gathering, Uncle Stuart had seemed vastly content with his choice of second wife. He always spoke warmly of her, at least, in their brief encounters.

"But you know, you must have seen her," Thomas was continuing, and Roarke realized he had blocked out much of their complaints.

He forced himself back to the present. "Er, no. I never met the lady, I'm afraid. Though you've made it no secret how little you three think of her, before or since your father's death."

"I should think we wouldn't," Philip said, his brow lowering. "After all she has taken from us. Her settlement was outrageous. Absolutely outrageous. If I had been in charge—"

"Philip," Thomas said sharply, and Roarke's younger cousin snapped his mouth shut with a sullen glare.

Roarke couldn't help but look around the opulent home they all sat in at present. He didn't think his cousins were hurting for funds, no matter how much their uncle had gifted for the widow he left behind.

"It has been three years since his death," Roarke said as gently as he could. "And it seems the lady is no longer in your lives. Thomas is happily in place as duke, so he makes the decisions for the future of the family, and there were no children from the second union to take anything from you. I am surprised you are still so bitter toward his second wife."

Thomas let out a long sigh and the three cousins exchanged a look heavy with meaning. It immediately put Roarke on edge. He knew that look, had seen it dozens of times as a child. It almost always meant his cousins had a plan of some kind, usually a cruel one, and they wished for him to be part of it. Probably so he could be blamed if the entire thing went wrong.

And once again Roarke cursed the fact that he had to grovel to them for money three times a year for the upkeep of his ill mother. Why had he not been more prudent? Why had he inherited his own late father's penchant for risk when it came to bright ideas of the future? There had been so little left to inherit, but perhaps if he had been prudent and guarded, he might be in a different position now.

"Well, I suppose we are thinking of the cruel grasping of his wretched wife all the more lately because of the terms of settlement we just discovered only this week," Thomas said.

"Only this week," Roarke said flatly. "You are telling me that you are still finding new terms of inheritance after all this time?"

"Yes," Thomas said, his tone getting a bit sharper. "You have no idea what we have endured. How hard it is to go through papers and papers, trying to sort out the whims of a father."

Roarke bit his tongue. They never had considered his father much of anything, despite his being their mother's brother, so of course they wouldn't see his death and the ripples that had come from it as the same thing.

"Hmmm" was all Roarke responded.

"Dearest Papa was far too kind," Gertrude continued, moving closer to Roarke. He realized they were all doing it, almost surrounding him, and his stomach turned. "There was an additional term in regard to our stepmother, and it will come into effect very soon if we do not stop it."

"And what is the term?" Roarke asked, trying to back away from the circling vultures, but only serving to edge himself farther into the corner of the room.

"Flora will inherit an additional ten thousand pounds if she reaches the third year of her widowhood without remarrying or taking a lover," Thomas said, his mouth twisting with disgust.

Roarke's head spun a moment. Ten thousand pounds. Great

God, he came to beg for one percent of that amount just to stay afloat, just to keep his mother fed and minded.

"It's not much of a sum," Philip sneered. "But that bitch hasn't earned it."

Yet again Roarke flinched at the crude language his cousin used to address his stepmother and in front of his maiden sister. "Your father seems to have felt differently," he said softly. "He must have cared for her a great deal in order to wish to protect her so thoroughly, as I imagine she must have inherited a tidy sum at this death."

"Fifteen thousand," Gertrude sneered. "Half again over what *I* inherited."

Roarke shook his head. Great God, but these people were so entirely separated from reality. They lived like kings and compared themselves to paupers. They hated a woman for taking from them, when it seemed there were unlimited resources available left to them by a caring father who had stewarded his unentailed finances carefully to protect his family. *All* his family.

Roarke despised them for it.

He smoothed his coat and then forced a sympathetic smile. "I am sorry to hear of your woes, cousins. I imagine you must feel great frustration over this news. I feel as though I am intruding now on your grief. Perhaps I should go and we can meet again another—"

"No," Thomas interrupted, arching a brow and glowering at Roarke in what he could only assume was his cousin's attempt at a *lord of the manor* expression. "You came here to ask for our assistance, as you do several times a year."

"The money is for my mother," Roarke began, but his cousin lifted his hand.

"I don't give a damn about your mother," he snapped. "*She* was not related to us through blood." Roarke clenched his fists at his sides but managed not to react in any other way as his cousin continued, "You receive a sum from the family at *our* pleasure. *Our* discretion. I've never asked you for repayment, have I?"

"No." Roarke managed the one word through clenched teeth. "You are very kind."

"Do you feel you owe me?" Thomas pressed, his eyes lighting with further cruelty.

Roarke bent his head, his breath coming rough. "You are talking about repayment, I suppose. I don't know how you expect such a thing when you are so keenly aware of my circumstances. I thought lording it over me would be enough for you, as it has always been a pleasure to you to do so."

"Watch your tongue, cousin, or it might be watched for you," Philip said, edging closer. "The duke is talking to you."

Roarke forced himself to lift his gaze back to Thomas's and held there. "What do you want?"

"Nothing dire," Thomas said, his tone dripping with false reassurance. "Nothing financial, so it will not be a trial to you. I am only asking that you investigate our stepmother. She didn't know you, so she wouldn't suspect if you did a little snooping into her life."

"Investigate what?" Roarke sputtered.

"She *must* be whoring herself out," Gertrude spat.

Roarke jerked his attention toward her. Here he had been surprised at the blunt language of his male cousins in front of her, but she was just as vulgar when it came to her stepmother.

"She has to have a lover," Gertrude continued. "She probably had one while she was watching my father die in the bed beside her. And now she hides his…or even *their*…existence just so she can milk a little more away from Papa's estate where it belongs."

Roarke pushed past his cousins at last, his distaste finally overriding any duty he felt here. "No," he said, walking toward the door. "Absolutely not."

"Five hundred pounds."

Roarke stopped as Thomas said the sum. He stared at the door, his escape. He usually got three hundred pounds a year from this lot, barely enough to scrape by and cover his mother's carer. With an extra five hundred he could make her more comfortable, even give her a few niceties.

He swallowed and turned back to stare at the vultures who called themselves his family. They were smiling at him now. They already knew the trap was sprung, and he hated them and himself for the fact that it was true.

"You cared for your uncle, didn't you?" Thomas asked.

Roarke pursed his lips. "Yes," he choked out, and it was true. As a child he'd been close to his uncle, who had always been kind to him. But once his aunt had died, all that had changed. Thanks in part, he believed, to the very cousins who he stood before now. They had pushed him out and he had lost the bond to his uncle, except for fleeting conversations when they found each other at the same club.

"Flora was a monster," Thomas continued, his tone serious. "Whatever you think of us, know that to be true. She took advantage of him in his old age, she played him for a fool all for what she could gain from him after his death. If you do this, you would be defending his honor."

Roarke drew in a long breath. He had to give it to his cousins, they were experts at manipulation. Yes, the money was a tantalizing carrot to dangle in front of him, but the idea that he could do the right thing was even more attractive. If they were even a fraction correct that his late uncle's young wife was using the situation for her own gain, then perhaps she *did* deserve to have her schemes uncovered.

And if not...well, at least Roarke knew he wouldn't lie about it. Not like some other investigators his cousins might hire if he refused them. He could be a dispassionate judge of the circumstances and either deliver the dowager from the lies her stepchildren told, or condemn her for being a mercenary and using his uncle.

Either way, when he told himself this, convinced himself, it made him feel a little less guilty. "When do I get the money?"

"I will put half in your account today," Thomas said. "Along with the other amount we agreed to earlier in our meeting. And when you have given me your report, you'll have the other half."

Roarke folded his arms. "What if I find that the lady is innocent of the charge that she has taken a secret lover?"

All three of his cousins scrunched their faces as if in disbelief. "There is no way she isn't," Philip said. "Not with her beauty."

Roarke's stomach turned as Thomas flashed his brother a salacious grin. "What if it's not true?" he insisted.

Thomas threw up his hands. "Then you get the rest, I swear it to you."

Roarke wasn't certain he believed that, but for now it would be enough. "Fine," he ground out through clenched teeth. "I will do as you ask. I will look into the activities of the dowager."

"Excellent," Thomas said with a smug expression. "You will find her on Kent's Row. At least she knew enough to deposit herself there with the other dried-up crones."

Roarke sighed. First the woman was a flagrant whore with a siren's beauty, now a dried-up crone. It seemed there was no consistency here except for their hatred of the woman. Which meant he had to be extra careful in any of his own judgements of her. That was the least he could do under the circumstances.

Out September 5!

ALSO BY JESS MICHAELS

The Kent's Row Duchesses

No Dukes Allowed

Not Another Duke (Coming September 5)

Not the Duke You Marry (Coming November 14)

Theirs

Their Marchioness

Their Duchess

Their Countess

Regency Royals

To Protect a Princess

Earl's Choice

Princes are Wild

To Kiss a King

The Queen's Man

The Three Mrs

The Unexpected Wife

The Defiant Wife

The Duke's Wife

The Duke's By-Blows

The Love of a Libertine

The Heart of a Hellion

The Matter of a Marquess

The Redemption of a Rogue

The 1797 Club

The Daring Duke

Her Favorite Duke

The Broken Duke

The Silent Duke

The Duke of Nothing

The Undercover Duke

The Duke of Hearts

The Duke Who Lied

The Duke of Desire

The Last Duke

The Scandal Sheet

The Return of Lady Jane

Stealing the Duke

Lady No Says Yes

My Fair Viscount

Guarding the Countess

The House of Pleasure

Seasons

An Affair in Winter

A Spring Deception

One Summer of Surrender

Adored in Autumn

The Wicked Woodleys

Forbidden

Deceived

Tempted

Ruined

Seduced

Fascinated

To see a complete listing of Jess Michaels' titles, please visit:

http://www.authorjessmichaels.com/books

ABOUT THE AUTHOR

USA Today Bestselling author Jess Michaels likes geeky stuff, Cherry Vanilla Coke Zero, anything coconut, cheese and her dog, Elton. She is lucky enough to be married to her favorite person in the world and lives in Oregon settled between the ocean and the mountains.

When she's not trying out new flavors of Greek yogurt or rewatching Bob's Burgers over and over and over (she's a Tina), she writes historical romances with smoking hot characters and emotional stories. She has written for numerous publishers and is now fully indie and loving every moment of it (well, almost every moment).

Jess loves to hear from fans! So please feel free to contact her at Jess@AuthorJessMichaels.com.

Jess Michaels offers a free book to members of her newsletter, so sign up on her website:

http://www.AuthorJessMichaels.com/

facebook.com/JessMichaelsBks

instagram.com/JessMichaelsBks

bookbub.com/authors/jess-michaels

Made in the USA
Middletown, DE
08 September 2023

38203869R00136